D0354610

This book is a work of fiction. Names, characters, places, and incidents are either the product of the author's imagination or are used fictitiously, and any resemblance to actual persons, living or dead, business establishments, events, or locales is entirely coincidental.

The author and the publisher do not have any control over and do not assume any responsibility for third-party websites and their content.

an Italian Adventure

**TO MY FAMILY,
SO FARAWAY, SO CLOSE.**

I left a few Italian words in the text because they really cannot be translated without losing some of the flavor. I hope you will forgive the fact that most of them are swearwords. I am sure you will get a sense for their meaning within the first few chapters.

The capitalization of God reflects the views, at times changing, of the characters uttering it.

— GBA

Part One

SPRING

1

Blame it on Nico

On that early afternoon in the April of 1988, I had no idea that I was finally about to shed some light on the mystery of sex.

Peo, Flavio, and I spilled out of our elementary school with the rest of the kids. We jumped on our bikes and headed toward Catechism, which we had to endure on every Tuesday to maintain our good-standing position in Jesus' fastidious notebook of sins.

I would have never suspected that I was about to add to it big time.

The sky was a promise of the summer to come, and the blackbirds celebrated it from the poplar and cypress trees surrounding the fields.

I made a sharp left, wrinkling my nose at the stench of the new road: a black, sticky, umbilical cord that connected the new church in the middle of a cornfield to the rest of Arese.

Our small town had originated a millennium ago as pile-dwellings overlooking swampy planes and was now a suburbanite heaven, close to Milan yet in the middle of the Groane Park.

I came to a full stop in front of the church, and Flavio and Peo skidded beside me. We were sworn brothers, always together. Teachers and classmates called us *The Trio*, but we really were the better version of the A-Team. Flavio was Hannibal, poised, charming, in charge. Peo was Mr. T, muscular and gruff. Because my teen sister beat the hell out of me I feared no pain, which had gained me my Howling-Mad-Murdock nickname.

"Lee, Peo! Check that out!" said Flavio in awe. He was the tallest in our class, while I was the shortest of all the almost-ten-year-olds in school, probably in all of Italy. His brown eyes rested on the huge puddle that had formed in the muddy parking lot beside the church. It had rained for seven days straight, like it often did in spring, and some of our classmates were already disfiguring the ground around the puddle, leaving tire marks to form an intricate lace of mud.

"Wow, it's like a lake!" I exclaimed.

Peo asked, "Can we fish in it?"

Our musings were interrupted by the argument escalating in front of us, which of course revolved around Nico.

Nico the Thug, as I had taken to call him in my head, had moved to our northern town from Sicily a few months ago. He was always by himself and didn't even try to make friends. It wasn't clear to me whether his hostile attitude was cause or consequence of his troubles, but every day he grew more aggressive and isolated. The aura of doom that surrounded him suited his gypsy looks, which would have been remarkable if not for the unsettling smile of the unrepentant.

"I dare you!" he yelled at Mario, my archenemy.

Because of the alphabetical order, Mario sat beside me in class—hiding my glasses, stealing my stuff—no matter how often I fought him to get it all back.

Flavio mused, "If only they'd kill each other."

No kidding.

Mario yelled back at Nico, "Why don't *you* do it?"

"You're a chicken!" Nico laughed.

All eyes stared at the two boys.

Mario shook his head of wild blond hair and grabbed his bike, pointing it toward the puddle. Nico performed an exaggerated bow, inviting him toward the water. Something big was about to happen.

Nico screamed, "I knew it! Chickeeeen!" He dragged the insult in a girlish voice, sending Mario in a rabid rage.

Mario shot on his bike and entered the puddle with an explosion of water that barely missed Nico who, startled, jumped backward.

Mario was going to wade through the gigantic puddle. We all watched breathlessly as the unusual aquatic firework dissipated, leaving Mario, trembling, stuck in the middle of the mire, water up to his shins.

He precariously balanced, while trying to push forward, for a handful of interminable seconds.

SPLASH!

Mario and the puddle became one, in mud and shame. Nico laughed out loud. Then he skidded on his bike, tracing wide circles into the slit, clucking like a hen.

Mario dragged himself out, and everyone looked away, afraid his demise might be contagious.

Flavio locked our three bikes together. "Let's go in. It's about to start."

I nodded and Peo shrugged, quiet as usual.

At the end of Catechism, Flavio suggested we explore the fields beside the puddle on foot. Homework could wait. Peo and I followed him along the path, cutting through young corn and poppies.

We rounded a bend and spotted Nico, squatting on his heels by a big poplar tree, poring over the ground.

Damn.

Flavio hesitated but kept walking; showing fear at ten is like painting a target on your forehead, and no one intimidated The Trio.

Nico lifted his gaze. "Guys! Guys! Check this out!"

What? Nico the Thug wanted *to share* something?

We looked at each other, and Flavio stepped ahead. "Check out *what?*"

Nico picked up a magazine from the dirt. "*Look!* Look what I found!"

It was a *porn mag.*

Wow.

I had only seen the covers at the newsstand: big boobs and raunchy poses in plain view, leaving the contents to my imagination. Now we had one specimen available, for free, and no one would ever know.

"*Put that down!*" Flavio growled, throwing an alarmed glance over his shoulder as if anyone could witness what was happening in the deserted middle of nowhere.

Nico dropped the magazine back on the ground not so much in response to Flavio's command but to keep poring over the forbidden pages. Peo and I hunched in the dirt beside him in awe.

The little I knew about sex came from a book on how children were *made* that had been passed down to me with a bunch of other youth titles, likely by mistake.

Sure enough, I knew everything about *uteri* and *sperm*, but I could not have been less prepared for the sausage fest disentangling beneath my bewildered eyes.

No one said a word while, dumbstruck, we stared at the images of naked people doing the weirdest things with the most unexpected parts of their bodies.

My curiosity grew tepid, then froze solid with the ice of a sudden realization. "Ah, *wow*, so…Our First Communion is in a couple of weeks…Um, do we have to confess about *this*?"

Nico rolled his eyes. "Such a dork. *That's* what you're thinking about?"

I retorted, "At least *I think!*"

Yet, Nico ignored me, stashing the magazine into a hollow in the poplar tree.

🍦

That night I lay in my bed and prayed, more flustered than usual.

"Dear Jesus, I am so, so sorry for the porn mag. I really didn't want to look at it but, I'm sure you know, it was all Nico's fault, right? Let's forget about it, okay? Please let me sleep well with no nightmares and make it sunny tomorrow. Amen."

🍦

Hours went by, yet sleep wouldn't come.

The porn pictures had etched themselves on the inside of my eyelids, and even worse, were branded hot onto my conscience. I wanted nothing more than to punch Nico on his dumb face. Our exchange replayed in my head as I came up with the vindictive comebacks I could have said and never would, till I finally drifted off into oblivion.

🍦

I slowly became aware of my bed and blinked to the darkness, where two huge, yellow eyes without pupils stared at me. My chest imploded, fear shooting me awake.

The devil himself has come to get me!

I rubbed my face, repeating in my head Mom's mantra, "Monsters don't exist! Monsters don't exist!"

Is this because of the porn mag?

Guilt, guilt, guilt!

Heart pounding, I gazed at the night again, and the night gazed back, unblinking. I screamed as loud as I could.

Doors slammed. Lights flicked on. Mom was on me. "Lee! Lee! What happened?"

"It's behind you, right behind you! Mom watch out!"

Of course, the devil had fled, and Mom wouldn't believe me.

As soon as she left me alone in the dark again, I turned the light back on and squeezed Hairry, my long-time blankie and the only sweater, rough and misshapen, Mom had attempted to knit.

Unless I wanted the devil to come back and drag me to hell, Nico's porn mag had to be destroyed.

🍦

On the following day, at recess, I loitered in the courtyard with the rest of The Trio beneath a scrawny pine, waiting for our turn to challenge Mario's team at soccer. An awkward silence weighed among us. Peo kicked a pine cone. Flavio unraveled a loose thread from his faded t-shirt (all his clothes were hand-me downs from his holder brothers).

I muttered, looking at my sneakers, "Guys, I don't feel so great about the porn mag."

Peo answered, too fast, "Me too." Unease bloomed into hope.

Flavio shrugged. "We can't *unsee* it."

I bit my lower lip and proposed, "Let's destroy it before *First Communion* and all."

Flavio frowned. "*How*? Nico has it."

I replied, "We saw where he hid it."

Peo asked, "Do you think it's still there?"

Flavio straightened up and answered, "There's only one way to find out."

🍦

After school, we biked on the deserted muddy path by the church.

Quieter than usual, the fields filled with the squelching of our tires until a knot of sparrows left the field, chirping in alarm in the leaden sky. The cold breeze smelled like rain.

We rounded the bend; crouched in the shade of the poplar tree, Nico welcomed us with a bitter grin.

"Here they come," he said. "Wanna see some more? 'Cos you might have to pay this time."

Torn in between guilt and temptation, I uttered, *"We don't care about the stupid mag!"* Unfortunately, despite a lot of practice, I was still the worst liar on Earth.

Nico scoffed. "Come on, four eyes, I know you liked it."

Flavio glared at Nico. "First Communion is on Sunday, and we're gonna get rid of it, period."

Nico scoffed. "The hell you are! It's mine!"

Flavio stared, unflinching.

Three on one; he had no chance. His face sagged. "ARE YOU OUT OF YOUR FREAKIN' MINDS? Destroy it? *Why?* This is *gold*! We will never be able to get one again! For free! In secret!"

Flavio said, "We all saw it. Big deal. Why keep it?"

Nico yelled, "You're a bunch of wusses!"

Peo strode forward and snatched the magazine from Nico's hands.

Nico pushed him, but Peo pushed right back. Nico then charged against me, the smallest of the three. I leaned forward, eager. I could not wait to unleash my frustration on someone *almost* my size, for once, rather than my seventeen-year-old sister. My famous mad grin must have surprised Nico because he hesitated, then stopped.

"Bunch of wusses," he muttered again, resigned.

"Go to hell, Nico!" I growled.

Peo stared at the cover of the magazine he had passed to Flavio. "Let's rip it to pieces."

Flavio objected, "What if they fly away with the wind? My house is just on the other side of the field."

Nico said, "Don't be idiots. If the cops come with the dogs, they'll track us."

I added, still glaring at the darn thug, "Or they could run fingerprints on the pieces."

"What would my parents—" Flavio trailed off mid-sentence, staring blankly ahead. I imagined the faces of Dad and Grandma, and my hair bristled.

"*Miii*," Nico added. *Miii* was short for *minchia*, a swearword apparently common in Sicily. "Let's burn it," he said. "Let's burn it to ashes." He pulled out a lighter.

I didn't know why he had a lighter, but I was not surprised. We burned a few pages at a time, careful not to start a fire, for the best part of an hour.

Yet, the sense of filth and contamination did not wash away, and with First Communion looming ahead in just a few days, all I had to blame for it was Nico the Thug.

He was still glaring at me, so I stared right back and said, "It wasn't right."

Nico snarled at me, "No, *Leda, you* are not right! Because you're a *damned girl.*"

His words dripped down on me like molten lead. Nobody called me *Leda*, ever, I was Lee. He had done it on purpose, and the anger triggered my instant transformation into my eviler self, Mr. Hyde; not like I had read the story, but it sounded so cool. I jumped toward Nico, but Flavio's big hand seized my shoulder.

Nico backed away, his face distorted with fury. "It's not over, four eyes! You'll pay for this!" He ran, but his words echoed in my flustered brain.

It was not my fault that I was born a girl; I had wanted to be a boy named Alessandro, not a girl named Leda.

Because boys pee standing, wherever they want.

Because boys play with robots and video games instead of stupid dolls.

Because boys don't have to wear freaking skirts and dresses.

Because boys climb trees and ride bikes and play soccer.

Because boys grow into firemen and jet pilots, not housewives.

Because Dad wanted a boy.

2

Miracles

On the following day at school, I could not focus, but my musings on monsters, guilt, and revenge were disrupted by Antonietta, our exasperated teacher, who burst out with, "Nico, *enough!*"

Morose, Nico replied, "*What?*"

Veronica the Airhead, sitting beside Nico, whined in a high-pitched voice, "He broke my pencil, *again!*" The jagged edges of a snapped, Rainbow-Brite pencil bled glitter on her desk.

Nico, rolled his eyes. "You and your f—"

Antonietta cut him short, "NICO! I said *enough!*"

Nico kicked his desk in warning, glaring at our normally sweet and imperturbable teacher.

She yelled, red-faced, "All right, this is the last time I move you around. Bother someone again, and you end up in the Principal's office. I'm *not* joking!"

The collective gasp did not affect Nico, who just stared at her, unmoving, arms crossed.

Antonietta ordered, "Veronica, swap with Lee."

I protested, "*What?*"

Antonietta begged, "Lee, *please.*"

Her move was smart because Nico was not going to budge.

Fine.

I turned to Mario, my hated neighbor, and said, "Good riddance, buddy. See you never!"

Mario's gaze widened with horror, since Veronica had a notorious crush on him since first grade. She sprung up gathering her remaining numerous, sparkly pencils with a huge smile.

I sat down at my new desk, brushing off the stupid glitter and glaring at Nico.

He smirked. "Hey, four eyes. It was meant to be."

I answered, "One more word, and I'll have you *eat* my glasses."

He flinched, possibly amused.

Nico and I had been neighbors for a week, his personal record, and despite his best efforts he still failed to intimidate me. Every time he poked me, I poked back, just like I had done with Mario or my sister for years. To my surprise, he reacted with a tacit gratitude.

Meanwhile, First Communion approached, and I still could not imagine confessing about the porn mag.

Stupid Nico!

The music teacher stepped into the classroom, yelling, "Quiet! Did you study for the spring concert?"

"Yes!" the teacher's pets answered.

I hadn't, and my conscience caught fire like hay. "Psst! Nico, did you study?"

Nico shrugged. The teacher raised his hands, and when he gave the signal, we blew madly into our plastic flutes. I certainly blew one note after the other.

The lanky teacher ran his hand through his graying hair. "ENOUGH! ENOUGH! You sound like cats in heat! You will make fools of yourselves and *me* at the concert!"

His gilded paisley vest made a fool of him already, but when his rabid glare scanned the terrified classroom, I wiped the smirk off my face.

He called, "Nico! Out here!"

A deathly silence befell the class, terrorized by our collective ignorance of the *Ode to Joy* and the notion that, as always, Nico was going to be the expiatory goat atoning for everyone's sins. Not like he didn't deserve it.

Used to being singled out, Nico stood up, walked to the front of the class and, without blinking, rose his huge, brown, angry eyes to the teacher.

"Nico, do me a favor, and show this bunch of oafish ignorants how to play the flute."

What?

Nico played the *Ode to Joy* without missing a note. Plastic flutes could apparently produce pleasant sounds.

When the teacher thanked him, Nico walked back to his seat, wordless and emotionless.

As the bell rang, the teacher added, "Next week I'll grade you! You'll be very sorry if you are not prepared."

"Who's the dork now?" I asked, smirking. "How long have you been a music freak, Mozart?"

"Forever," Nico answered, leaving me dumbstruck. "I've played the sax since I was three. This stuff is easy, and by the way, four eyes, Mozart was a pianist."

At recess, The Trio made a mission out of exploring the mysterious (and forbidden!) schoolyard slope that disappeared from view underground, behind a colorful wall painted with murals.

The teachers chatted beside the building on the opposite side of the lawn, so Flavio whispered, "Three, two, one..." and we bolted, disappearing swallowed by the secret ramp.

Exhilarated, bent over double and catching our breath, we found ourselves facing a huge metal gate. Patches of orange paint had escaped the rust, which made a filthy, big padlock look relatively new.

The noise of the kids above us was muffled by the wall and the change in level. We were not supposed to be there: exciting!

I approached the big gate like a ninja, listening for any noise on the other side. Flavio put a hand on the gate, which was resting on a track. He pushed, and it slid as much as the padlocked chain allowed, making such a ruckus that we fled halfway back up the slope, where I ran smack into Nico.

"Chickens!" he taunted us.

I rubbed my neck. "Dude! Are you following us?"

Nico looked away. "Of course not! I always hang out here."

Peo growled, "Yeah, right."

We turned back to the gate, dark and silent, now slightly cracked. Strangely, I got the feeling that rather than light seeping in through the crack, a beam of darkness, dust, and silence spilled out on the cement.

I crawled closer. "I think I might be able to squeeze in."

The other three trotted behind me.

Flavio blurted, "Are you crazy?"

The gate was eerie. The darkness ate the indistinct noise of the children above us. A strange smell exuded from the secret basement, of something old, worn out, and forgotten. I pushed my head through the slit in between the gate's doors, peering inside and holding my breath to keep out the musty smell and evil spirits.

You never know.

Nothing: dark, dark, dark and quiet.

Nico whispered, "Anyone inside?"

I shrugged. "It's dark, but I don't think so."

The light from the opening above and below my head had carved away a slice from the dark floor, revealing the dusty concrete on which my shadow melted into black. Indistinct shapes, maybe old desks or stacked chairs, teased the edge of the darkness.

To show everyone I was no chicken, I stepped inside.

The other three asked in a frenzy, "Are you crazy? What do you see? Anyone there?"

I whispered back, "It's pitch black, guys. It's impossible to see the back wall."

I swallowed, entranced by a very bad feeling, remembering the Nothing that had enveloped Fantasia in *The Neverending Story*, one of my favorite books ever. Maybe this was where the Nothing had fled after Atreyu and Bastian had kicked its butt.

Nico chuckled. "Do you think that there *is* a back wall?"

I answered, "I'm gonna find out!" I took one step forward. They laughed nervously. I took another step into the unknown.

Flavio whispered, alarmed, "Lee, come on! You made your point, come back!"

I took another step with their concern weighing on my back, but distress was evolving into excitement. "What do you see? What's there?"

I couldn't see a thing, so I focused on crawling forward with my arms stretched ahead to feel for possible obstacles, which never came.

The cold engulfing me made me more aware of the sweat beading on my face. My heart was pounding.

Around me, huge piles of unidentified, luckily inanimate objects, were stacked ceiling-high—if there was a ceiling.

On edge, I couldn't shake the feeling that someone lurked in the darkness, ready to pounce as much as I was.

When something cold touched my hand, I immediately screamed, scrambling backwards.

Flavio yelled, "EVERYTHING OKAY?"

Tachycardic, I pondered; nothing was moving. I stepped forward again and reached out with my hands, yell-whispering, "Yeah! I found the back wall!"

"You rock, Lee!"

A sudden thump from my left caused me to scream again. My friends quieted. A noise scuttled closer. My adrenaline, already high, skyrocketed in a hot wave. I bolted back to the door with the scurrying *thing* at my heels to drag me into the Nothing forever.

Panic.

Ragged hot breath scratching my throat.

The light grew bigger. Yet, to my surprise someone was pushing against the gate, trying to get in.

Am I in trouble?

I yelled, "Go, go, GO!"

Nico moved away and I squeezed out of the secret basement, running up the slope where Flavio and Peo had retreated, terrified. I pressed on, dragging my friends up the slope with me.

The harsh daylight, even in the shadow of the wall, hurt my eyes. Fresh air filled my lungs with relief, claiming me back to the kid's screaming above us, life, normalcy, The Trio…and Nico, the only one who had stayed behind to…*help* me?

"Dear Jesus, please let the monster in the basement stay there and not be angry that we bothered it. I promise I'll...*try* to confess about the porn mag before First Communion. Please let me sleep well with no nightmares, and make it sunny tomorrow. Amen."

Sunday was going to be the most important day of my life, at least according to Grandma.

She was all dolled up, no gardening boots or flowery muumuu. Her unruly curls were leaf-free, permed, and dyed into a festive hue of blue. No dirt underlined her many wrinkles. "Aren't you hot in that sweater?" she asked.

I knew that what really upset Grandma was not the sweater, nor my diplomatic, blue, wool pants, but the fact that I was not wearing a ridiculous meringue-dress like the other girls, who crowded the black road in front of the New Church like waterlilies would paint a dark river.

Mom said, "Grandma, forget it, please! She wanted to wear jeans and sneakers."

I muttered, "Do you think that Jesus cares what I wear?"

Mom answered, "*I* do."

"But Mom! You don't even go to church, ever!"

"Exactly! Once that I do, we're not going to look like beggars."

Mom was a petite woman with long, auburn, wavy hair, huge brown eyes, plump lips, and high cheekbones, complemented by coordinated designer outfits and heavy makeup.

I brooded silently in my umbrage while Grandma droned, "Oh, *Leda*! Today is a very important day. You did well taking Mom's advice and dressing, um, *almost* appropriately. First Communion is like a marriage with Jesus!"

Indeed, most of the boys crowding the *piazzetta* outside the church looked like little grooms and the girls like brides. My whole family was gathered for the occasion: Dad, Grandma, my sister Viola, Uncle Bedo—lurking behind Dad like a big bear—and of course Mom, who was still mad because her sense of fashion disagreed with my dignity.

Nico, at ease in jeans and shirt (damn him!), stood by his older brother, no parents. The thug steered clear as I fidgeted with my glasses, pretending to not see him.

We entered the church, and soon, the hubbub subsided; Mass began.

I sat and stood, then sat again at the right cue, wringing my hands, waiting for the miracle of Confession, when the priest would turn into Jesus (not physically, just inside).

If I repented and had the courage, or rather *the humbleness*, to confess my dirtiest deeds, Jesus would forgive them, but what about Don Aldo?

How could an *almost* ten-year-old *girl* confess to watching *pornography*? I imagined wearing a meringue dress and catching fire under Don Aldo's condemning glare.

Would they ship me away?

Gah.

A fattening worm of guilt kept feeding off my shrinking confidence that burning the mag was enough for the sin to be forgiven.

Beside me, Dad's black eyes twinkled under his widow's peak. Intimidating as he could be, he was the one who had been taking me to church every Sunday. This was as meaningful to him as it was to me, and I had no idea how to not disappoint him.

He startled me with a gentle pat on the shoulder. "Lee, it's your turn." He nodded, beaming, toward the confessional of doom.

I swallowed and stood up on shaky legs, sweating.

3

Viola

The open curtain beckoned me to enter the wooden closet they call confessional, and I kneeled, squeezing everything but the porn mag through the cross-shaped grating that separated me from Jesus himself.

As I finally got to meet him in person, I thought how ironic it was that I couldn't even give him a hug.

The priest—and Jesus within him—listened to me nodding, measuring the extent of my shame. After mentioning my occasional swearing.

"Well? Is this all?" Jesus asked.

I knew Jesus was *omniscient*, and I knew what was missing, too, but the words just didn't come out.

To break the guilty silence I added, "Um, I fight with my sister a lot, but she's always wrong."

"That is for God to decide." I thought I heard him chuckle (most definitely not Don Aldo, then) before he added, "For these and *all the sins you might have forgotten*, I forgive you."

My heart exploded with happiness and relief: he had known and had forgiven me! He started the conclusive rite: "Oh dear Jesus of blazing love—"

I continued reciting the magical formula I had learned by heart, "—I wish I had never offended you. Oh my dear, good Jesus, I will never offend you again!"

Jesus, through the lips of the priest, forgave me provided I said ten Hail Mary's and four Lord's Prayers to atone for my sins. I went back to my seat, where Dad greeted me with a huge smile. My soul was bleached clean as the day I was born, the porn mag forgotten.

After reciting the prayers, came First Communion. Don Aldo, the priest in charge most of the time, turned the wine into the blood of Jesus and then the host—a thin, white wafer—into his flesh in front of everyone's eyes.

Yet, grown-ups did not believe in monsters.

Go figure.

To me, the whole thing seemed a little gory. I still didn't understand why we were eating Christ now and every Sunday.

Everyone agreed that crucifying him in the first place had been a mistake. Yet, Dad told me it was not like that, and the host did not really turn into his flesh. Then he said it did, but it did not look nor taste like it, and I should stop asking questions. I should just have faith.

So I did.

A bit intimidated, I lined up with all the other kids in front of the altar, but when Don Aldo, three meters tall on the altar's step, put the host into my mouth I did feel the magic flowing through my veins, and my spirit sang, uplifted to the seventh heaven with Jesus, Mary, Joseph, Grandpa, the angels, and all the clique of the apostles.

Take that, evil monsters!

🍦

To celebrate, Dad drove Mom, Viola, her bestie, and me to Como Lake for dinner. The *lungolago*, the promenade along the lake, was an explosion of azaleas, lavender, and geranium, and yet it was a mere forty-five-minute drive from our more rural reality.

Here, palm trees lined the cobblestone walk that wrapped around the calm dark waters of the lake, pierced by the characteristic posts painted in white and blue swirls.

Scattered on the slopes of dark mountains, pastel-colored houses with white or dark shutters challenged the lush forest around them with their red-tiled roofs.

My sister Viola, a lean girl with big hazel eyes, had pale, delicate features that contrasted with her marked cheekbones and black hair.

She would have been beautiful if huge iron braces didn't fill her mouth to the point of making her upper lip protrude.

As we made our way to the restaurant, she joked around with her best and only friend, Marta. Both were seventeen.

Viola, wary of people and way too smart for the world to understand, had spent her childhood with a marmot-like imaginary friend, mostly torturing me, at least until Marta had come along. They had been inseparable since their first year of middle school. I was quite jealous of their friendship.

Some of my parents' friends waved at us from a bench by the water.

"Wait," I asked. "Weren't we celebrating *my* First Communion?"

The grownups ignored me, greeting their friends and moving to the restaurant's courtyard, in view of the lake.

My excitement over pizza petered out into boredom. For my parents, food was an excuse to talk forever, and their chatter, mixed with the sweet scent of azaleas, lulled me to sleep.

Viola and Marta went for a walk.

The sky glowed red and dimmed before goodbyes were finally uttered.

Dad left money on the table and stood up. "Where is Viola?"

Mom shrugged. "They should be back any minute."

Dad mussed his receding black hair, fuming. "She's late! So much for letting her roam around."

"Come on, Carlo! It's only fifteen minutes—"

Dad interrupted, raising his voice, "*Only*? It's not like we're all here waiting for her!" Which was exactly what we were doing, if you ask me. Dad added, "If she's not in trouble, I'll give her some—"

Viola crossed the *piazza* in front of the restaurant, running in her white Run-Dmc t-shirt, wearing the sleeves of her sweatshirt but not the rest of it, which was stretched over her head. She was shouting, "MOONSHIELD! MOONSHIELD! MOONSHIELD!"

She disappeared at the other end of the *piazza*, laughing like a madwoman.

It was the most un-Viola behavior I had ever seen.

Mom and Dad stared, dumbstruck, in the direction in which Viola had dissolved, then Dad ran after her, growling, "VIOLAAAAAA!"

Mom and I exchanged a concerned glance.

When Dad emerged from the night a few minutes later, he was dragging Viola by one arm. She waved goodbye to some indistinct friends. Behind her, Marta chuckled.

Mom blurted, "What happened?"

"Moonshield?" Viola winked, giggling. Dad jerked her arm.

Viola, smooth black hair now messy, held back giggles, but her effort caused her to blow a raspberry through the braces, making Marta explode in laughter and causing my sister to lose control as well.

With a badly concealed grin, Mom asked, "Did you…drink?"

"A little?" Viola chuckled.

Dad glared at Mom, who was trying to keep a straight face. "Oh, don't *you* start as well!" He continued, "They stole—I said *stole*—the leftovers of a bottle of white wine from a table at a restaurant. I cannot even believe it myself…" He turned to Viola, disappointment in his eyes, "Didn't I teach you anything?"

"Moonshield?" Viola looked at him with regret, pulling the sweatshirt over her head with her free hand, to apparently find shelter from the moonbeams, or Dad's anger, or both.

"You're grounded!" Dad yelled. "Two weeks, at least!"

"Moonshield?" Viola replied.

Viola's punishment meant that torturing me was going to be her only source of entertainment for two weeks.

I was watching cartoons, when she seized the remote and turned to theVideo Music channel.

"Hey!" I yelled.

Dad peeked into the living room ."Don't you two start. Mom and I need to go shopping in Milan—not so fast, Viola, wipe that smirk off your face—we'll drop you two at the movies."

"Can we watch Top Gun?" I asked, eager.

Viola rolled her eyes. *"Top Gun? Really?"*

Dad squinted. "Viola, be grateful I let you out of the house at all. Not to mention we watched *Labyrinth* last month, now it's Lee's turn to pick a movie."

"Well, it's not my fault if the chicken was too scared to watch the goblins take away the young obnoxious sibling."

I protested, repeating Mom's refrain, "I'm not a chicken! I'm just... impressionable." The yellow-eyed demon had not been my first monster sighting.

"*Impressionable...*" she echoed in a dumb voice supposedly imitating mine.

She always made fun of my extensive vocabulary, gained by spending sleepless nights reading. Yet, she wasn't as intimidating with her mirror-lens sunglasses that read "I ♡ Michael Jackson" on the top of her head.

I retorted, "And didn't the old sister save the little brother from the goblins, after all? Dad told me!"

"Yes, because she was a loser. I would have gladly run away with David Bowie."

Dad cut us short. "Enough! We're almost ready—" He stopped mid-sentence, staring at the TV.

Viola nodded toward the screen and said, "Cool, huh?"

Mom's heels clicked down the stairs, awakening Dad from his catatonic state. He belittled, "Not a big deal, it's all a big show. I bet you, it doesn't take much to do that stuff. I could do it any day."

"That *stuff*, Dad, is called *breakdance*, and I would really love to see you try."

Dad replied, "Not now. We have to go. But later, when we come home, I'll give you a little demonstration. Hurry up, now. Actually, go open the garage door." Dad disappeared jingling the car keys in his pocket.

"Odd or even?" Viola asked. "If you lose, *you* go open the garage."

"But you cheat!"

"You can't cheat at odd or even, knucklehead."

Yet, a minute later, I was opening the garage door.

🍦

Back from the movie, I ran out in the backyard, pretending I was a jet pilot. The late May sun was still bright on the grass covered with daisies. I hopped on one of the two swings. The movie had been grand, except for the yucky part where Tom Cruise made out with his blond instructor.

Viola had made fun of me when I had turned away, and then she told Mom, who had bent over double laughing and had started calling me, "Oh, chaste one."

Viola turned around the corner. She picked up one of the silver maple's helicopters, those seeds that fall from the tree spiraling down. "Did you know that these are pistachio nuts?" she asked in her mean voice.

Anxiety, fear, and sadness filled me up like a thick fog. "They're not."

If I didn't believe her, I'd be an idiot. If I believed her, I'd be an idiot. Frustration suffocated me because I was torn between the unwavering need to impress my big sister and her unwillingness to comply.

She peeled off the shrunken shell and fanned the green seed so close to my face that I couldn't have seen it even if I wanted to. "See?"

Then she grabbed a handful of my short hair, taunting, "Eat the pistachio, come on!"

I wriggled out of her grip and half fell out of the swing, running away.

Unfortunately, just like with wild animals, running triggers chasing, and I didn't stand a chance.

Did I? Maybe I could reach the birch tree and climb it before Viola caught me.

I shot toward the tree, but she was already on me, screaming, "Little brat! Where do you think you're going? Come eat your pistachio!"

She threw me on my back, and the impact with the ground winded me. My glasses flew off, so that I scratched blindly, pleading, "Stop it! Let me go!"

"Oh, shut up! Let's make this quick before the goblins get you!"

Viola blocked my wrists one-handed, sticking the seed in my mouth and then choking me to force me to swallow. Terrified, I wheezed for air.

This time, she was going to kill me.

4

Revenge and Other Disasters

Powerless, immobilized, at Viola's mercy, *again*. My throat burned; I could not breathe.

Mom's voice, coming from around the house rescued me. "Hey, you two, what's going on?"

Viola sprang to her feet while I half-chocked on the seed, coughing the darn thing out.

My sister called back, "Hey, Ma, nothing, just playing." She wiped her jeans.

Tears rolled down my face. I yelled, outraged and humiliated, "You, LIAR!"

Strangely, I could see quite well even without glasses but Mom wasn't around yet. Was she coming at all? I took my chances and kicked Viola's shin as hard as I could.

She winced. "You *brat!*" and reacted by slapping my face as hard as *she* could, which was quite hard.

That did it.

Viola had, once again, triggered my transformation into Mr. Hyde. A confusion of red, hot lava, destructive and relentless, was rising inside of me suffocating everything else.

Losing control over my body, which was now launching on my sister, I screamed, "YOU, *STRONZA!*"

I sunk my teeth into her arm, inflicting as much pain as possible, ignoring the blows that kept raining down my face.

Mom bellowed, "STOP! STOP IT!"

She had come after all. Her voice brought me back, causing my anger to pop like a bubble, revealing its contents of shame, rejection, and humiliation. Snot leaked from my nose.

Viola was furious. Cradling the arm I bit, she yelled, "This psycho assaulted me again!"

"It's not true!" I sobbed, face on fire for the slaps. "Viola was forcing me to eat the tree seeds!"

Viola gave me a killer glare that promised revenge. She yelled, "What a liar! Why do you always have to lie?"

"But I didn't lie! Mom, she tried to force the seed into my mouth!"

"ENOUGH!" Mom yelled, paler than I remembered. "Lee, you know about Chernobyl, right? You didn't put the seed into your mouth, did you?" Mom looked at me as if I had just committed murder.

I shook my head, dropping my eyes in resignation to pass once more for a liar because I didn't know if I was more afraid of Viola's glare, Mom's concern, or the Chernobyl nuclear disaster.

Radiations had crawled over from Russia about two years earlier. I picked up my glasses.

Mom sighed and pushed some hair behind her ear with perfect, orange-glazed nails. "I thought so. Out of the grass. Viola, let's go get some ice." She added in a glacial tone, "Lee, go to your room."

Mom walked away leaving a trail of cigarette smoke, her sandal heels clicking on the stones around the house, Viola in tow.

At the last minute, when Mom entered the kitchen, Viola turned to face me. "Are you ever gonna grow up, Lee? All you can do is cry and snitch!" She stuck her tongue out and disappeared after Mom.

I could not win. Even when Viola was wrong, she held the whip hand, and the whip hurt...a lot. She left me with a broken heart and a radioactive taste in my mouth.

My first reaction was to run, disappear, hoping they would grow worried and come looking for me, apologizing and showering me with attention like in *Noisy Nora*, one of the first books I had ever read.

I leaped up to the lower branch of the birch tree and pulled myself up. Determined to leave my broken heart behind, I climbed higher and higher, where the branches became thin, and you had to know where to put your feet.

I did.

At the top, the view was breathtaking. The little red-roofed houses were huddled in the middle of a patchwork of fields, stitched together by rows of cypress, poplar trees and dirt paths. A few *cascine*, the typical farmhouses built around an inner courtyard, guarded the many browns and greens of the countryside, hues changing with the light.

The birds resumed their bickering, and I found my peace again, like I always did, in the rustling of the leaves, while the sky ripened gold and pink.

How many others had enjoyed such a spectacular view?

Lonely was safer, sometimes.

For some reason, I thought of Nico.

Then I promised myself that I would grow up and never, ever cry again.

My wounds grew distant, small, down there where Viola was certainly looking for me, worried sick, and torn by guilt. Dusk brought a certain chill with it. I was getting hungry, too.

I climbed down.

The house was quiet.

On the following Monday, Antonietta did not come to school. Maybe she was sick.

The sub teacher looked too young. The more she screamed, slamming her hand on the teacher's desk, the more it was obvious she had no control over the situation. "QUIET! SILENCE, NOW!"

Everyone ignored her. We were old enough to know that she couldn't hurt us. At most she could write a note to someone's parents, but in that case her victim would have been Nico, for sure. He was running down the hallway chasing after Laura the Gorgeous, from the neighboring classroom, to slap her butt, disregarding the escalating, dire cries of the sub.

Accustomed to the sweetness of Antonietta, we somewhat behaved not to disappoint her, but in front of the screeching woman, we had nothing to lose, nothing to prove.

Personally, I was aiming paper balls at Peo and Flavio in a war that, as much as chaotic at least was silent. In the general pandemonium, the sub's screams stopped; she had collapsed in the chair, face buried in her hands.

Apparently you didn't have to be a kid to feel helpless and hopeless.

Two paper balls hit my temple in rapid succession. I motioned toward the undone teacher. Flavio clenched his teeth, bending his lips downward.

"Enough of this mess!" I yelled, just as Nico fell into his chair (Laura's class had begun as well).

The serendipitous conjunction between my unusual screaming and Nico's appearance froze the class into stillness.

The adult mind works in unpredictable ways.

When the sub's hands slid off her face, two icy eyes, everything but grateful, scanned the classroom.

Her gaze stuck on me.

Her pupils were beads of hate while, with a poisonous voice, she hissed, "Shame on you! *Mess*? Who raised you, savages? What is the proper term to use in this context?"

The unexpected turn of events threw me off and, despite my vocabulary prowess, the challenge remained suspended between her anger and my disbelief.

"Um...Bedlam?" I mumbled.

"Bedlam is an asylum for the insane, where you all belong. The correct word is chaos, confusion. Thank you for the demonstration of ignorance."

Mario whispered, from his desk beside Veronica the Airhead, "Ignorant!"

Everyone heard him, but the witchy, ungrateful sub pretended not to.

Some people are born into misery and in misery will die. Not only they are not able to help themselves but if someone offers them a hand, instead of climbing out of the mud, they drag their victim into their filth with a grin. A lesson I had not yet learned.

At recess I stared out of the hallway window. The silvery back of the poplar's leaves on the big hill beyond the courtyard flapped in the wind against the sky, stormy like my mood. The green shoots of the willow tree and the yellow blossoms of the forsythia, bright against clouds of lead, fought against the wind.

"Should we key the *stronza*'s car?" Nico's low voice startled me, and I gasped.

I hadn't noticed him at my side, hands in his pockets just like me, black hair covering one eye, while the other, lively as ever, was fixed on the window, either looking outside or at my reflection in the glass.

Flavio and Peo were my sunshine friends, normal and happy. Nico was dark, sad, and angry, fearing nothing and caring for even less. He was Mr. Hyde's buddy; bonding with a dark side I was ashamed to even acknowledge.

I sought his eye in the window's reflection. The sweet prospect of revenge transformed my humiliation into the power to punish, to exact some justice for once.

...but that was *wrong*, right?

"We don't even know what she drives," I said.

Flavio, behind us, chimed into the conversation, "Peo saw her from the window, dropping some books in an old blue *Lancia* car in the parking lot."

Nico and I turned to find Flavio and Peo, who nodded to confirm.

"And if we get caught?" I asked.

"Suspension, no doubt." Nico shrugged as if it was no big deal.

"We have to be smart, then," I said, hatching a plan.

When school let up, Flavio, Peo, Nico, and I ran out to set our plan in motion. We weren't guilty yet, but all four of us were edgy, acting way too casual amidst the hordes of parents and pupils leaving the grounds.

When most bikes, cars, buses, and scooters faded into the distance, we traced back toward the parking lot with circumspection.

"What are you doing?" Mario asked, walking out from behind a bush.

I exclaimed, "You've got to be kidding me! Mario, mind your own —" but Nico stepped defensively between us, and dragging, maybe on purpose, his Sicilian accent, he growled, "You've gotta get out of my way, ah?"

The two squared off for a few seconds. Mario leaned back but stood his ground. "Easy, huh? Four against one!"

Nico hissed, "Why, do you think I need help, ah?" He stepped closer.

Mario faltered but didn't retreat. Nico started forward as if to strike him with a backhand, finally causing him to gasp and run for his life without looking back.

Nico lowered his hand. "Why is he always around?"

I shrugged.

The blue *Lancia* car was still in the parking lot. Some teachers stayed the afternoon with the few *after-school* kids who had both parents working, but we had no idea if the sub was one of them, so we tried to hurry.

Peo approached the car and looked through the window, where the books were in plain sight on the front seat. "This is it."

"Okay then." I summarized our plan, "I'll be on the lookout. If someone comes our way I'll clap my hands and run toward you. We hop on the bikes and disappear through the fields where cars cannot follow. Understood?"

Nico rolled his eyes."Miii, Lee, can't you learn to whistle already?"

"Nico, I *can't*. Get over it, I'll clap and that's that."

I crouched behind a blue Panda, just like Mom's, staring at the school's entrance, while Flavio, Peo, and Nico pissed with gusto all over the *Lancia*.

And then the school door cracked open.

I forgot to clap my hands and ran, yelling, "GO GO GOOOOOOO!"

Nico, Peo, and Flavio zipped up their jeans, and in a moment we were flying through the fields. Nobody looked back to see if it was the evil sub leaving the school, if someone followed or recognized us. We stopped only at the church, past the very much shrunk big puddle, collapsing on the grass by the poplar tree, laughing like mad kids.

Nico caught his breath. "We should have keyed it. She might not even notice we blessed the old crock."

"Yeah, right! It's gonna stink like hell!" Flavio laughed and Peo grinned.

The blue sky peeked through the foliage. "Look!" I pointed up. "There's something up there!"

Everyone looked up, and Flavio squinted. "Some kind of platform. Maybe a tree house?"

"The last one's a *picio!*" Nico screamed pouncing up the trunk like a leopard. I was surprised at how quickly he had picked up the northern slang.

In spite of Nico's head start, I gained the lead. The others followed in a whirlwind of comments, laughter, frights, a couple of blasphemies on Nico's part, always segued by everyone's indignant remarks. A few broken branches later, we were at the top, safe and sound, sitting on the platform.

Sitting on the few remaining planks that maybe once were a treehouse, Flavio said, "We found a base!"

Flocks of swallows bathed in the early summer above the countryside, which was plowed in elegant patterns of brown and green. The little church hung in the middle of the field. I half expected to see the feet of the Wicked Witch of the East sticking out from it. Even if the view did not match the one at the top of the birch tree where I promised myself I'd never cry again, now I had my friends to share it with and that made it so much better.

Nico turned to me and *smiled*, startling the shit out of me.

Weren't there four A-Team members? Nico fitted perfectly the role of Faceman, the handsome bad boy.

"What's there?" Flavio asked, pointing at some grassy knolls that rose hap hazardously in the middle of the otherwise flat and square fields.

Tombs? Treasure? Tectonic plaques clashing?

We climbed down the poplar tree and, below the shrubs, discovered a thin line of compact, dry mud that ran toward the odd hills.

The mounds were covered with tall grasses and weeds, except for a peculiar baldness, producing the ridiculous effect of an inverse Mohawk.

"I heard about this!" Flavio, who lived close by, declared. "These must be *the hillocks*! They're made with the debris leftover from the construction of the new church. My brothers come here with their motorbikes to jump and stuff! They talk about it all the time."

We challenged each other on our bikes, up and down slopes so steep that we had to drag ourselves up on foot to then rush down headlong. Two knolls were particularly huge, towering against the deep blue sky.

Nico dared us, "Wanna see who makes the whole circuit without ever stopping?"

This implied enough speed to crest the two bigger hills and yet, somehow, managing enough control to keep to the narrow trail at the curves. The consent was enthusiastic, and I, Howling-Mad Murdock, was drafted for the first trial. I pumped on the pedals with all my might, gaining speed, avoiding rocks and the occasional hole as the first mother-hill approached full of threat.

The others cheered, "Come on, Lee! Kick its butt! You can do it! GO! GO! GO!"

I had no doubt I could make it. However, the closer I got to the first huge hill, the more it grew, swallowing me in its ominous shadow. The slope challenged my ascent and the pedals became cement-like as the giant mountain laughed at little old me falling backward from my bike.

The loud teasing of my friends, running toward me to assess the damage, hurt more than my leg. I swallowed my tears. For the second time in a few days, the world was in perfect focus, even if my glasses had fallen off.

"All right," Peo cut us short, preparing to go next.

Flavio shook his head. "You're out of your mind, guys!"

Nico said, "Come on Peo! Go for it! We want more blood!"

My leg indeed was scratched and bled a little. Straightening the handle of my bike I followed the others to the point where the trail from the poplar tree joined the circuit, but Peo continued all the way to the base.

He climbed his bike, the air tensing. The silence was torn only occasionally by the call of a bird, a fly, or leaves rustling in the breeze. Peo shot forward, standing on his pedals, pushing the bike left and right with a murderous determination in his eyes.

"He's gonna kill himself," Nico whispered, for once without any mockery.

Peo tore by at the speed of light, the fierceness of Francesco Moser plastered on his face, raising a cloud of dust.

"Slow down!" I yelled.

He did not relent, already facing off the first big hill, climbing it like a rocket but slowing down fast, fighting against the pedals. The effort twisted his face into a grimace of pain.

"He's going to fall," Flavio muttered.

Stuck in a standstill with his front wheel at the top of the hill, Peo balanced precariously, but for how long? He screamed like McEnroe in a last supreme effort, boosting up his bike to clear the hill.

What power, what determination, what a hero! All his physical training for basketball had paid off.

"PEOOOO YOU ARE AWESOME!" we all screamed.

But the challenge was not over. Peo continued pedaling like crazy to conquer the second big hill and finish the circuit. Unfortunately he did not realize that the descent from the first one was as steep as the ascent and that the second hill was not quite as tall. In fact, it barely slowed him down at all.

Everything happened in an instant. Peo reached the top of the second hill, triumph on his face quickly replaced by dread as he took off into the air, just like the kid in the movie E.T. the extraterrestrial, high, very high, but unfortunately with no alien in his basket to keep him afloat.

5

Bam! Bam!

The serenity of the fields was torn by Peo's cry, louder and louder with his approach, still in flight, to our position. Flavio, Nico, and I stared, paralyzed, powerless, for a very long instant.

CRASH!

Nico screamed screamed a profanity as we ran toward the accident; Peo was scratched, sore, and scared out of his mind but in one piece. His bike...not so much. It was split in two, the front wheel bent out of shape.

I pretended not to see the tears brimming in Peo's eyes, while Flavio gave him huge pats on the back, assessing the status of his aching bones.

Our voices all mixed together:

"Miii you were going at least *thirty*, no *forty* kilometers per hour!"

"You must have been at least two meters, no, *three meters* in the air!"

"Are you crazy? At least ten."

"But how do the guys with the motorbikes do it?"

"Better shock absorbers," Nico explained.

We backtracked to the poplar tree and then the church, pushing the bikes by hand because Peo was dragging the useless carcass of his ride.

He wondered, "What am I gonna say to Mom? She'll kill me."

The scenario was possible. Peo's Mom was the parents' representative at school: a strong, independent woman, weird enough to keep her last names after getting married and to have a job despite two kids.

Flavio shrugged. "Tell her the truth. You fell, it's not your fault."

"Yeah, right..."

We all exchanged a somber look behind Peo's curved back.

🍦

A few hours later, right before dinner, Mom yelled from the kitchen, "COME SET THE TAAABLEEE!"

I switched off the TV only when I heard Viola stomping down the stairs with Marta.

My sister commented, "Sheesh, Lee, it's not like you're gonna die if you start setting the table one minute before me."

"Right."

Viola had a knack for lingering upstairs until the job was done. We got in the kitchen where Mom, instead of setting out the usual milk and cookies that she called dinner, was actually pan-frying steaks. A bowl of tomatoes drowned in mayo was already on the table.

"Wow," I let out, while Viola and Marta sucked in some air, surprised.

"About time," Mom said, curtly. "The dishwater needs unloading, too."

Huffs and eyeballs all around as I grabbed the silverware and Viola pulled out the dishes.

Mom asked, "So, Marta, what did you two do last night?"

"Er..." Marta replied, her big nose peeking out of her big black curls.

"Nothing," Viola mumbled, sullen as usual.

Mom forced a smile. "And who did you do *nothing* with?"

"The usual crowd, Mom." Viola huffed, setting the tablecloth. I gathered the silverware from the dishwasher.

"Marta, were you there, too?" Mom insisted.

"Yes, ma'am," Marta answered setting down the plates.

"And *where* did you go?"

"Mom *enough*! Some bar...I don't remember!" The drinking age in Italy was sixteen, not like anyone ever bothered to check. "Wait a second. I'm a genius!" Staring at the silverware I was sorting out, my sister elaborated, "If when we put the cutlery in the dishwasher we divide it by type, it would be much quicker to sort it out, wouldn't it?"

Marta's tight black curls bounced all-over her face. "Brilliant, Basty!"

Basty was the mysterious, endearing nickname my sister and Marta reserved for each other.

"But," I started without knowing how to discredit her yet, "they would get stuck into each other and not get cleaned properly," I concluded with little conviction, just out of spite.

Instead of starting an argument, Viola's shoulders slumped. "I guess."

High school had been awful to Viola. She had wanted to attend art high school with Marta, but Dad had forbidden it. Apparently, art was only a hobby and didn't pay the bills. Not like Mom worked, anyway.

Mom called, "CARLOOOOOOOOO! DINNER'S READYYYY!"

After a minute of silence, Dad's chair screeched in his home office announcing his imminent arrival. "It smells good," he said. "Are those *steaks*?"

Mom rolled her eyes. "It's not like I never cook, you know?"

We all knew better than to reply. We sat at the table, and at the collective *"Buon appetito!"* we dug into our food, passing around the tomatoes and bread.

I was babbling about our adventure at the hillock when Viola interrupted me with, "I have great news!" Mom's and Dad's faces wrinkled with concern. Marta kept chewing on her steak. "I became so good at it that they decided to move my radio show on Sunday morning, from nine to eleven!"

Followed an explosion of relief, congratulations, and felicitations.

Viola had become a DJ at Radio City Arese, which was run by the church, a few months earlier. Dad had agreed to Viola's DJ career only because she would have seen a lot of priest.

Dad shrugged. "Well, how hard can it be? It's not like you're playing the instruments…"

Viola scowled. "Are you kidding me? I have a cassette player with the ads and two record players for the LPs, and I have to drop the stylus not at the beginning of the vinyl, like I normally would at home, but right at the point where the music starts—"

Wow. "And how can you tell where that is?" I asked.

"I *can't*. And I have to do that while I'm talking, and the music from the two LPs has to overlap, without ever stopping."

Dad sighed. "Fine. But you'll better improve your grades or you'll have to quit. Understood?"

Mom lit up a cigarette. Dad waved the smoke off his face and added, "You know, when I was young I was quite musical myself. I used to play guitar, and I even learned to play the trumpet when I was in the army." Like any able man, Dad had served one year, right out of school.

Mom rolled her eyes, puffing on her cigarette, but Viola asked, "Really, Dad? Were you any good?"

"I was all right," Dad reminisced, eyes aglow with memories despite the cigarette smoke.

"As good as with breakdance?"

We all laughed, but Dad protested, "Make fun of me all you want! One day I'll show you who can breakdance!" He retreated to his studio, grumbling.

Viola and I were clearing the table when Dad peeked back into the kitchen. "Lee, a word with you, when you're done."

"*Me?*" But he was already gone.

"Uh-oh. Are you in trouble?" Marta asked.

"I don't think so."

Mom chimed in, "Maybe he just wants to show you something."

Yeah, right. "Speaking of seeing things...Mom, can we schedule a checkup with the eye doctor?" She frowned and I beamed at her. "I don't think I need glasses anymore."

Mom scoffed. "I will, honey, but I've been wearing mine all my life. Don't get your hopes too high."

I finished clearing the table and rushed to Dad's home office in a mix of excitement and fear, knocking timidly on the doorjamb, then peering inside.

"Come in."

I stepped in his lair. Dad was an engineer by day, but he spent all of his free time painting, which made his recommendations for Viola's education a lot more heartfelt.

He spoke without lifting his eyes from the canvas, "Lee, I know you think that nothing can ever happen to you. At your age I thought so, too."

I was blown away because that was *exactly* what I thought. Jesus kept an eye on me; I *was* special. It moved me that Dad bothered to know what I thought.

He continued, "When I was eighteen I lived in Milan. I was walking down the street when I saw this truck lurch as if it had hit a rock or an open manhole. BAM! BAM!" He paused, looking at me, and then carried on, "It was no rock. It was a child, more or less your age. It was a horrible accident. There was nothing to do."

He looked at my vacant, stricken expression. "I will never, ever forget that awful scene, and the sound...BAM! BAM! I am sure the kid thought nothing was ever gonna happen to him as well, and yet..." Dad grew quiet for a moment, his words sinking in.

I asked, "Why would God let something like that happen?"

Dad scoffed. "Do you know the saying: *help yourself and God will help you*? Jesus is busy. He cannot fix every distraction of every human being on Earth. Plus, didn't you learn about free will in Catechism?"

I shook my head. I was learning more in this ten-minute conversation with Dad than I had in years of Catechism.

He continued, "Free will means that God granted us the freedom to make our own choices, good or bad. That comes with a price though. We have to assume responsibility for the consequences."

I looked at Dad, wide-eyed.

He added, "Be careful with your friends. We all can die. Peo was lucky, but it could have ended very differently. Don't push *your* luck. Understood?"

I nodded slowly; Peo could have died, and apparently I was mortal too.

"Scram now," he concluded with some warmth in his voice.

I hurried out. My swagger was gone, but Dad's concern was wrapped around my heart, warming it like only Hairry the magical blankie could have.

A few days later, on a sunny afternoon, I met with Flavio, Peo, and Nico after school and we set out to climb the highest tree that we could find in Arese. The poplar tree in my front yard was unapproachable, the lower branches far too high, the trunk too wide, so Flavio suggested some tall pines at the big hill, not far from school.

Indeed, a few majestic pines grew on the hillside facing the fields. Each one of us climbed a different one.

Nico yelled, "The last one's a *picio!*"

"That's getting old, Nico!" I teased.

The pine trees were easy to climb because of their many thick branches. Sure enough Flavio, who was not the most skilled climber but was definitely the tallest, soon announced, "*First!*"

I got second place, and Peo qualified third. The view was breathtaking. The fields, the hillocks, and the school seemed so tiny in the blazing spring light.

Nico struggled in the ascent, and Flavio taunted, "Guess who's a *picio* after all?"

Profanities raised from the thick boughs of his tree. Soon our jokes became advice, but just when he was almost at the top, the unthinkable happened; Nico slipped.

His eyes went wide, arms flailing. As I watched him fall backward, Nico screamed.

Then we only heard the sound of the branches slamming against his back while he dropped to the ground.

BAM! BAM!

He lay face up, still.

My heart stopped.

Flavio's voice, low and uncertain, broke the silence. "Nico? Yo, are you okay?"

No answer. Nico didn't move.

Adrenaline filled me with heat up to my ears, suspending me in a loud, roaring silence, like the sea's. Its waves crashed on the inside of my forehead, oozing redness and sweat, leaving my head utterly empty.

We stared at the body that used to be Nico's, and the obvious escaped my lips: "Oh my God; Nico's dead."

The words echoed in my empty head, pushing tears to well up. Stuck in a limbo of disbelief, I finally recovered from my trance. "No, no, no, no," I muttered, rushing down the tree, plummeting from branch to branch. Flavio and Peo descended behind me. Just a few weeks ago I had hated Nico! So many things had changed and now...BAM BAM!

When I reached him, Nico was still on his back, unmoving, eyes closed. I didn't know what to do because if he were dead for real I couldn't help him, but if he had broken his back I should not move him, they taught us so in school. So, I remained transfixed, brain numb, heart aching, despite the reeling emotions wreaking me.

Someone kept repeating, louder and louder, "Nico? Nico? NICO?" Then I realized it was me. My voice became a scream, hoping to reach him wherever he was to bring him back.

Nothing.

BAM BAM! Hadn't Dad warned me?

6

Starry

I leaned over Nico's body, barely touching his face, his arm. Of course he was still warm, and everything seemed normal. If only he had been sleeping! If only we had never climbed the stupid pine trees! I wanted to go back in time and change this ridiculous moment that should have never happened.

After what seemed like an eternity, someone touched my arm. "Lee?"

I turned, tears streaming down my cheeks. Peo and Flavio had reached me, as horrified as I was.

"Is he okay?" Flavio mumbled.

"He's not moving," was all I could say, choking on the words.

Peo suggested, "Maybe he's just passed out. Is he breathing?"

We all leaned over to check, when Nico jumped up screaming, "AAAAAAAAAAAAHHH! *Coglioni*, I *so* fooled you!" All three of us fell hard on our butts. Nico exclaimed, "Lee, are you *crying*? What a *wuss*!"

I didn't know which was stronger, my desire to hug him or to punch him in the face. Peo beat me to it. He leaped forward tackling Nico to the ground.

"Easy, *easy*! I did just fall out of a tree, ya' know? I'm hurting!"

Peo thundered, "Not enough!"

They rolled to the foot of the hill, Peo punching him hard, Nico yelling, "Ow, ow, ow!"

I wiped my face, grinning, and felt Flavio's hand on my shoulder. I turned to find my relief mirrored in his eyes, and we both laughed.

A few minutes later, all four of us lay on the grass watching the clouds evolve in the blue sky, exhausted and happy to be alive, four friends for life, even if Nico was a definitely a *picio*.

Once back home, I barged into the house and into the kitchen, where Viola was saying, "Slimy creep!" Her brow crumpled in disapproval, and her mouth settled in a thin line."Who would have expected *that* from a *priest*?"

Mom replied, "I would have."

"Hi!" I said.

Mom greeted me with a hug, while Viola, ignoring me, added, "Of course you would have expected it, you must have smelled it with that nose of yours!"

Mom's nose wasn't *that* big, but she was so sensitive to any comment about her appearance that we mocked her on a regular basis.

Dad entered the kitchen taking everyone by surprise."What behavior?" he asked. "Which priest?"

Viola froze in place, allowing Mom to reach her and administer one of her much-feared side pinches in retribution for the nose joke.

"*Ouch*! Ah, hello Dad…no, nothing really," Viola stuttered, but since Dad kept staring, she confessed, "Uh, Don Aldo…he kind of… felt my butt."

"*Nonsense*!" Dad laughed. "I'm sure it was just a good-natured gesture of affection." He poured himself a glass of soda. "He's a priest and you're a child, how can you even think that way?"

He disappeared again into his studio, while Mom and Viola exchanged a meaningful look.

"Anyway," Mom resumed the conversation. "Going out tonight?"

"Yeah," Viola answered. "The usual," she added before Mom could ask.

Mom sighed and sagged in her chair.

"Dear Jesus, Please, keep in check that priest of yours. I don't like him getting fresh with my sister. And have her become a famous DJ, so she doesn't need to study math anymore. Thank you so much for the base up in the poplar tree, it's *awesome*, and thanks for keeping Nico alive because as of now he would definitely go to hell."

I paused, considering how I had always asked God for a sunny day and had taken completely for granted my life. "Thanks for keeping me alive as well. And please, let me sleep well with no nightmares, and make it sunny tomorrow. Amen."

On the following day, Viola was sent home from school. It was a first. Mom had tried to figure out what had happened beyond what the principal had relayed, but once again, Viola had put up a wall. Thank goodness Dad was at work.

After a very silent lunch, Viola, morose, reached me in the backyard.

"That's not how you walk, kiddo," she said. "You've gotta look tough if you don't want to be bullied."

"But I don't—"

"Shush. Quiet and watch." She walked toward me, hands in the pockets of her brand new, black leather jacket, staring me in the eye.

"A real punk never yields," she declared. Boots and skintight, gray jeans that she and Marta had filled with drawings and quotes completed her outfit. She had finally removed her braces for good.

I asked, "But what if you run into someone who doesn't yield either?"

"You slam into them without hesitation."

She demonstrated by hitting me with her shoulder and sending me tumbling into the grass.

Mom, who was watering the flowers outside the kitchen, interjected, "A real punk will end up serving *paninari* at Burghy if she gets suspended."

Viola hated *paninari*, loosely translated as burger-eaters, the name of the latest fad in Italian youth trends. They were mostly teenagers dressed in designer clothing gathering at Burghy joints: a hamburger chain modeled after the American ones.

Viola retorted, "Ma, it wasn't my fault! That *stronza* of Monica was looking for trouble."

Mom replied, "Viola, *language!*" Then she added, "And how was it Monica's fault? She didn't *yield*, maybe?"

Viola, furious at Mom's comment, said, "If you really want to know, that...*idiot* suggested I've been sleeping with the psych professor, and that's why I do so well!" Tears welled up in Viola's eyes who did not excel in many subjects.

"What did you just say?" Mom replied, dumbstruck. "Is she out of her mind? Come here."

Viola did not get any closer to Mom, reminding her that physical contact was not a good strategy with my teenage sister.

Mom continued to water the plants as if she hadn't noticed Viola's rejection and added, "What a bunch of rubbish, right?" Her pitch was a little too high.

"Of course!" Viola replied. "My grades are deserved! Why can't anyone believe that I'm actually *good* at something?"

"Of course you are, honey!"

Viola made a gagging face, as always when someone called her anything endearing.

Mom carried on, "You're just girls, and I can't fathom how this Monica even thought about these...*things*. She sure *is* an idiot, like you said, but why are you so angry, then? Who cares about what *she* says?"

At the comment *you're only girls* Viola had turned her back to Mom to walk away, but now she stopped.

She said, "Well, just because I hate math it doesn't mean that I'm dumb."

"No one thinks you are dumb, honey."

"Enough with the *honey*, it makes me want to vomit!" Viola snapped.

Mom continued her thread of thought, unfazed, "And how did Monica's pearls end up on the bathroom floor?"

"Because she's a moron, I told you! *She* has a crush on the teacher! I was in the bathroom, um, washing my hands. She came in with two friends backing her up and messed with me. I totally ignored her, ready to walk away. The bitch—ahem" She rolled her eyes. "Anyway, she got so frustrated that she pushed me. Can you believe her? *She* pushed *me*. I lost it and pushed her back but caught her pearls. Her necklace broke and she had a full meltdown, hysteria and all. And who ends up sent home? *Me*, of course! *So* unfair!"

Mom replied, "True, but think about it, is she worth being sent home for? Maybe suspended the next time? With your grades, you would have to repeat the year for sure. Next time pay her no mind. She's just jealous. Walk away."

"You think she's *jealous*?" Viola seemed surprised and almost hopeful.

"I'm certain," Mom answered.

After a little pause, Viola added, "Who the hell would wear pearls to go to school anyway?"

Mom sighed. "Not you, for sure."

She had always wanted a princess for a daughter and instead she had ended up with a punk and a tomboy. Tough luck.

Viola retorted, "Yo, *Starry*, stop complaining. It could've been a lot worse."

Mom asked surprised, "Starry? Starry who? Where did that come from?"

Viola giggled. "Haven't you read *A Clockwork Orange*?"

"A long time ago." There weren't too many books Mom hadn't read.

"Well," Viola explained, "remember how the characters in the book speak Nadsat, that weird slang? 'Starry' is how they call old fogies like you, *Starry*." She laughed at her own joke. Starry didn't comment. She simply moved over the garden hose, drenching her irreverent punk daughter.

When I came home for dinner on the next day I heard, right from the foyer, Starry, AKA Mom, knocking insistently at Viola's door.

Starry begged, "Viola, *please*! Open the door, already!" Then, with more authority: "Viola! Enough is enough! Open the door, *now*!"

I ran upstairs skipping the steps two at a time. "Starry, what's wrong?" Probably *because* of Mom's initial resistance the nickname had stuck.

Starry sagged back from the door sighing, fist still hanging in the air. "Nothing. Go to your room."

43

A couple of hours later, Starry called me from downstairs, "LEEEEEEE! It's time to set the table!"

When I got to the kitchen, Starry was by herself. I asked, "Ah, shall I call Viola?"

"Good luck."

Instead of shouting, as I would have normally done, I climbed back up the stairs. I knocked on Viola's door with all the kindness I could muster. "Viola?" Just like I expected, no one answered.

I remained awkwardly still in front of her shut door, uncertain. Then I leaned closer and muttered, "Viola, I don't know what happened, but I'm sorry. I'll set the table tonight. Don't worry about it."

I walked away, but the key clicked, so I turned back. Viola's door was ajar, and her puffy eyes stared at me askance from the narrow opening. I raised my hands, but she didn't yell nor shut the door.

My big sister sniffled. "You really don't know what happened?" I shook my head, bewildered. She actually *meant* to speak to me. "Mom came into my room while I was at school, and searched for my secret diary."

"You have a secret diary?"

"I *did*. She found it."

"She didn't read it, did she?" Viola, who would have normally rolled her eyes, just nodded emanating sadness. "*Why?*" I asked.

Starry would have never done such a thing, but I knew better than contradicting Viola.

She shrugged, while her lower lip tensed with a new harshness. Not like she smiled a lot, but this was different.

"I'm not having dinner tonight," she said. "If you have a diary, burn it." Her door slammed shut again, sealing Viola's wrath within.

I stared at the white, wooden door with the sticker that read *Viola's room*, cheerful with mushrooms and squirrels. Her sadness hit me, and I thanked the heavens that I had never thought about having a secret diary.

How serious was the offense, if what Viola said was true? Our parents had given her the diary, the room she was locked in, and even her life. Yet, if the people who birthed you couldn't trust you, then no one could, and you could trust no one back.

When I got back to the kitchen, Starry was adding to the pasta some pre-made sauce she had bought at the store.

"Nothing?" she asked, sadly.

I shook my head, studying her pale, worried face behind the heavy makeup.

She added, "Did you at least hear something? Is she awake?"

I nodded. There must have been either a misunderstanding or a very good reason for Mom to violate my sister's privacy.

I asked, "Why did you read her diary?"

"She talked to *you*?" Starry blurted, dropping the spoon into the pasta bowl.

"Why wouldn't she? For once, I didn't do a thing."

Starry's face, clouded with anger and regret, resembled Viola's, as she justified herself. "She forced me to! She's out almost every night and there's no way of knowing where she goes, with whom, or what she does. I ask her where she's been and she says she doesn't remember. *She doesn't remember!* Can you believe her? She's so unhappy, but she doesn't say a word. She locks herself up in her room, and spends hours on the phone talking, with *Marta*, she says, who knows."

"Yes, but that's *her* choice."

"*Fine*, but I'm her mother, right? And what do you know anyway, you're just nine!"

"Almost *ten*."

"Well, smarty pants, as it turns out, I was very right to get worried! Did you know that she *smokes*? That's what she was doing in the bathroom at school when she had the fallout with the pearl string classmate." Mom scoffed. "And this is just the tip of the iceberg. And *she* dares not talk to *me*. *I* should be the one not talking to *her*. I swear she's grounded for a month! Forget the radio show!"

"NO WAY! You're gonna have her quit the show? And what about her school trip to Vienna? And not to be polemic, but you're quite the smoker yourself, aren't you?"

"I'm a grown-up!"

"How old were you when you started?"

"This conversation is over."

I knew she had been sixteen. Starry knew it too.

The Quartet

A few days later, when I ran back inside from the garden for dinner, the classic *hiiiiii* got stuck in my throat, as I heard arguing from the kitchen.

Mom was saying, "Carlo the kids are growing up. I gotta do something or I'll lose my mind!"

Dad taunted, "Oh yeah? I would love to have your options! Nails or coffee? Maybe some shopping?"

"Well, *you* try, then! I'm done staying at home!"

"But back to school at your age, Silvia? Don't be ridiculous!"

"I'm only thirty-eight!"

Normally, my parents did not talk. Dad came home from work at 5 p.m. and Mom made sure his drink of *Aperol* on ice was ready in a glass rimmed with sugar and garnished with a slice of orange, like in the ads. Dad would seize his *aperitivo*, undo his tie's knot and retreat into his studio to paint watercolors till dinner.

I cautiously stepped into the kitchen. "Hello?"

They froze in place.

Dad barked, "Lee, what are you doing here? Can't you see we're talking?"

Rather than remind him I lived at the house, I opted for an appalled silence.

Starry said, "Come on, Carlo, we'll talk later. Let's toast some bread fro dinner or something."

When called, Viola came to set the table, but that didn't ease the tension since she hadn't talked to Starry in days, since the diary incident. Thankfully, her long-awaited school trip to Vienna had not been pulled from the table.

The punishment for whatever Starry had found in Viola's diary had been limited to being grounded for one week, likely because Starry didn't have the courage to share her discoveries with Dad, and she didn't want to pique his curiosity with out-of-the-ordinary extreme measures. The diary's contents, paradoxically, remained a secret between Starry and Viola who, for the whole week, left the house only for school. She had to cancel her show. She told the radio staff that she was going to be away for her school trip, but it didn't look like she was going to forgive Mom anytime soon.

🍦

Viola had been in Vienna for three days, when dinner was interrupted by a phone call. Starry trotted to the entrance to answer.

"Hello? Yes, speaking. Who is this? PROF. POLENGHI? VIOLA? WHAT?"

Dad and I dropped our forks and ran to the foyer, where Mom was staring at the phone's base, gripping the handle and twisting the cord, wide-eyed. "Is she okay? But...*how*? I understand...Thank goodness! I'm so sorry. True. Of course. Thank you very much. See you tomorrow."

She hung up, white as a sheet, and said right away, "She's fine! Everything's fine!"

Her shoulders slumped as she exhaled. Then she lit a cigarette. We followed her back to the kitchen, where she crumbled on her chair, pushed away her half-eaten sandwich, and massaged her temples before adding, "They went to the Prater, as planned—"

I interrupted, "What's the Prater?"

"A huge amusement park in Vienna." I burned with envy, while Mom continued, "Viola went on the pirates' ship with her classmates —"

I asked, "What do you mean *the pirates' ship*?"

"Leda, stop interrupting for goodness sake! Viola was on a ride and passed out, but it's nothing!" She rushed to the end of the sentence, looking at our horrified faces. "They did the full blood work and she was absolutely clean—no drugs, *of course.*" She looked at Dad, who still seemed terrified. "And she's not pregnant either. Long story short: it's not her fault! Apparently, something's wrong with her inner ear, nothing serious. The doctor said she has to avoid extreme rides."

Dad sucked in a breath of relief.

I had barely understood a few words."What inner ear?"

Dad rolled his eyes. "Gee, Silvia, could you not smoke at the table?" Mom rolled her eyes in turn and left the kitchen. Dad turned to me. "The inner ear has to do with balance."

We finished the rest of our dinner in an unnatural silence.

🍦

On the following day, my anxiety eased as soon as I heard the front door opening and Viola's voice pervading the foyer, "...and the *Sachertorte!* I bought a little one for you guys to try!" She babbled about the trip for a while.

When Starry went upstairs to change into sweats, I asked Viola, "Did you forgive her for the diary?"

Her face turned to stone and I regretted my question. "I never will, and you'd better mind your own business."

Beyond the sting, I felt reassured that even if the bitterness of betrayal was going to stain Viola's rational thoughts for a long time, routine and affection buried it quite deep into her heart, in a place that we didn't get to see very often.

🍦

"Jesus please, have Starry and Viola make peace. And have Starry stop smoking if you don't mind. And please let me sleep well with no nightmares, and make it sunny tomorrow. Amen."

🍦

I had worn glasses since I was three, when during a routine examination in preschool, I mistook a fish for an umbrella. It was determined that I had an almost blind, lazy left eye. I had to wear an eye-patch for a few months and then my hated glasses, ugly and always in the way. For once I was excited about my upcoming eye-examination because I was hoping to get rid of the darn things once and for all.

The ride to Milan was going to take half an hour. The *Varesina* State Road cut through the fields. The monotonous sequence of light posts was interrupted by colorful prostitutes in unlikely, scanty garments. Uncle Bedo had taught me that the more their clothing was flamboyant, the higher was the chance that they were *trannies*: men dressed like women.

I took it all in as a matter of fact. Regardless of their sex, the prostitutes, supposedly illegal, marked the passing of the day by exposing more and more of their bodies till being all but naked, late at night. I found them fascinating. In a country where sensuality was pervasive yet publicly frowned upon, they seemed like the only honest people.

As we got closer to the city, the occasional industries grew in number and size, forming organic tangles of pipes and cisterns, sprouting from crumbling walls taken over by layers of weeds and graffiti. To make time go by Mom and I sang all of our favorite songs: from *Fabrizio De André*, a family favorite, to the Plasmon biscuit ad.

Mom complained, "Gee, Lee, you're tone deaf!"

Too bad because I loved singing.

"Mom, what does it mean 'women, grab a hose'?"

"In which context, honey? Where did you hear that?" Mom answered lifting an eyebrow, hands on the wheel, eyes on the road.

"On the school bus. I think it's a dirty song, but I can't understand what it means. It says, I think, 'Women grab a hose for cream will come out to quench your thirst.'"

It was a dirty song because Mom blushed and tried not to burst, I am not sure if in laughter, anger, or indignation.

Eventually she gave me the customary answer I had heard a million times, the same one that made prostitutes so interesting. She said, "Forget it. It will all make sense when you grow up."

Right.

I was not dumb and I was pretty sure that the hose was a penis, but the cream made no sense to me, whatsoever. Every word in the Italian language had some sort of recondite sexual meaning: from potatoes to birds. No wonder genitals are also called gen*italia, Italia* being the name of my own hypocritical country.

The eye doctor determined that even though my sight was perfect, it was better if I kept wearing glasses, *just in case.*

"If she doesn't," he said to Mom as if I were not there, "Her lazy eye might slack, and she might lose her sight again."

I did not understand.

The way back home was sad and quiet.

Mom parked and left me to close the garage door, while she brought groceries into the kitchen. Nine years (almost ten) of Dr. Jekyll had led to nothing.

For nine years (almost ten) Dr. Jekyll had meekly worn glasses, even an eye-patch for a while, and endured visits. With one hand on the open garage door, I removed the darn spectacles and looked at the magnificent poplar tree that took up most of our yard, its leaves playfully rustling in the breeze. I could see each and every one of them in detail.

Mr. Hyde took over and hurtled the glasses on the floor tiles of the garage and crushed them with his foot, stomping hard, three times. Then he left as quickly as he had come, leaving me horrified with the disaster.

What am I gonna say to Mom?

I picked up what was left, mortified, thinking about how much they cost, Mom's disappointment and anger, Dad's wrath. I entered the kitchen, defeated.

Mom took me in: my face, my hand, and the smithereens of my glasses."What happened?" she asked.

"Um, they broke."

To my amazement, she answered, "Oh well. Maybe we'll see how you do without." She walked toward me, picked up the pieces from my hands and threw them in the garbage.

This was why, even if she couldn't cook and never cleaned, my mom was the best mom in the whole world.

The following day I biked to Catechism with my friends. Flavio was unusually quiet and Peo never spoke, which left Nico to ask, "So… what the hell happened to your glasses?"

"I don't need them anymore."

Swerving left and right on his bike, beside me, Nico said, "Oh, wow. No more four eyes?"

"No, but I can still kick your *culo*."

Everyone snickered, even Nico. All that remained of the puddle was a dusty ghost in front of the church. We locked our bikes and went in for the last time since school was over in a few days.

🍦

After Catechism, Peo, Flavio and I sat on our secret platform at the top of the poplar tree, waiting for Nico, who had detention for an extra fifteen minutes for saying the umpteenth blasphemy.

I said, "Nico's always around lately. Sometimes he behaves like a *coglione*, but it's all for show. Now we even share a secret base with him. Don't you think he should be officially part of The Trio?"

"Maybe," Flavio replied. "He is practically already part of the group."

Peo growled, "No way! What would we call ourselves then, 'the quartet'?"

I burst out laughing because it sounded more like a string ensemble than a gang.

"IT SOUNDS AWESOME! A VERY APPROPRIATE NAME!" screamed Nico, who had snuck up on us, ninja style, from the back of the tree.

Peo almost fell off.

I had never seen Nico so happy, and I wondered if it had to do with the feeling of being wanted, to be part of something, to belong somewhere. Peo mumbled a curse under his breath, but Nico ignored him.

"So, when's Confirmation?" Nico asked, still giddy with the wind at the top of the platform ruffling his black hair, always a bit too long.

Peo answered, "For you, *never*."

Nico scoffed, and I asked, "Really, what's the point? Did you ever go to Mass after First Communion?"

Flavio said, "He did not. If he walked into a church, the cross would fall on his knucklehead."

Peo concluded, "For the rest of us it's next year, *coglione*, just like Don Angelo said today."

"Who's a *coglione*, huh?" Nico protested. No one took his bait or seemed intimidated, so he continued with a slight pout, "I have to say forty Lord's Prayers and thirty Hail Mary's. That priest is insane!"

I rebuked, "Dude, you said blasphemy *in a church*! I thought Don Angelo was gonna have a stroke or something."

"I wish! And not like the priest will know how many prayers I've said, anyway."

Maybe it was a lost cause. "I can't believe you, Nico! Do you want to lie to the *priest*?"

Peo added, "And *God* knows anyway. You might fool the priest but—"

"Wouldn't God tell the priest?" Flavio interrupted.

Nico retorted, "Miii, what a drag, you guys! God is infinite and forgives."

I added, paraphrasing the title of my favorite Bud Spencer and Terence Hill's spaghetti western, "Don Angelo, however, does not." Everyone laughed.

The wind rustled the leaves of the poplar tree. Flavio looked distant, with a faraway look in his eyes. I nudged his side and asked, "Hey, you okay?"

Startled, he replied. "Who, me? Yeah…Yeah."

He was acting so weird that we all stared at him. He bit his lip, working his fingers around a splinter stemming from the board we were sitting on. He mumbled, "My dad…I heard him say that things at his job are not peachy. They're cutting personnel again."

Flavio's Dad had been working at the Alfa Romeo car factory. In our town of eighteen-thousand, the plant had been a monster of nineteen-thousand employees. After selling to FIAT in 1986 workers had been laid off in rounds. In spite of strikes and protests, the number of employees was now down to six-thousand.

Nico shrugged. "Want to go check it out? We can ride there and see if there's a strike. We can ask around."

We all agreed, even if I was not allowed to bike toward the industrial area, where cars drove faster toward the highway.

Once we made it there, it was apparent that there was no strike, in fact it was a ghost town. I tried to see a future in the semi-deserted parking lots, cracked by the roots and the sun of too many summers. Surrounded by the hum of the road tumor, the beast of concrete and chimneys slept, necrotic, like the cement carcass of a prehistoric mammoth.

"Well," I said. "If something happens during the summer give me a call."

Nico shrugged. "I'll be in Sicily."

Flavio said, eyes downcast, "Everyone will be away."

He was right. We had no control over our lives, summer uprooted us every year to take us wherever our parents thought we should be. We were not going to see each other for three long months.

Nico said, "Dude, my dad was fired. We moved. We're…okay."

I wondered about the significance of Nico's hesitation before uttering the word 'okay.' When I turned, Peo was staring at me, the funeral gaze in his face reflecting my mood like a mirror.

Another year was over.

Part Two

SUMMER

Drowning

Like every summer, the end of school meant saying goodbye to the quartet, but I looked forward to the long days at the pool with Luca, my neighbor, who was one year younger than me. An only son, Luca adored me, very much like I did Viola.

The Pro, short for prototype, was the name of our small, gated community, the first of many identical ones built throughout Arese, yet the only one with an outdoor pool. Every home in the Pro was made of brown masonry topped by an odd, big roof of gray shingles that encased the whole second floor, making the homes look like mushrooms. In the seventies, the architecture must have been futuristic, but now it seemed outright ugly. Each property was surrounded by a garden encircled by a light brown wall, about one meter tall, sometimes surpassed by tall hedges.

Luca and I biked through the Pro to call on our third partner in crime, Francesco, one year younger than Luca. When we rang at Francesco's nothing happened at first. Then his terrifying Grandpa opened the door.

"*What?*" he growled.

"Hello, sir." My voice trembled while Luca, much taller than me, failed to hide behind my back. "Is Francesco at home?"

"Of course he's at home and not wandering around like you, brats!" he barked, chewing on his pipe.

I felt like Atreyu from *The Neverending Story* dealing with Morla, the grumpy old turtle. It was nice, for once, not to feel like scrawny bookworm Bastian. Maybe because rather than being the smallest member of the quartet I was the eldest in my summer gang.

Francesco stomped down the stairs and his smiling face peeked from behind his grandpa. "I'm off to the pool, Gramps!" he chirped while hobbling his chubby frame past his grandfather, who had not budged and still stared at us.

My good manners forced me to say goodbye to the old man, who mumbled to himself and disappeared inside the house, slamming the door.

Luca and I exchange a mortified look. I never reacted well to the unprovoked rudeness of adults, who arrogated to themselves the right to yell at us for no reason.

Francesco joined us on his bike. He said, beaming, "Man, I'm so glad you guys came!"

We both looked at him. In our eternal struggle to look cool and prevail on each other, we were always taken aback by Francesco's shameless and genuine profusions of affection, dependency, and friendship.

"Yeah… It's good to see you too," I managed to say, biking away with the other two in tow.

My leadership was soon going to be put to the test.

🍦

Luca, Francesco and I dropped our towels and clothes on the grass that surrounded the pool. We put on the mandatory swimming cap and stepped toward the water. The first day was always a tragedy since the water was so frigid.

"Do you think Roberto can swim?" I wondered out loud looking at the huge, hairy lifeguard. Under the one umbrella, his fat spilled over the only lounge chair on the otherwise bare lawn. As usual, he was busy with crossword puzzles.

Luca surmised, "I think he'd sink."

Francesco chimed in cheerfully, "Hey, if he can be a lifeguard, so can I!" He wobbled his own rolls in an awkward little dance and then trotted toward the water.

Luca and I exchanged a skeptical glance. We knew how this was going to end…or begin, rather. Francesco, inexplicably jolly and unsuspecting, was going to be thrown in just like every year. Yet he smiled, watching the water and giving us his back.

I silently mouthed to Luca, "One, two..."

Each one of us grabbed Francesco by one arm. The joy had barely time to drain from his face before he splashed in. His head emerged, a hurt look of betrayal spoiling his happy features. His voice wavered toward a whiny prelude to crying. "You, you...why—"

We both cannonballed at his side. When we surfaced, Francesco still seemed a bit off kilter.

I said, "Oh come on, quit it! We threw you in because we knew you could take it!"

And that was that. Turning a perceived weakness into a declared strength caused a smile to break Francesco's resentment. We splashed around, and Luca ran out of the water to get the ball.

The afternoon went by without a worry. We had just invented the *composite-missile-dive*. I stood on Luca's shoulders at the edge of the water, he jumped in as high as he could and I leaped off him. We both opened up our arms and entered the water head first, one in front of the other, like two twin missiles looking for an enemy submarine. In our dreams.

In reality, we just laughed and kicked each other in the face. Francesco graded our performance. We were up to a five out of ten, steadily rising.

I entered the water in front of Luca with my arms opened wide, just as planned. I wondered if he did as well. I was hoping for a seven. Within the blue, I filled with joy, finding myself in my favorite element. Out of momentum, I swiftly turned around to hit the pool's floor with my feet and to propel myself upward. The beautiful silvery surface separating water from sky was above my head. I let out all the air from my nose to get rid of undesired liquid and no longer essential oxygen, like always marveling at the mercury-looking bubbles floating above me to their freedom.

Sometimes seconds unexpectedly dilate and stretch into hours.

As my head broke the surface and I opened my mouth for a fresh breath, something went really wrong. At first I didn't understand what was happening and I drank a mouthful that should have been air. Like a real expert, I managed to send the gulp into my stomach rather than my lungs, in spite of my surprise and the awful taste of chlorine and who knew what else. Pool in Italian is *piscina*, little piss, and sure enough we peed in it every time we needed to.

In my shocked stupor, I realized that someone was keeping me underwater, pressing on my shoulders. I didn't find the joke funny, at all. I pounded on the hands keeping me under to communicate my urgency, to let me go, that the joke was stupid, that I was going to be mad.

The hands did not relent.

I had no idea what had gotten into Luca. With my lungs ready to explode, I kicked back as hard as I could, wriggling myself out to the side and reaching a distant present where, thank goodness, I could take air for granted again.

I was furious. I coughed hard clinging to the pool's edge. "Are you out of your freaking mind, *coglione*? I had let all of my air out to come up and—" I turned around and froze.

It wasn't Luca. My throat closed in a tight knot, air not so much for granted anymore.

Alberto's grin welcomed my astonishment. "Go on. Go on. You'll pay for each and every word later."

I jumped out of the water and stalked toward our towels, sprawled on the lawn where Luca and Francesco waited for me, a deep concern painted on their faces.

Luca whispered, "Lee, what did you do? What does *he* want with you?"

I had no idea. Alberto lived right behind my house, on the opposite side from Luca's. I knew him only through his reputation, a bad one. He was huge, at least five years older than me, and a renowned bully.

Of course, we had never played together. For some reason, in a pool full of people, he had decided to pick on me. It felt weird to be so powerless, with no one to back me up. Well, I was not going to give up that easily.

The episode at the pool was not isolated, just like Alberto had warned.

Time after time, while underwater, I would suddenly feet his damned claws on my head. I couldn't do a thing. I couldn't bite him or hit him in any way, because he had learned to keep a safe distance from me, stretching his arms out to keep me under.

Once again, the future trickled out of my hands. I had no control over my life. The more I wriggled, the quicker I used up air. I tried not to oppose him, thinking he'd get bored or worried. But seconds passed and nothing changed, at least one minute went by, it seemed like a year.

I soon reached my limit and gulped in some disgusting water. I twisted: nothing. I had no more air. I couldn't hold on anymore. Everything inside of me was burning with urgency and need. My lungs exploded and my mouth opened wide, greedy for oxygen and tasting water instead. I was going to die.

He let go.

I barely had the strength to swim to the surface, opening my mouth to life. The jerk was ready just for *that*. As the cat with the mouse, he was waiting for my open mouth to splash a wave at it. I swallowed more. He pushed me under, again, and everything went dark.

🍦

A sudden, strong grip ensnared my arm and hauled me out of the pool. I shook with an intense fit of coughing, half vomiting water.

I couldn't see. My throat burned like hell. I slowly felt the oxygen going back to normal, while my surroundings came into focus, again. I was sitting on the edge of the pool.

Roberto, the huge lifeguard was examining me. "Are you okay?"

I could breathe, I could see. My throat hurt, but I was okay. "Yes," I confirmed, grateful to my unlikely hero.

Alberto's head peeked from behind the lifeguard's impressive back. "See? We were just playing! I told you!"

I glared at the bully with a look I don't think you would find often on the face of a ten-year-old. With the chill of winter in my voice, I gave him a piece of my mind. "*Really*? You almost *killed* me. Play your idiotic games with your friends, possibly twice your size."

The words burned my throat and my head throbbed. I got up. I did not feel humiliated, on the contrary. I felt the outrage of injustice with such an intensity that I think my words conveyed it to all the people who had gathered around us, and now stared at Alberto with a bit of disgust, or at least so I hoped.

I grabbed my stuff and left, dripping water along the way and coughing. It hurt. In the distance I heard Roberto lecturing the monster.

Luca and Francesco caught up with me. "You're a legend! Man, you told him off!" Their voices crowded my ears, but all I wanted was to go home. They let me.

As I entered the house Mom intercepted me right away.

"Lee! What happened?"

How do moms always know?

As I told her what had happened, Mom listened keeping her hands on my shoulders, nodding in understanding, anger, and outrage. She asked me to repeat myself to Dad. Surprised, I complied. It had never occurred to me that they could help me. Alberto was *my* problem, but Dad thought otherwise.

"Couldn't you tell me before, Chubby? Alberto won't bother you anymore, I promise."

Dad called me Chubby when he felt affectionate, which was as rare as funny because I was quite the scrawny kid.

🍦

"Dear Jesus, please make sure that Alberto forgets about me while I'm gone at Grandma's in the mountains. But before he forgets, make him remorseful and unhappy, as much as you can, I would really appreciate that. And please make me sleep well with no nightmares and make it sunny tomorrow. Amen."

9

The Valley of Not

Transshipments, as Dad referred to moving the whole family to our holiday destinations, were a curse to us all. Usually, Dad's intense stress subsided once the reservation was made, about ten months before the scheduled departure. The angst became tangible again at the moment of loading the car, six hours before leaving, and it would escalate exponentially through the various phases of the journey, infecting the entire family.

On these occasions, it was impossible to assist or console Dad in any way. For example, there was only one winning combination for stowing the luggage into the trunk of the car, and Dad was the only one to know it, even if it took him several heroic, angry attempts to remember it.

As we all stood in the garage watching him struggle with Mom's suitcase, she whispered to Viola and me, "He's an Aries; there's no fixing *that*!"

At least, no reservations were needed to stay at Grandma's. She had been at the mountainside in Afes since May and, according to her, she had been missing us every day since. The three-hour drive stretched in a rain of swearwords and insults directed at the summer traffic. Given Dad's rigorous education, his swearing was never vulgar, at least in front of us.

"Look at that mother FU...SSER, son of a...witch!"

Viola couldn't hear anyway since she was glued to the headphones of her brand new *Walkman*, a portable cassette player that repeated in her ears all of her favorites —Spandau Ballet, Madonna and Michael Jackson— anywhere and anytime, even when Dad put on the upbeat *Mixage Summer '88* by Baby Records instead of the usual, melancholy cassette by *Fabrizio De André*.

The landscape became familiar. We left the highway behind, buried in a valley between two big mountains, and ascended through the small towns where I recognized a big tree by a church, a red house here, a broken window there.

Afes, my Great-grandma's native village, was located in the *Valle Di Non*. Valley Of Not, a place with a name like that could only be magical, although Viola had tried to convince me that it was 'Viola of Not' and that she owned the place.

A rusty sign read: "Afes, 575 m.s.l.m., population 454".

Dad had already explained that m.s.l.m. meant *metri sul livello del mare*, meters above the sea.

I asked, "Did they count Grandma when they wrote 454 inhabitants?"

Mom chuckled. "I don't think so, she's not a permanent resident, you know, and that sign has been there as far as I can remember. There are probably fewer people now."

Everyone knew everyone in Afes, and everyone spoke an incomprehensible dialect called *Noneso*. We were considered *foreigners* because we weren't born there and came only on vacation a few months per year. Our house was emblematic of this situation. Out of town, along the state road that split Afes in two, it sat just before the other rusty sign that marked the end of town.

Also, while Afes comprised mostly very old homes and stables, our house had been rebuilt in the '50s, big and beautiful, surrounded by a huge, fenced yard. It was stark white, with two floors, a large basement for laundry and preserves and a mysterious attic, which we were forbidden to enter.

Dad parked on the cobblestones in front of the garage and walked out of the car to close the big metal gate behind us. Viola, Mom, and I climbed out after him. All around us, Grandma's gorgeous garden exploded with life. In spite of her seventy-five years, Grandma was strong and healthy. When she was not gardening, she spent her time cooking, embroidering, and watching soap operas. Grandma appeared from around the house, arms open wide. She squeezed me, filling my face with kisses.

"Eeew, Grandma, not on the ear! I can't hear anymore!"

Grandma glared at me. "Oh, don't you tell me you're turning out like your sister. I haven't seen you for three months. Now I do as I please."

Viola stepped back, horrified, protesting at Grandma's effusions. Mom and Dad joined us, and the house became alive with uncles and cousins, either coming out to greet us or waving from the living room's windows.

The house and the whole town of Afes were perched on the side of the valley, overlooking a green expanse of apple orchards. Grandma said it was a spectacle when they all bloomed at once in spring. Higher up in the mountains, the darker evergreen woods were interrupted by the brighter hues of a few bare pastures. Higher still the vegetation gave way to sheer cliffs of rock that met in the harsh summits. The whole scenario turned molten pink as the sunset retreated its gown across the valley, disappearing behind the mountains.

Everyone hugged and greeted each other. Then I saw Uncle Bedo, the eldest of Grandma's five children, gigantic and gruff as always, slumped against the house's wall. I ran to him.

"UNCLE!"

He grinned almost imperceptibly with his eyes, his lips tight around the iconic cigar.

He swung me in the air exclaiming, "Cochi!"

He was the only one to call me Cochi. It was the name of his favorite stand-up comedian and he said that I made him laugh, just like him. In spite of being well over fifty, Uncle Bedo still lived with Grandma and gravitated around her even in the summer. He had made it clear that he had no interest in getting married, and no one had ever seen him with a girlfriend, or a friend, for that matter.

Uncle tossed me around the way I liked. I hoped Starry was not watching.

He asked,"You know who missed you?"

"You, Uncle?"

"No, not one bit. Assenzio!"

"Oh, *come on*, Uncle!"

"It's true! I saw him just the other day on his spaceship. Just to play it safe, I fixed our old anti-alien alarm." He put me down. "DON DON DON. Oh, it's going off right now!"

"UNCLE! I'm ten already. I'm not afraid of Assenzio anymore."

"DIN DON, DIN DON, DIN DON...He's getting closer."

We stared each other off. Then I ran as fast as I could toward the kitchen doorsteps, the only place where Assenzio couldn't catch me. Just then, I heard the alarm announcing the alien's arrival: "DINDINDINDINDINDIN!"

Uncle glided past me with his arms open like an airplane, cigar in place. I had barely escaped Assenzio, the evil alien who had wanted to kidnap me since I was a toddler.

Viola stepped out of the kitchen with our cousin Elli, two years younger than her.

Viola barked, "Back off, brat! You're not invited."

"Who cares? I wasn't following you," I lied.

Elli smirked and my sister explained, "See that door?" She was pointing at a small square trapdoor on the outside wall of the house by the kitchen. "It's the entrance to their magical world of the fairies of Afes, but you're not invited and if you hang around we can't go either."

"Yeah, right." I snorted. I wasn't five anymore for Viola to fool me.

"No, for real," she insisted. "Adults can't even see the door, but if you behave you might get an invitation. Just get out of our way."

"Whatever," I answered, not so sure anymore. I hadn't seen monsters in a long time, but I could give Viola the benefit of the doubt. I walked away to leave them alone with the magical door.

Uncle Bedo was in the garden with someone I didn't know, a *woman*, who had likely just arrived. I pretended to snub my cousin and sister and ran to spy on my Uncle from behind a tree. He puffed on his cigar and the lady laughed.

I walked closer. "Hi?"

Uncle Bedo turned toward me. "Uh, Cochi. This is, uh, Teresa."

I did not understand Uncle's embarrassment. Teresa was not pretty. She had thick glasses and a big hairy mole right by her mouth, but when she smiled to introduce herself her face lit up and she looked beautiful.

She said, "Lee, it's so nice to finally meet you! I heard so much about you!"

I wished I could have said the same. "Thank you, it's really nice... to meet you, too," I answered.

Uncle had been a misanthrope for his whole life. If he had found love, well, maybe so could I, one day.

On the following day, I came back from the garden to find the house in an uproar. The whole family was in the foyer, crowded around Viola and Elli. Both stared at the floor, abashed.

Did the fairies let them down?

Grandma dragged them into the small piano room with Mom and aunt Mallia, Elli's mom, who was still shouting, "What the hell were you thinking? You could have gotten yourselves killed! What if a car —"

BLAM!

The door slammed and Aunt's voice became unintelligible. The crowd dispersed.

What the hell?

After dinner, everyone gathered to watch TV in the living room. Only Uncle Bedo was missing. I spotted him in the garage, where he was grooming his Cagiva 650cc, an aggressive dirt bike with huge shocks, shining white and red even under the mud Uncle hadn't cleaned out, yet.

"Uncle, is Teresa your *girlfriend*?"

He jumped, startled. "None of your business."

Witnessing the massive blushing that overtook my Uncle was more than proof. "Wow! And you're getting married?"

"Shhhh!" Uncle whispered, looking around. "Next spring, actually, but don't say a thing. On a different topic," he smirked, "Did you hear what happened to your dumb sister and cousin?"

I shook my head. Dinner had been tense and quiet, Viola had shifted uncomfortably the whole time.

Uncle puffed on his cigar. "Those two idiots went to the sports center and decided to go down the slope...in roller skates."

I didn't have time to express what a great idea that was because Uncle continued, "They took such speed, they couldn't stop. Just before the crossroad, Viola threw herself down on her *culo*, Elli on her knees. Grandma got the tweezers to pick out pebbles from their wounds. Your sister will not sit still for a long time!" he added, amused.

My knees turned to jello. They would have been better off sticking with the fairies of Afes.

Uncle threw the rag he was using to clean his motorbike into a bucket. "Want to go for a ride?"

"YEAH! But—"

"Oh, your mom doesn't need to know. We'll be back in no time."

The relationship between Starry and Uncle Bedo was strained at best. She claimed he had no common sense whatsoever but she had a tendency to get worried, no matter what.

Uncle lifted me on the big saddle behind him and we snuck out into the dusk.

Oh, the exhilaration of the wind in my face, the smell of summer! Uncle accelerated full throttle, winding through small towns pregnant with the fragrance of hey and manure.

Uncle asked, "Are you ready for a little off-road track?"

"YEAH!" I screamed. I was born for speed.

He took a sharp turn down one of the countless apple orchards that covered the Valley of Not, and we found ourselves bouncing on a rocky steep path. Uncle maneuvered the bike deftly till we reached, way too fast, an unexpected ledge. Rather than braking, Uncle accelerated and the bike leaped off. I screamed and so did he. But while I was afraid, he was happy, like I had never seen him, and my terror turned into exhilaration. We landed in one piece and kept going till dark.

When we crawled back into the garden Uncle whispered, "Lee, you can't tell anyone, understood? This is going to be our little secret. Otherwise Assenzio will come and get you while you sleep."

"Sure thing, Uncle! Will you take me again?"

He smiled, walking away and lighting up another cigar.

A few days later, I was watching TV in the living room when I noticed with the corner of my eye Viola spying on me. She never cared for what I did, so I assumed that *she* was up to something interesting, and I snuck after her.

I was sure she had run upstairs, but the second floor was deserted, only the breeze and birds' songs pouring in from the open windows, animating the curtains dancing in the golden afternoon sun. As soon as I dismissed my weakly sister jumping off the second floor, I noticed the door to the forbidden attic, ajar.

I peered inside. It was a tiny shaft, big enough for the door to swing open. The rungs of a metal ladder were cemented in the wall to my right. I scampered up into a dark, huge space filled with dust and what looked like rubble. Elli was staring at my sister, balancing on a pile of roof shingles to reach a filthy skylight she had somehow managed to open.

Viola screamed toward the forest, "Ahh-woooo! Ahh-ahh-ahh-wooooo!"

What the cazzo? I almost fell off the ladder. Surprisingly the forest answered. Were there wolves in Afes? Were they friends with my sister?

Viola jumped down and saw me. "What the *cazzo* are you doing here? One word and I'll kill you!"

I scrambled down the ladder, panicked. Fairies and werewolves, what was my sister up to?

The mystery thickened. I had heard Viola make her wolf-call almost every day, before disappearing with my cousin into the forest.

In front of the garage, I asked Uncle, "Are there any wolves in Afes?"

"No," he answered. He loaded me on his motorbike for what had become our evening habitual adventure then patted his pocket. "I forgot my lighter. I'll be right back." He trotted back into the house.

Viola's voice startled me. "Starry will kill you."

Tears worked their way to my eyes, but she wasn't going to ruin this, too. "I wondered what she'll think of your werewolf friends. And by the way, Grandma can see your secret fairy door quite well. It provides access to the kitchen pipes, just so you know."

"You told Grandma? What a *loser*! Now you'll never get the invitation to fairyland!"

It didn't matter who was right or wrong. What mattered was that I wanted my sister to like me and she didn't. That always made me wrong by default.

Uncle Bedo stepped back in the garage. "Viola, you didn't see wolves for real, did you?"

Viola rolled her eyes. "Of course not. I howl to let the Ramallis know we're ready to go out. If they're ready, too, they howl back." The Ramallis were some kids from Trento that came to spend the summer at their Grandma's farm, right in between our house and the forest. Both our Grandmas were rather stingy with phone expenses no matter how cheap local calls were (200 liras every few minutes).

I chuckled and Uncle Bedo stared at my sister, considering his options. "Want to join us?"

Viola answered, "How?"

"Just jump up behind me, Cochi in front."

She pondered and I taunted her, "Look who's the chicken, after all!"

She huffed. "Is it safe?" Thick dark scabs from her skating debacle were visible on her backside, below the hem of her shorts.

"Like anything," answered Uncle Bedo. "I mean, planes crash, don't they? And if you walked you could still be hit by a meteorite or something. Not to mention skates…"

"*Fine*," Viola conceded.

Uncle climbed up and Viola followed him. I was in front.

We took off. Uncle was not as reckless as usual, but we had fun. Viola was screaming most of the times, making me feel brave even if she was more likely complaining about her aching butt. When we pulled up in front of the gate, she couldn't wait to get down, her butt likely sorer than ever, but when she hopped off something went wrong. She screamed, crouching on her ankle.

Oh, cazzo.

Uncle urged, "What's wrong? What's wrong?" as Grandma and Mom left the house in a hurry to reach us outside. Uncle pulled me off the bike, but it was too late; we were caught.

Viola whined, "My ankle, I freaking burned it!"

Grandma yelled, "Bernardo! What happened?" Starry rushed to Viola.

Uncle Bedo, aka Bernardo when he was in trouble, answered, "Nothing Ma, nothing, just a burn on the hot muffler, that's all."

That was when Starry lost it. "ARE YOU OUT OF YOUR MIND? You took my kids onto that thing of yours?"

She nursed Viola, hugging her. For once, my sister did not protest.

"Mom," I intervened. "It wasn't dangerous, it was just bad luck! We ran around all summer!"

Somehow, that was *not* the right thing to say. Everyone yelled. As the discussion escalated into full-blown drama the topic shifted under Grandma's angry impetus.

She yelled, "See, Silvia? You raised these children without any guidance and now they're fearless! They can't tell good from bad! You have to take them to church every week!"

Starry, aka, Silvia, exploded. "*What*? If I'm not mistaken, Bernardo is *your* son, and quite Catholic, too! He almost killed *my children* on that bike of his!"

Grandma retorted, "But he didn't because God's looking out for him! Didn't you see all the signs? The snowfall of '85, the hailstorm of '86…hail as big as tennis balls! What else do you need to believe?"

Starry glared. "Frogs. If it rained frogs I'd give you the benefit of the doubt."

Uncle Bedo snuck behind them, putting his bike back in the garage and nodding for me to follow him away from the furious arguing.

Unfortunately, when the news reached Dad we were forbidden to get even close to a motorbike ever again. I wanted nothing more than owning one, one day, but girls didn't own motorbikes, did they?

"Dear Jesus, please make Starry forgive Uncle Bedo and convince Dad that motorbikes are awesome, even more so for *girls*. Please make sure that we have a blast at the seaside, make me sleep well with no nightmares and make it sunny tomorrow. Amen."

10

Transshipments

Once back from Afes, after a few days to do laundry and repack, we left for Genoa to take the overnight ferry to Sardinia, the pearl of Italy, the gorgeous island with Caribbean-like waters west of the motherland.

Most Italians spent all of August *in ferie*, on holiday, and all the stores were closed except in touristic locations. Since we always left several hours early, we usually ended up stranded on the cement of the endless Genoa harbor pier under the hot sun of August for at least three hours.

Nonetheless, we were typically never first, a few cars already lined up under the grilling heat. This always made Dad's blood boil. Formula One is huge in Italy, and he craved the *pole position*, to be the first car in line to start or, in our case, to get onto the ferry. His reasoning failed me, since the earlier we got there, the longer we spent under the pitiless sun, but I assumed he knew best. Yet, every year, we got there earlier to wait a little longer.

However, the time had finally come. After years of trying, Dad's dream had come true. As he pulled into the deserted parking lot, a wide, joyful smile spread on his face. Four hours early: we were the only witnesses to the harbor's dirty waters.

The joy of victory waned by the hour, tempered by the heat. Air conditioning was almost unheard of in Italy in the 80s. After two hours of baking, our Audi was still the only vessel in the sea of asphalt. Starry, Viola, and I studied Dad's internal struggle with apprehension. He seemed torn between the need to go ask for information and the inability to abandon the historic, much-deserved pole position.

"It's guaranteed, the moment we drive away, they will all come flocking down like vultures," he explained with the air of the expert. So, we baked by ourselves on the deserted pier a little longer.

Eventually, only one hour from the scheduled departure with still no one in sight, Dad hatched a plan. Unfortunately, he did not share it with the crew. We watched him walk away in a real sour mood, swearing and sweating in the sea of concrete, his shrinking silhouette distorted by the fumes of summer's mirages till it disappeared swallowed by the heat.

Left in the car, we sweated and worried even more. Something was very wrong.

The time for departure came and went, and still the Audi was the only vehicle melting on the grill, no news from Dad.

Finally, I spotted a mirage growing within the heat, Dad was coming back. Our joy was stifled the moment he was close enough for us to see his face, as dark as the asphalt on the newer sections of the never-ending pier. He got in the car and started it, driving away without one word.

Slightly miffed, Mom eventually asked, "*So?*"

Dad looked like the Etna, the Sicilian volcano, before an explosion. He mumbled, "It's tomorrow."

"What?"

"The ferry. It's tomorrow."

"You mean we came *the wrong day*?"

While Starry's essential sense of humor spread a wry grin on her face, Dad didn't reply, wounded in his pride of engineer and master planner.

I genuinely tried to comfort him. "Well, Dad, come on! At least we were the first in line!"

My words did not break Dad's obstinate silence, but Viola exploded into an unexpected roar of laughter, making me very, very happy. Our little snag was about to turn into a major adventure.

There was no way we were gonna drive the whole three hours back home to return on the next day. It was not acceptable by Italian standards for which a three hours drive compares to traversing the United States. Therefore, we searched for accommodations.

"This could turn out to be fun!" Starry exclaimed. "Why don't we take a walk along the beach and eat some focaccia and gelato? We could stroll into Genoa's alleys and window shop, and—"

Dad cut her short, nowhere near cheerful, "Nonsense! Along the beach? Are you out of your mind? Without a reservation, they are going to rip us off, for sure!"

Starry threw her latest cigarette butt out of the car's window. "So what do you suggest? Waiting on the pier till tomorrow so we are the first in line?"

Dad cowered. "Would that be so bad? It's already late afternoon. Can't we sleep in the car?"

Mom and Viola exclaimed at once, "NO!"

Dad sighed. "Gee, fine! Let's drive out of town and get a cheap place or something."

"At least let's drive along the coast," Starry chided, exasperated.

Dad complied, begrudgingly. "They will rip us off, I'm telling you," he muttered.

They were both wrong. All the hotels on the coast were full, and we kept driving: Savona, Finale Ligure, Albenga, Alassio, Imperia…

"It would have been faster to go back home." Starry, sarcastic, had completely lost her cheer, but she was actually right.

Dad was furious, all of us exhausted. Past Sanremo, what began as a joke —we are going to end up in France— was not so funny anymore. We didn't have our passports anyway, so we had to stop right before the border, dead-tired, in a squalid Motel by the highway. It was almost midnight.

Even though we were still in Italy, the concierge spoke only French and crinkled his nose at Mom's linguistic efforts. He lifted a disgusted eyebrow and handed her two keys. I trudged behind Viola with the last bit of my energy. I was not prepared for Viola's scream, once she opened the door to our room.

"WHAT? YOU'VE GOT TO BE KIDDING ME!" she yelled.

I peeked past her, at the full bed that we were supposed to share. While she stood frozen on the door, hands in her hair, I dragged my feet to the mattress. As I slumped on it my head hit something hard; the pillows were not pillows at all, but very hard cylindrical rolls. "What the—"

Viola loomed closer, disappointment emanating from her every feature. "Great. French pillows. Just great." She turned around and marched out.

She was back within a few minutes. "Apparently they have no other pillows. I don't know if he understood what I was saying, or maybe he pretended he didn't. He looked at me as if I were an idiot."

I would have never expected Viola to say something like that. She had just finished her fourth year of high school and she didn't do very well, not only in French. She had to remediate three subjects in September to be admitted to her fifth and final year. It looked like the experience had gnawed at her soul and confidence maybe she would have been better off in art high school with her best friend Marta.

I dozed off while she went to the bathroom to change.

When we were finally in the dark, I found it impossible to sleep. The pillow was uncomfortable and Viola, as always before she fell asleep, kept swaying back and forth on her side with the headphones in her ears. The music was muffled further by the noise of her rhythmic rocking. After about an hour, she stopped moving and I heard only Madonna's faint howling. I threw the pillow on the floor, trying to find a more comfortable position, but the light flashed on.

"ARE YOU DONE OR WHAT? It's impossible to sleep if you keep moving!"

"Sorry," I blurted, not daring to mention her incessant rocking habit nor Madonna, "but these pillows are impossible."

"They sure are," she conceded leaving me astonished because Viola never, ever, agreed with anything I said.

She asked, a bit less aggressive, "Is that better?" throwing her own pillow on the floor.

"No," I answered. "Hem, Viola...how...you... " She looked at me quizzically and I managed, "Why do you rock back and forth before falling asleep?"

Believe it or not, Viola blushed. She switched the light back off. Then, when I had already given up on an answer, I heard, "It... it helps me fall asleep. I—" she stopped, but fortunately, for once, I kept my mouth shut and she carried on. "You know, when I was little...I had terrible nightmares. I used to dream that Pinocchio was in my room...and that...he was eating me alive."

I swallowed, starting to break into a cold sweat. "Pinocchio? Eating you...*alive*?"

I didn't love the guy either. He seemed slightly devious, but a jolly, harmless fellow. Viola shifted. After a few seconds she added as if every word cost her a big effort, "Yeah...eating me...piece by piece. And you know how you normally wake up from bad dreams when pain is involved? In these dreams the pain...the pain was unbearable. But I never woke up..." her voice trailed off.

"And do you still have these nightmares?"

Viola snapped back into the present. "No, of course not. But I still have the habit of rocking back and forth before falling asleep, so that Pinocchio can't catch me."

I confessed, "You know, I also used to have nightmares...at least Mom says that's what they were." It had been a while since the last monster sighting.

"*Chicken!*" Viola taunted me. After a couple of minutes though she added, "If I tell you something, do you promise to keep your mouth shut?"

"Of course."

"Do you remember Chiara and Argo, Mom and Dad's old friends?"

"Ah, maybe?" I was surprised because we hadn't seen them in ages.

"Did you ever wonder why we stopped going over at their place? They were so close."

"Sometimes," I lied.

"Well, years ago, when they were young, they did séances. Chiara was a *medium*."

"*Séances*? *Medium*? What are you talking about?"

"Geez, Lee, you *are* a bit slow, aren't you?" I could picture Viola's annoyed face, even if I couldn't see it. "Séances are when you try to talk with the dead, and a medium is a person that can do that."

"*What*? Aren't the dead... *dead*? What do you mean, talking to the dead? Like ghosts?"

"Chill, kiddo, yes, ghosts, let me finish." I *was* chilled, to the bone. Viola continued, "They used to get together with Mom and Dad and sit around a table with a glass on an alphabet board. Chiara summoned the spirits to ask questions and the glass moved by itself to answer—"

"You've got to be kidding me." Ice dripped from my words.

"I swear. Ask Starry if you don't believe me." Since I was speechless, she kept going, "The sessions became more intense. Mom told me she saw Chiara levitating on her stool. Can you imagine how scary?"

I could imagine, way too vividly.

She continued, "One day the spirit said that he wanted to enter Chiara's body. Of course Chiara said no, but the glass moved again, faster and faster, spelling 'CHIARACHIARACHIARACHIARA'. Argo lost it. I don't know if he was more angry or scared, but he threw the glass on the floor, which was probably a terrible idea. They never had a session again and the friendship with Mom and Dad became increasingly awkward, till they lost sight of each other. But it was when Argo broke the glass that I started having the nightmares. When we moved to Arese, fortunately, the nightmares stopped. It was such a relief."

I wanted to cry. Monsters were real. My sister had been haunted before I had been born and Starry knew it all along. She had lied to me. She let me sleep in that room, alone, knowing what I had seen. Why did adults always denigrate the fears of children? Was that a way to feel superior, stronger, and find the courage, or the cowardice rather, to deny and bury the same monsters that terrified them as well? I tried to deny the horrific story clinging to denial with all I had left. Maybe, I was growing up, too. I had just turned ten, after all.

I said, "It doesn't make any sense. Why would Starry ever tell you any of this?"

"Well, last spring Marta and I got the idea to have a séance. We didn't think much of it, just being silly. But when I joked about it with Mom while looking for candles around the house, the color drained from her face. She had me sit down and told me the whole story, just like I told it to you today."

After a pause I wondered, "And you think that's why you had the nightmares?"

"Yes, but Starry didn't think there was a connection. She said they were only nightmares."

At least Mom was consistent.

Eventually, I fell asleep in spite of all the monster-talk, thinking that I had found something that Viola and I had in common even though she didn't seem to agree.

11

What a Shame

For the first time, our destination in Sardinia was a seaside all-inclusive resort, rather than an apartment rental.

I commented, "Wow! Look at the pool, it's gorgeous!"

"Yeah, gorgeous," Viola echoed, ogling a guy on the other side of the pool, carrying some cumbersome lights through a side door into a white-washed building.

Dad rebuked, "You go to the pool at home, every day." He would have much preferred the rental.

"But Dad! This pool has islands in it! And there are stepping stones to cross it!"

He grumbled, "A pool is a pool. I can't fish without my dinghy."

On every seaside vacation I remembered, Dad had gotten up at dawn to go fishing on his dinghy.

Mom said, "Oh come on, Carlo, there are plenty of activities. Look on that board: tennis, archery, volleyball…"

Dad tried to *not* look excited and failed.

"What's that?" Viola asked pointing at the building that had swallowed the guy with the lights.

Starry answered, studying the map we had received at check-in, "Mm, I guess that's the amphitheater where they do the evening shows. The restaurants must be nearby."

"Restaurants!" Dad exclaimed, sounding less grumpy.

Starry beamed. "Yes, so I won't have to preoccupy myself with cooking."

Viola countered, "Starry, I don't think you *ever* preoccupied yourself with cooking."

"True," Starry conceded. "But at least we'll get to eat!" She pointed at the flyer and added, "Viola, look! There's a junior club, says here, age fifteen-eighteen."

"Mm. Not interested," Viola replied.

"Why don't you check it out? Maybe it's not so bad. And Lee, there's a mini club—"

"No way!" I protested.

"Okay girls, chill. Check it out, if you don't like it, you don't have to go, but give it a try, it's included in the, ah, hefty price."

At the mention of the hefty price, Dad's mood plummeted again.

After five days at the seaside, Starry had still to leave the room, a strange ailment afflicting her ankle. She had been lying on the bed for days, her red swimsuit the only clue of our summer location.

"Come on, Starry, come to the pool at least!" I tried to persuade her. "You can lie down in the shade to read your books!"

Starry put down *the Adventures of Monsieur Poirot*, and answered, "No, Lee, thanks. The heat makes it so much worse. And I really don't want to walk on that darn foot."

I studied Mom's foot, identical to the healthy one, nails perfectly glazed in orange, while Dad mumbled in a sour mood, "We might as well have stayed at home."

I asked, "Gout, you said?"

"Apparently," Starry confirmed. "Our diet of salami and cheese might have to change."

Viola peeked in from our room, adjacent to our parents'. "Yeah right, like you're going to cook."

"I won't have time to, anymore," Starry announced, her face lighting up with a big smile. "I decided to go back to college in the fall."

"*What?*" Viola and I exclaimed, completely taken aback.

"Yep. I had been thinking about it for quite a while. I'm going to get a degree in psychology."

"Psych is awesome!" Viola exclaimed.

Dad scoffed rolling his eyes. "Waste of time."

We all looked at him surprised, and he stormed out.

Pointing at the door from which Dad had just left, Viola asked, "What was *that* about?"

Starry sighed. "Dad doesn't approve. He thinks it's just a whim, and that psych is useless anyway." She scowled. "If it were for him, everyone would be an engineer." And with that, she buried herself back into the adventures of Monsieur Poirot.

🍦

The first week flew by with Mom mostly reading in the room. I was sitting at a table by the pool's snack bar with Viola and Dad, who was moody and lost in his own thoughts. Viola chewed on her Bounty coconut bar staring towards the amphitheater. She was smitten with Renzo, the light technician she had seen on our very first day. It was the classic impossible love, given that he was twenty-eight and she was just seventeen. Viola sighed.

A headband held back her brown permed curls. Even in her swimsuit and coverups, she wore makeup. Like Starry, she never got into the water anyway since it was too cold for her. Viola had become more and more like Mom, both of them incredibly beautiful, I noted with a tinge of envy.

As she raised her glass of Chinotto soda to her plump lips, eyes intensely fixed on the light technician of her dreams, I yelled, "Viola stop! Don't drink!" She barely acknowledged me but Dad seized her wrist staring at me. I continued, "There's a wasp in her glass!" I was so proud to have saved my sister's life.

She didn't even thank me, nor Dad, who threw away her soda offering his in exchange. She was back to staring at Renzo and Dad was back in the doldrums.

I. Was bored. To death.

"I might as well give the mini club a try," I announced. Since nobody paid me any attention, I stood up and left.

🍦

A few hours later Ezio, the most handsome guy I had ever seen, asked me, "And what's your name?"

He looked just like Chris from the movie *Stand by Me*, for whom I had developed a remarkable crush. I loved bad boys, maybe they reminded me a bit of Nico.

I stared at gorgeous Ezio, wondering about protocol.

Should I give him the stink eye and ignore him, kick him in the shins just in case, or simply answer his question?

The only guy older than me that had ever paid me any mind was the bully who had tried to drown me. Repeatedly. The longer it took me to utter anything, the more the words got stuck in my throat. Instead of leaving me be as I expected, Ezio leaned his head sideways and kept looking at me with a smile in his eyes.

I answered, "I'm Leda, but everyone calls me Lee." I immediately cursed myself for not kicking him in the shins. So, to make up for it, I tried to stare him down and found myself looking at the ground instead, since I was blushing like the hopeless dork I truly was. While I waited for the inevitable banter or, better, for the earth to swallow me whole, he added without batting an eyelid, "Well, Leda, you have the most amazing eyes that I've ever seen."

The earth did not swallow me. Worse yet, I felt myself blushing more, in spite of my *amazing eyes* being glued to the tiles around the pool.

I managed to reply, "I said that everyone calls me *Lee.*"

"I heard you the first time, *Leda.*"

Just then, a friend called Ezio back for his turn at Ping-Pong. I hoped no one noticed my embarrassment.

Pathetically, Ezio was fourteen. Only a few hours before I had laughed at Viola for her decrepit light technician and now…Since the entire mini club was staring at the two Ping-Pong players, I took the liberty to glue my *amazing eyes* on Ezio. He was wearing blue swim trunks and was shirtless.

Shirtless.

Shirtless.

Like everyone else since we were at the pool, I had to remind myself. Yet only *his* bare chest bothered me.

He didn't look like Flavio, Peo, or Nico who were still kids, (like me. Again, mental note to self). His shoulders were wide over his narrow waist, his muscles more defined than those of a ten-year-old.

"Lee, I think you've been in the sun a bit too much."

The mocking remark woke me up from my trance. I peeled my gaze from Ezio to glance at the staff girl who ran the mini club. She winked at me and burst out laughing. A few kids turned to look at us then back at the game.

The staff girl whispered in my ear, "Actually, you look really smitten...by the sun, I mean."

I growled, "Oh, shush!" but she looked even more amused.

I was losing my intimidating ability which, sadly, was the only modality of interaction I knew. I felt safe only if I hid my weaknesses by making people around me feel more scared than I was. Without my tough-cookie reputation and without the rest of the quartet at my side, I was a fish out of the water, a ten-year-old, short, skinny, and rather shy...*girl*.

What a shame.

Ezio won the match, which meant that I had to face him in the final. I was pretty good at Ping-Pong. I had grown up playing against Dad who had defeated me with no mercy since the dawn of my childhood, hoping to raise a champion. I was no champion but usually destroyed my peers.

Nonetheless, Ezio was much older and had the physical advantage of height and strength. Just thinking of the word *physical* associated with Ezio got me in a tizzy. *Merda*. I reached for my racket. If I caught even so much as a glimpse of him, I was at risk of missing the ball altogether. This was going to be awful.

The more I lost, the more I got furious.

Mr. Hyde stirred beneath the surface of my skin scorched by the sun, shyness, and anger. Yet, I couldn't throw the racket in the pool, like Mr. Hyde suggested, not in front of everyone, most of all not in front of Ezio.

The more I got furious the more I lost.

"Twenty-one to thirteen! Ezio wins the gold medal!"

What a shame.

I didn't know what burned more: the defeat (I would have loved to bring the gold medal to Dad for once) or that Ezio saw me so weak, a real sissy.

Ezio said, "Good game, Leda. You have an incredible energy for your size."

He shook my hand, and I didn't understand anything anymore, dazed by the sun, the handshake, the compliment, and the reference to my quite negligible size.

I let his hand go and stalked away without a word. All my friends treated me like a boy, and if they didn't I beat some sense into them. Ezio had no idea that he was not supposed to treat me like a girl, and it wasn't something that can be explained, especially to a fourteen-year-old for whom you have a ridiculous crush.

What a shame.

Later that afternoon, I was sitting on the beach in the shade of a eucalyptus tree, ruminating on my misery, while stealing forbidden side glances at Ezio.

The fine, white sand formed a small bay between two big boulders of brownish-red rock. Eucalyptus trees and pervasive pink oleander bushes separated the bay from the dry brush behind it. Cicadas were the soundtrack to the massive, dry heat that baked the few plants that survived the Sardinian summer, spreading their pungent aroma to meet that of the seawater. The island could be quite windy, but the sea was more often a flat overlay of crystal in shades of aquamarine, emerald, and topaz, through which you could see the soft ripple marks on the sandy bottom. It was heaven and yet I was in hell. Everything inside me was roiling and churning.

I looked again at Ezio. He was playing monkey-in-the-middle with his best friend Franco in the shallow bay, water to their waists. A girl I didn't know was the monkey. She was slightly shorter than Ezio, meaning a lot taller than me. Whenever she jumped out of the water trying to catch the ball, her huge boobs bounced up and down in her tight yellow bikini, between spraying and laughter. She looked like the bodacious pin-up, Carmen Russo, all smiles and curls. I could even see her dark nipples through the wet fabric.

Stronza.

With a critical eye, I looked down at my own torso without encountering any hindrance. I was still as flat as an ironing board.

Ezio urged, "Leda, come on! Come out and play!"

I couldn't believe my ears. "Who, me? Well, I—"

Carmen Russo in her yellow bikini chimed in with a big smile, "Come on, I can use some help!"

I suspected they were out to tease me but concluded I would have looked even dorkier skulking by myself under the eucalyptus tree. I waded into the water and joined forces with Carmen (whose real name was Dora).

I didn't know if Franco, Ezio's friend, underestimated me or if he shot low on purpose, but with one feline leap I intercepted the ball on my first try.

"Holy crap!" Franco uttered, startled.

When I splashed back into the water, Ezio and Dora were staring at me, mouth agape. My heart split between the triumph of victory and the shame of my obvious display of non girly-ness. I know it's not a word. In my vocabulary, neither was girl.

What a shame.

At dinner I shared my day with the family. Of course I avoided the topic dearest to my heart and, to fill the silence that remained when I omitted Ezio from my report, I announced, "Dad, I won the silver medal at the ping pong tournament!"

"What happened to the gold?"

"Carlo!" Starry glared at Dad, who rolled his eyes and blurted, "I'm just saying, geez! Lee, that's great."

I knew that in his eyes silver and bronze meant having lost to the gold. Truly, I shared his feelings, which was probably why I tried to justify myself telling him that I lost against a fourteen-year-old. Then the conversation ended abruptly because I thought about Ezio again, I sighed, and turned all shades of pink. What the heck was I going to do?

12

A Very Long Night

That night I was all but sleepy.

I seized *The Bengal Tiger*, stolen from Starry's pile of thrillers, and I lost myself in the book crunching on a packet of orange-flavored Polo candy. After a couple of hours Viola, who had a midnight curfew, came back to our shared room.

"How come you're still up?" she asked, surprised.

"I can't sleep," I answered, munching on another orange candy.

Viola changed and hopped in bed with her Walkman, as usual. I couldn't contain the commotion that shook my guts, sliding up my mind and taking far more room than *The Bengal Tiger*.

Eventually I blurted out, "Do you think that an age difference of four years is too much?"

Viola stopped rocking on her side. "It depends. For what?"

"Hem, between a boy and a girl."

Viola propped herself up on one elbow. "Actually, Renzo is eleven years older than me."

"*Porca vacca*! I mean, ah, wow, but…actually, I wasn't talking about you."

"And who, then?" I immediately regretted having started the conversation, but my silence betrayed me. Viola blurted, "You? *No way*!"

I tried to back out of the situation as my face turned crimson. "No, no, it's nothing," I said.

I crunched more quickly on the candy, hiding behind the worn pages of the thriller. This did not discourage my big sis, staring at me with half a silly smile. I had never had her attention before, but right now I could have done without.

"Speak," she ordered from her bed. I peeked at her from behind my book, unsure. "Speak," she reiterated.

I took a deep breath and mustered my courage. "Well, long story short, I like a guy."

"*You do?*"

"Yes."

"And he's fourteen?" Viola seemed as excited as surprised.

"Yes."

"Mm, he does seem a bit too old, to tell you the truth."

My heart fractured because I knew that Viola was right. There was *no way*.

Maybe she did notice because she added, "If it's true love it will last forever, and ten years from now a four-year difference will be perfectly legit. Dad is almost nine years older than Mom."

My heart filled with new hope. "Really? Wow, I had no idea! Is this your plan with Renzo? To wait ten years?"

"Well, to be honest…you're not gonna say a word, are you?"

"Of course not!"

"Well, Renzo and I are *together*."

"NO WAY!" I exclaimed, concern mixed with admiration. "But, aren't you afraid? Do you trust him?"

"Afraid of what? Renzo is the sweetest guy. I've never been happier, but if Dad finds out he's going to kill me, so…lips sealed!"

I couldn't blame her. Relieved, uplifted, and with a thread of hope, I dared to ask a question that had been bothering me for a long time: "Viola, uh, do you cheat at odd or even?"

Viola laughed. "Of course not! How could I?"

"But then, how come you always win?"

Viola snickered and said, "Lee?"

"What?"

"You always put down two. *Always*."

I fell asleep feeling like the dumbest dumb on earth and dreaming of Ezio and *The Bengal Tiger*.

A few days later, after dinner, we watched the baby-dance at the amphitheater, waiting for the show organized by the staff.

The night always brought with it a gentle breeze, tinged with the sweet scent of oleander and the spicier aroma of the Sardinian brush, baked by the intense sun of a whole, long, summer day. A pomegranate tree in the *piazzetta*, the little square in the middle of the touristic village, still blushed with a few orange blossoms mixed with the first ripening fruits. Viola was hanging out with her friends from the junior club since, just like me, she had turned out to enjoy the experience a lot more than she had expected.

Dad, who had been sitting beside me eating his *bacio gelato* in peace, suddenly exploded,"WHAT THE HELL IS SHE DOING NOW?"

I almost fell off my chair. He threw off the remainders of his waffle cone and bolted toward the indoor amphitheater.

Oh, merda.

Starry and I exchanged a worried look.

Dad emerged from the theater dragging Viola. His yelling preceded him, "I told you to stay away from that flirt! He's thirty, and you're just a girl! Shame on him, and shame on *you!*"

Viola replied, furious, struggling to free her wrist from Dad's clutch, "He's not even twenty-nine, and you're a hypocrite! It's almost the same age difference that there's between you and Mom!"

My jaw dropped, Starry's too, our eyes almost out of their sockets. Dad froze in place and then turned toward Viola slowly, maybe contemplating the slap that he had never given her. Yet.

Viola looked at him straight in the eye, wounded by the humiliation of being dragged away right in front of her prince, likely confirming to his eyes that she was no more than the schoolgirl she had sworn not to be.

Dad balked at Viola's unexpected fierceness, then spoke, his voice frigid and measured, "Yes, but I *married* your Mom. That scumbag will find another girl as naive as you are as soon as you're gone, if not sooner."

Viola teared up. I don't know if it was the humiliation, the frustration of not being understood by Dad, or the fear that his words might be true, perhaps all three things together. It broke my heart and Starry's, too. I could tell.

Indeed Mom and Dad had gotten married when Starry was just twenty, but I didn't see Viola on the altar too soon, much less with Renzo, the light technician.

When Dad and Viola reached us they both looked livid. Viola glared at me. "Of course you couldn't shut up, could you?"

"But I—"

Dad interrupted me, "Enough! Viola, you're grounded. You're not to leave our side or your room in the evenings. Are we clear?"

"But Dad—" Viola tried to utter.

"ENOUGH! I trusted you and I was *wrong*. From now on I'll keep an eye on you until you prove to be a bit more mature."

The conversation ended leaving Viola and me in total despair. I was bewildered. Love must have gotten to her brain. How could she think I had snitched? And why would she talk to Dad that way? Was this true love? Or was Dad right? I had at least to convince Viola that I had no part in her big blow up.

Back to our room, Viola rocked back and forth on her bed in the dark listening to music through her *Walkman*, creating the characteristic soundtrack of the summer nights I shared with her.

"Viola?" Silence. "Viola?" She kept rocking back and forth. "Viola, I don't know if you can hear me, but I didn't say a thing. I'm really sorry." Viola kept rocking back and forth. Madonna sang *Papa Don't Preach* muffled through her headset. "Well...goodnight."

"We were kissing," Viola said when I had given up all hope of interaction. "Dad saw us."

Kissing? I thought. *The decrepit light technician? Eeew!* Astonished, I didn't say a thing.

Viola continued, "Renzo is not like Dad said. He's a nice guy, sweet, honest. He could lose his job if Dad reports him. And he is in love with *me*."

I felt myself blushing in the dark. I understood then that what hurt Viola the most was Dad disbelieving she could be unique and special, irreplaceable.

"Ah, you'll see," I said. "Everything will work out, eventually."

"Yeah, right," Viola growled, restarting her rhythmic rocking, indicating that the conversation was over. Soon I drifted off to sleep.

I woke up at half past eleven PM, according to the Casio digital watch that had recently replaced my old *Flik Flak*. The dark room seemed quiet, too quiet: no rocking, no music, no breathing.

"Viola?"

I turned the bedside light on. Viola's bed was empty, as was the bathroom.

Merda.

I started to worry. I turned the light back off and I tried to fall asleep again, smothering in common sense the doubt that Viola had run away with the dazzling light technician.

I woke up again in a daze, several hours later, or so it seemed. Someone was in the room. "Viola?"

Silence, just rustling. I turned on the light.

Viola whisper-yelled, "SSSSSSSSHH! *Merda*! Turn the light off already! If Dad catches me he'll kill me!"

I turned the light off, but in that flash of light I had gotten a pretty good idea of the situation. Viola was plastered. She had been slouching against the wall, her yellow sweater stained with wine. This time she had really started a war with Dad.

I rolled my eyes in the dark hoping Dad wouldn't hear my sister slumping around the room. What could he do next to punish her? Have her arrested? It was almost 2 AM. I put my head on the pillow and soon all of my worries (Dad, wine, the light technician, Viola, and Ezio) were mixed in a vortex of dreams.

When I opened my eyes again, Viola was rising, but the night was far from done.

"*Cazzo*, Viola, what's up now?" I whisper-yelled.

"I can't take it anymore," she whimpered. "I'm gonna call Dad."

"Are you still *drunk*?"

She fumbled to the door that separated our room from our parents' and knocked, then opened it. I heard whispering. She went in. What the hell was happening?

Then I heard Dad yelling, "WHAT?" Their light flashed on.

Viola hadn't even changed clothes, her red and yellow sweater clung around her, blatant proof of her guilt. What was she thinking? How was she going to explain *that*? Dad jumped out of bed. Viola cried, fidgeting, beside it. Dad seemed more terrified than angry.

"What's wrong?" I asked from my bed.

Dad, white as a sheet, thundered, "Go back to bed. We're going to the hospital."

Starry hugged Viola. Both of them were crying. My family took off in the heart of the night, leaving me behind to wonder what the heck had happened.

Of course I couldn't fall back asleep. How much wine did it take to put you in a hospital? What had Viola done? Did the light technician assault my poor sister?

With the rest of my family swallowed by the Sardinian night, the darkness pressed on me, scary and empty. I turned the light on and looked at Viola's bed. The wine had stained her sheets too, but it seemed a little too dark. Didn't red wine stain pink? I stepped over and touched the stain to realize that it was *blood, a lot* of blood.

WHAT THE CAZZO?

When my family came back from the hospital it was dawn, and I was almost rocking back and forth with anguish. I jumped up to greet them. My sister was in one piece, helping herself with crutches, a huge white cast around her leg. When our parents crawled back to their room, Viola lay on her bed.

I asked, "What the hell happened to you?"

She muttered, "Nothing. We fell off Renzo's scooter." Then she rolled over to give me her back.

So many things were wrong in those few words. Viola had *snuck out*, on a *scooter*, of all forbidden things, with *Renzo*, the decrepit light technician, and she had *fallen off*, apparently *breaking a leg*. I was surprised that Dad hadn't finished her.

She added, suddenly emotional, "I ruined Mom's bracelets too." She lifted her right arm, where the bracelets must have been, earlier. It was patched with bandages that could not cover a red stain of mercurochrome, the nasty disinfectant. The arm must have been the source of all the blood I had mistaken for wine on Viola's once yellow sweater. I thought she drifted off to sleep, but in the light of dawn she added, half mumbling, "Lee, there are three days left. Tell Renzo I'm okay and give him our address."

"Sure."

I doubted that she was ever gonna hear again from her beloved light technician.

13

When Dad Disappears

The morning after Mom and Dad tried to yell some sense into my broken sister. I thought that there could have been nothing worse than Dad's wrath, but I was wrong. The huge baggage of sad disappointment that Viola had to bear on her conscience every time that Dad didn't smile or didn't joke with her was far heavier. Rather than getting better with time, Dad's mood deteriorated by the hour. He barely spoke to my sister and at times it seemed like he couldn't bear to look at her.

In my eyes, she had gauged the breadth of her transgression only *post-facto*. With so many rules to follow, many nonsensical, it was hard to ascertain when Dad was actually right. Viola had snuck out to run after happiness, a happiness that Dad had deemed wrong and shameful. Everyone expected Viola to screw up and so she had. In all of this, I had never considered the actual impact of what was happening on Dad until he went missing.

It was the morning of our last day, and my sleepiness evaporated in the heat of an escalating fury at a persistent noise. Viola was snoozing unaware of the odd commotion. Her leg was huge in the white cast. I padded to the veranda in front of the two rooms my family occupied. The dry, yellow, and fragrant Sardinian bush extended as far as the eye could see under a deep blue sky. The dirt path behind the low constructions that served as rooms dove down toward the beach. Bunny tails crowded the fields around the buildings. I loved bunny tails, pervasive in Sardinia. I had never seen them anywhere else with their fluffy white top, crowning an apparently dry twig. They waved all together in the breeze like a magical sea of tiny clouds.

Mom was pacing around the plastic table on the patio in her red bikini, smoking a cigarette and wearing a concerned look on her face. When she spotted me, she blurted. "Oh thank god, you're up early! Dad got up at dawn to rent a boat and go fishing, like in the old days, but he never came back."

The last few words sank in like bricks. Dad was missing.

"Ah, he'll be back any minute with a ten-kilo sea bass, I'm sure!"

She nodded and sat back down, the plastic chair making a hell of a noise against the terracotta tiles. She put out her cigarette butt and lit a new one.

🍦

When Viola and I came back from the breakfast buffet at ten, there was still no news of Dad. His absence was tangible in the stack of cigarettes piled in the ashtray in front of Mom's chair.

Looking more and more disconsolate, a sudden resolution crossed her face. "That's it. I'm calling the police."

She leaped up from her chair, putting out the latest butt, just as I yelled, "DAD!" because I had seen his head bobbing up from the narrow dirt path coming from the sea. Dad hugged me, still in one piece, not even a scratch, actually.

Yet.

Mom yelled, "Where were you?"

Dad and I looked at her. She was standing in her bikini in front of the entrance, legs apart, hands on her hips, a deathly glare on her dark face, a new cigarette squeezed tight between her lips. No matter what might have happened to Dad, it was clear that his troubles had only just begun. He put me down without taking his eyes off Mom.

She broke the awkward, tense silence. "It's half past ten! Do you have any idea of how worried we all were?" A deep hurt was showing on her face and in her shaky voice.

Dad climbed on the veranda, dropped his gear on the floor and collapsed on one of the plastic chairs. Viola and I said nothing, torn between the comfort of seeing Dad alive and the fear of the explosion of the maternal volcano, as infrequent as destructive. Dad sighed. He didn't seem ready to fight this battle, just very tired.

He said, "I went fishing a bit farther than usual, toward Tavolara." He threw his thumb at the sea, toward the island clearly visible even from the veranda.

Mom couldn't hold her angst anymore. "You could have at least told me that you were going to be late!"

Dad huffed. "When I swam back a second boat was beside mine. I hopped on board and found two machine guns pointed at my face."

"GASP!" We collectively dropped our jaws as Mom crumpled into a chair, lighting up another cigarette.

"Good god, do we have to pay a ransom? Did they kidnap you?" Mom had been quite impressed by the kidnapping of her favorite singer, Fabrizio De André, which happened right in Sardinia a few years before.

Annoyed at Mom's lack of logic, Dad spurted,"What kind of kidnappers would send me back to ask for my own ransom? They were *Americans*!" he continued, "Apparently there's a military base on the island and I trespassed. I had no idea, not like they could post it underwater… I was arrested and questioned."

"What? *Arrested*? Is it *legal*?"

"Well, they said so. America works differently than here, you don't have to be guilty to be arrested. They arrest you first and then ask the questions. Luckily with my brilliant English—" he paused to stare down our skeptical glances, "I cleared the misunderstanding. They released me with a few pats on the back."

Dad's self-proclaimed linguistic fluency, very much like his break-dancing ability, was still unverified, but Dad was back, out of the clutches of the American military police.

🍦

With Dad safe and sound, I threw on my monkey backpack and got ready for my last day at the pool with the mini club. I tried to disguise my complete lack of curves with a one-piece swimsuit. I would have been ridiculous in a bikini, and it would have been humiliating to walk around bare-chested like the child I was pretending not to be. My swimsuit was white, with a tropical flower print, and it had a frill on the sides hinting at some kind of skirt. I had never worn it since Starry had bought it in one of her crazy shopping sprees, where she forgot I was no dumb princess.

I had decided that for Ezio I was going to try to be a girl. One more flower would have made me vomit, and I felt very self-conscious. This was not me. While padding to the swimming pool in my flip-flops I vowed to never wear the frilly swimsuit again. Then I decided that in fact I was not going to wear it ever, and turned around to go change.

"Forgot something?" Franco's voice took me entirely by surprise.

At the sight of Ezio's best friend, I froze mid-step. "Hem, yes… no."

"If you want, I can walk back to the room with you. Ezio is late."

"Ah, no!" I replied, a bit too curtly. "It was nothing, really."

We sat on the short stone wall, waiting for Ezio and chatting. Franco was nice, two years younger than Ezio. They were neighbors and grew up together, like Luca and me. He was in middle school.

"Is it much different than elementary school?" I asked.

"Yes, I don't mind it. You have to call the teachers by their last names, like *Prof so and so.*" He moved his head sideways forcing a formal voice. "And you have to stand up when they walk into the classroom as a sign of respect. There are more courses and more homework, too. I like history, and you?"

I laughed. "I *hate* history! I really like reading and writing, art, and math."

"Look at these two," Ezio's voice interrupted us. "Franco, are you stealing *my girl*?"

Ezio's voice would have been enough to turn me eggplant-purple, and his comment made me internally combust.

"Don't be a moron," Franco protested. "Not to mention that Leda is not your girl *at all.* Why do you always have to make her uncomfortable?"

"I'm not uncomfortable," I lied. "I really don't care. And by the way, I'll show you the *girl!*" I waved a threatening fist in the face, alas incredibly handsome, of Ezio.

"Oh, yeah?" Ezio smirked. "And what would you do? And please, stop touching the frills of your swimsuit, I'm getting all hot and bothered!" He dodged my half-hearted punch, amused.

The truth was that I had no idea how to deal with this situation. I couldn't hold his gaze, nor could I stop thinking about his comment, even though he had meant it as a joke. So I turned away from him, stalking toward the pool, and starting a monologue on my ninja combat skills.

Franco and Ezio laughed. They wouldn't believe me and wanted a demonstration. More at ease on the familiar turf, I exhibited myself by popular demand.

Since we had reached the pool anyway, I dropped my monkey-backpack and prepared to show off my famous *combo move*. Ezio volunteered and pretended to throw a punch at me. I dodged, moving aside and starting the sequence without ever touching him, of course: elbow in the stomach pivoting a backhand that would have been on his nose, if he had been my size, and final body twist with knee raised to the groin. A masterful execution, Nico would have been proud.

"Wow!" Ezio and Franco laughed and applauded my demonstration.

"You were not kidding!" Franco added.

A spark lit Ezio's eyes. "And now a demonstration of the *secret move à la Ezio!*"

Quite unexpectedly, Ezio seized me and threw me on his shoulder. His hands on me, the feeling of his bare back, the smell of his skin, the sea and the sun: it all mixed together in my overexcited brain.

Followed utter confusion: the unexpected move, being so close to him and, way too soon, being thrown into the cold water of the pool. Maybe it was not a bad thing since I could use some cooling off. I stayed underwater longer than needed to bring my face back to a color justifiable by the sun.

When I emerged I protested, "Hey, I just pretended!"

Ezio winked and opened his arms as an invitation."You can always make up for it…"

He had no shame, while I had enough for both of us.

I tried to spray him, but Ezio jumped back, unscathed. I couldn't believe my eyes when he offered me his hand to help me out in a gesture of peace. How naïve! Before a satanic grin of satisfaction could give me away, I seized his hand, planted my feet against the wall, and dragged a bewildered Ezio into the pool, t-shirt and all.

Agile as a cat, I leaped out of the pool.

Ezio surfaced, spitting water like a cartoon. Bent over double, laughing at his friend's dismay, Franco exclaimed, "You found your match, man!"

Franco and I walked away toward the meeting point, leaving Ezio to soak.

You found your match, man! I mulled over Franco's words giving them a new meaning as triumph evaporated, and I wondered if I had just committed a huge strategic mistake from the romantic point of view.

That night the moon bleached the sky a sweet silver, shining on a thousand bunny tails that argued with the breeze. The sound of the waves breaking on the shore filled my ears but not my pining heart. It was my last night in Sardinia.

Ezio, unexpectedly emotional, handed me a piece of paper. "Leda, give me your address and promise me you'll write!"

Franco added, "Yes, but write to me, too!" Ezio threw him a punch.

There was no doubt in my heart that Ezio and I would have met again, maybe in ten years, like Viola had said. It was half past ten, my curfew.

Ezio suggested, "Can't you stay out a little longer? It's the last night! Even if they ground you tomorrow, who cares?"

"The punishment is not the problem. You don't know my Dad."

"I would have loved to meet him! You refused to introduce me," Ezio reminded me while Franco whispered (making sure to be heard by Ezio as well), "Of course, he wanted to ask for your hand!"

I felt myself blushing for the last time, while the two friends kept up their bantering. I put their addresses in my pocket, and I walked toward the room, hoping for something to happen.

Now Ezio runs after me and stops me.

Now he jumps out from behind that bush.

A nuclear emergency forces us together, in a cave, for months.

Maybe he'll wake me up in the middle of the night, throwing pebbles on my window like in the movies.

I crossed the threshold of my bungalow as if I was stepping out of a dream.

14

The Zombie Dog

Back in Arese, school was not going to start for another couple of weeks. I couldn't wait to see Nico and the rest of the quartet. A premature note of fall could be detected in the crunching of the first falling leaves, in the ripening color of the sun, projecting longer shadows in the evening. Luca and I were playing a one-on-one soccer challenge on the street. I placed myself at a good distance away from him, and we kicked the ball as hard as we could, trying to get through each other's defense. Above the shoulder was out. Anything else was legit: bouncing off sidewalks, walls, and even parked cars.

There is such a beauty in children's games, an ability to enjoy life one second at a time that adults often forget. Incredibly, some grown-ups are resentful of this ability. Most fail to see that, even though less experienced, children are actually smarter than adults, because they are able to imagine a future that is not limited by what is likely and possible. Only people who remember how to do that become true leaders and innovators, constantly moving the thin line that divides the present from the impossible.

"STOOOOOOP! STOP EVERYTHING!"

Startled by the yelling, Luca blocked the soccer ball under his foot. He stepped aside, just in time to avoid his crazy neighbor, Marcus, zooming past him on his bike. Marcus hit the brakes coming to a full stop right past Luca, but it was clear that he could have stopped sooner without putting up such a show.

Marcus was a lanky, forty-something-year-old, the head of the Fachuskiches, an odd family who lived at the end of the street. We had made up their last name because their Austrian origins made their real one unpronounceable. Our parents were friends with them, but Luca and I were wary of the family, mainly because they kept their dog, Doggy, locked in a cage on the back of the house. Doggy barked continuously, even at night, waking up Luca.

Marcus yelled, "WHAT THE HELL DO YOU THINK YOU'RE DOING IN THE MIDDLE OF THE STREET?" He turned around to loom over Luca. He was so lanky that he could do so even sitting on his bike.

Luca stepped back and started the stutter he typically reserved for his Dad, "Bu-bu-bu-bu-but-"

"Bu-bu-bu-but *what*!" Marcus mocked him. "It's dangerous!"

To us, all adults were the same. As we were constantly reminded, they were right and we were wrong. Yet, I couldn't stand Marcus. Marcus saw me approaching and directed his anger at me.

"You're older, you should know better, Leda! Standing in the middle of the road is outright *stupid*!"

"And why is that?" I challenged him, furious at his offense.

"You know cars? Broom broom?" He pretended to steer a wheel with his hands as if he were talking to a dimwit.

I tried to keep my cool, this was no place for Mr. Hyde. "Yes, Marcus, I do know, but cars *broom broom* make noise, unlike bikes, and they don't come out of a curve at full speed going the wrong way. *You* should be the one to be careful."

Marcus laughed. He always took me aback. He snapped, "Such a smart mouth! You sure take after your mother!" It did not sound like a compliment.

I was about to retaliate, but Luca interjected, changing the topic, "Ma-ma-ma Marcus, what happened to Doggy? He-he-he he's been real quiet, lately."

Marcus's face darkened. "Doggy died. Poisoned."

"NOOOOO!" we both let out in disbelief. "Who did that?"

"Probably some neighbors," Marcus accused, turning his eyes into slits and fixing them on Luca.

"NO-NO-NO-NO-"

Marcus looked at Luca askance. "I hope not."

Luca continued to stutter no-no-no-no-no, while I added, "I'm sorry, Marcus."

"Mm." He jumped back on his bike and disappeared from sight without another word. Who would murder Doggy in our quiet, safe, gated community? It was only the beginning of a spooky mystery.

🍦

"Dear Jesus, please make sure that no one kills any more pets around the Pro, it's way too sad. And please let me sleep well with no nightmares, and make it sunny tomorrow. Amen."

🍦

I buzzed Luca after dinner a few days later. He jumped out of his door and ran to the gate, soccer ball in hand, and told me, "Doggy is back!"

"What do you mean back? Back from the dead?" I smirked, mocking my friend. I basked in the subtle pleasure of playing Viola's part, for once, since Luca had no siblings.

"I don't know. It doesn't make sense, but I heard him barking last night."

"Couldn't it be another dog?"

"It was Doggy, no doubt. I heard him every night of my life. I'd recognize him in a thousand!"

We looked at each other, lost. "A ghost, maybe?" I suggested, materializing Luca's thoughts and my worst fears.

It was up to Luca, to play the part of the grown-up. "Of course not! Ghosts don't exist, right?" He looked at me for a reassurance that didn't come and added, "The barking is real. Want to go check it out?"

I nodded, while a shiver ran down my spine. As we walked toward the Fachuskiches', I was not sure if I should be more afraid of a ghost or the real Doggy. I said, "If it really *is* Doggy, we start running the moment he starts barking."

"Sure thing," Luca agreed.

Doggy had never been friendly. Indeed, as soon as we were in sight of the gate, the familiar, hateful, relentless barking started. My jaw dropped, but we didn't start running.

"*See*?" Luca looked at me.

In spite of our fear and our deal, we approached the main gate to look through the bars. Doggy, supposedly, was a mad dog. Marcus kept him locked behind a wooden fence a few meters away from the tall iron gate we were trying to peer through. The barking became more frantic as we tried to take a look at the zombie dog.

"Could it be another dog?"

I didn't even finish the sentence that a frothy black muzzle of wrath and shiny fangs poked from behind the wooden fence, as the crazed dog jumped higher and higher, slamming its whole body against it.

"It's him all right," Luca declared, as we stepped back ready to run for our lives. The only thing scarier than Doggy was Doggy back from the dead.

Right then, the Fachuskiches' front door slammed open behind the impetus of Marcus.

"*What?*" he yelled. "If your soccer ball went over the fence it's doomed. Doggy already ate it, for sure. Get lost."

Trying to be heard over the loud, uninterrupted barking, I asked, "But, wasn't Doggy…*dead?*"

"Ah, yes," Marcus replied, lost in thought. "This is another Doggy, Doggy-two."

"Same as the first?"

"Yes."

"With the same name?"

"Yes."

"And this one is crazy, too?"

"Yes, I *had to* lock him up. See? But what the hell do you want? I'm busy, you know."

He glared at us, waiting for an answer. Luca was petrified. I tried my best, "Hem… I… We—"

Marcus rolled his eyes. "*What?* I guess stuttering is contagious! Go play elsewhere before Doggy slams the gate down and comes to get you!"

The dog banged as hard as ever against the wooden gate, Marcus slammed his door shut, and we ran for our lives.

After we caught our breath we resumed playing soccer. Since I always won, Luca declared that the slight downhill was to my advantage, and we swapped places. I was already winning two to zero. I took a couple of steps back, then ran and kicked the ball as hard as I could, aiming at the wall to his left, hoping for a killer bounce. The kick did not turn out great, but Luca froze, and the ball shot by his side.

"Three to zero! Screw the downhill! Get over it, I'm just better than you!" I teased, but Luca did not get angry.

He didn't even seem to hear me. He lifted his arm, shaking, his face distorted by a grimace that didn't bode well, and his finger...his finger pointed at me.

I grabbed my chest shouting, "What? *What?*"

Then I sprung around, finding myself face to face with Doggy-two: black, huge, its fangs exposed in a growl.

Luca couldn't take it. He screamed, "RUUUUUUUUN!" just as he did just that.

Doggy-two pounced forward passing me by, launching in Luca's pursuit, while I yelled, "STOOOP! Luca, stop! He's gonna come after you if you run! STOOOOOOOP!"

Luca did stop, oddly feeling safe standing on the one and a half meter wall surrounding one of the properties. He obviously was *not* thinking that, to escape from his prison, Doggy-two had crashed through the wooden fence and jumped over his own wall. Luckily, Doggy-two didn't seem to be thinking about that either, because rather than hopping on the wall and devouring Luca, he stopped dead in its tracks and turned its big head to look at me.

Oh, *merda*.

Doggy-two did not seem friendly, maybe amused, wagging his tail a little. He was a gorgeous beast.

I smiled tentatively, crouching on my heels holding out my open hands to get rid of any possible inkling of threat, and I timidly called, "Doggyyyyy! Doggy-twoooo!"

Doggy-two trotted over and sniffed my hand. He wasn't growling anymore, and I caressed his big head, hoping he wouldn't snatch my hand off. His hair was long, black and thick.

I felt special. I had always hoped to have a superpower like on TV shows, to be able to talk to animals and plants, to read people's minds, teleportation, anything. It didn't matter what. What mattered was that someone —an alien, a secret agent, a talent scout— would finally find out how unique and irreplaceable I was and then told Viola, Mom, Dad, Nico and the rest of the world.

I looked at Doggy-two, who rubbed his big head on my hand. He didn't seem *that* crazy. Maybe he was all show, like Nico, Alberto the bully, and…well, *me*. It broke my heart to think of him locked in a cage. Unfortunately, there was not much else that we could do but bring him back to his master.

Luca approached us, but Doggy-two snarled.

"I think he feels that you're afraid," I murmured to Luca not to startle the beast.

"He-he-he-he he feels right," Luca confirmed, walking a few meters behind us, as we approached the Fachuskiches' property.

Reluctantly, but also with a bit of pride, I rang the doorbell. The door flew open, as always when Marcus was behind it. The moment he saw us with the dog, his dashing smile disappeared, replaced by blatant panic, and he rushed to the gate shouting, not asking, "What happened!"

He opened the gate, dragging inside the terrified dog that whined, staring at me, while Marcus shouted, "You all right! You hurt! Any bites!"

"No, no, no, no," we reassured Marcus.

Nevertheless, he grabbed the dog by the collar even tighter and slapped him hard on the muzzle, scolding him, while the poor wolf yelped. I felt like Judas.

Marcus's wrath turned to us. "And you two! I told you not to play around here! You instigate him! Shoo! GO!"

We ran away once again. It seemed apparent that Marcus was driving the poor beasts to madness by lack of love, isolation, and who knows what else. Exasperated, the poor wolves could only bark their brains off, and maybe the brain of some sleep-deprived neighbor. At least now we knew whom we should be afraid of.

Francesco ambled down the street. He was tanned and had lost quite a bit of weight through the summer. "Hey, guys!"

We welcomed him with big pats on the back. He was now a full head taller than me. I was still waiting for *my* growth spurt.

We sat on the sidewalk telling each other stories from our vacations. I watched Luca and Francesco and I thought of the quartet. I suggested, "Why don't we form a group, like a gang?"

Luca answered, "Awesome! And what would we call ourselves?" Everyone stared at me expectantly.

"How about *the Wolf Gang*?" I raised an eyebrow waiting for my friends' response. The Wolf Gang cheered unanimously.

15

The Lone Wolf Gang

School was about to start. I planned to spend the last few days of vacation with the Wolf Gang at the pool of the Pro, but something was off. Francesco was not his usual jolly self. His friend Mauro lagged behind him.

While Luca and I were ready to shed our stuff and start the rite of *who gets in the water first*, Francesco blurted, "I just don't get it, Lee. After all, you're a tiny, little girl. How do you get the guys to respect you and do what you say?"

His comment rekindled the forgotten pain caused by the incident of the porn mag, which had been buried under a year plus a summer of happiness. While Nico's rudeness had seemed out of place at the time, Francesco's words resonated with something new. My crush on Ezio had unveiled to my own eyes that I was a girl indeed, a strange one maybe, but a girl who had liked a boy. Completely taken aback, I turned to stare at Francesco, my heart hardening into granite.

I asked, glaring as threateningly as I could, "What do you mean?"

Unfortunately, he didn't seem intimidated at all. His weight loss had been compensated by a new swagger. "Well, I just think you're all talk," he answered.

"Really?" I snarled.

Francesco was not stupid. Although I had two years on him, he was taller and wider. Luca was even taller than Francesco, but he was as skinny as a pole, and not quite the daredevil. Still, if glares could kill, Francesco would have been dead.

Mauro, who was new, observed his friend's display of cockiness. I was quite sure that this show had been set up solely for Mauro's benefit. Francesco remembered well the Alberto incident for which I had gained the respect of the entire pool. He didn't know that what had kept the bully away since had been a phone call from my Dad and not my public-speaking skills. Or had Francesco found out?

He pressed, "So, tell me. How do you do it? Or are you just a bluff?"

"With teeth and nails," I answered, thinking about all the times I had fought with Viola.

Nonetheless, I pondered his question for real. Why did my friends keep me around, even if I was a girl? I guessed it was because I pretended not to be one, because I pretended to be like them. I looked Francesco straight in the eye.

He flinched, caught himself, and carried on, "I don't believe you. Your nails are short."

True. Actually I had never scratched anyone in my life, but I retorted, "What matters is how you use them, not how long they are."

"*Stronzate*. I think you're full of it. Scratch me then. Show me."

"Are you out of your mind?"

"No, for real. Scratch me. Here's my arm, go ahead," he incited me, mocking, reading in my hesitation a statement of weakness.

Mr. Hyde rose to the surface, but I tried to fight him and keep my cool instead. "You're not going to cry?" I asked.

Francesco burst out laughing, "Of course not!"

Amused, he offered his arm, leaving me no choice. So, be it. I pinched his arm with the tip of my thumb and forefinger's nails, staring in his eyes, without betraying the emotions that crowded the other side of my pupils: the fear of ridicule and of losing my friends, the hatred of being a girl, the sense of guilt for hurting him, the anger at his affront, the desire to see him cry.

I increased the pressure of my pinch.

His gaze held mine, till his initial impassiveness cracked letting me glimpse his worry. It poured into my eyes, giving me a new gale of courage and bravado. I was hurting him, I was stronger.

He crumbled. "OUCH! OOOOOOW!" he howled.

I let him go, surprised, seeing the old Francesco, more child-like and quite humiliated, watching his own arm and wailing. "You made me bleed! I cannot believe it! Why did you hurt me so bad? I was just joking!" he whined.

Why did I?

I knew he had not been joking, but did I really *have to* hurt him? A minute ago the confrontation had seemed inevitable. Was I so different from Viola? From Nico? From Alberto?

Bewildered by his reaction and feeling awful about hurting him, I used the technique that my sister had imposed on me for years: I blamed *him*. "You looked for it, *coglione*! What a wimp, you swore you wouldn't cry!"

"But you pierced all my *seven skins*! You made me bleed!"

"I *what*?" I asked, bewildered.

Luca and Mauro gaped at the exchange, eyeing Francesco's arm where a tiny red spot signaled my ruthlessness.

"I saw it in a documentary." Francesco sniffled, cradling his arm and not looking me in the eye.

I had thought that hurting him would have shown everyone how strong I was but, at least to me, it had only shown how weak and scared I could be. Incapable to deal with my guilt and Francesco's numerous layers of damaged skin, how many ever they might have been, I walked away mumbling, "Well, you got what you asked for."

I marched off toward the pine trees at the end of the lawn, kicking the ball. Luca and Mauro trotted behind me, thank goodness.

"Wow, you're tough, Lee! You made him *bleed*!" Luca claimed with adoring eyes, soon joined by Mauro, our new acolyte.

"He left me no choice," I lied, mortified, trying to hide my own doubts.

We kicked the ball around and, after a couple of minutes, Francesco joined us, too. He was still holding his arm, but he seemed determined to never speak of the incident again. When we were sweaty enough, we got the courage to face the frigid shower and jump into the pool.

We didn't throw Francesco in, this time.

On the next day, Luca asked on our way back from the pool. "Hey, Lee, wanna come eat at my house?"

"Sure! I'll tell Mom and be right over."

I hopped up my front steps and yelled into the entryway, "MOOOOOOM! Can I go to Luca for dinner?"

Starry walked out of the kitchen, huffing. "Hi to you. Don't they get tired of feeding you?"

"I don't think so. His mom always says she wishes Luca were like me."

"In front of Luca?" Starry arched a disapproving eyebrow.

"Uh, yes. I don't think he's doing too hot in school."

"Mm. Did Alberto ever bother you again at the pool?"

"No, I guess he doesn't come to the pool anymore."

"That's good."

"Right. Do you know what Dad said to make him disappear like that?"

Mom shrugged and then smiled, changing the topic. "Apparently Luca told his mom you're all in a gang or something."

I thought it was supposed to be a secret although, I realized, I had just assumed so. "Yeah," I replied.

Starry seemed amused. "And what is it called again?"

"The Wolf Gang."

"Right! The Wolf Gang! So, Luci asked Luca how come you're part of the Wolf Gang, given that you're a girl. Do you know what he answered?"

She had no idea about the amount of angst her words caused me. She hurried to answer her own question, "Luca answered, *but Mom! She's the boss!*"

Starry cracked up, and a wide smile tore through my anxiety. I laughed with her even though I was not sure what was so funny. But Luca was the best.

When Starry recovered she prodded, "So, fearless leader, may I ask what is it that you do with the Wolf Gang, anyway?"

"Well, nothing. You know, we ride our bikes, play soccer, and go to the pool, like we always did."

"You're a hopeless tomboy," Starry declared, but she said it with affection as if she was finally getting used to the idea. I gave her a kiss and ran to Luca's to eat dinner and play on his Atari.

The next day was cloudy but warm.

I asked the Wolf Gang, "Wanna get in the water?"

Francesco and Mauro answered in choral enthusiasm, but Luca hesitated.

He studied my face then said, "No, I want to play soccer."

We were all taken aback by his strange behavior.

"Alone?" I joked, but he had lost all humor.

He snapped, "How come we always have to do whatever *you* say? Francesco was right, you *are* a girl, after all!"

"So what?" I protested, "Do you want to get in the water or play soccer?"

But that was not quite the issue, was it? My being a girl was not going to go away and as much as I tried to ignore it, my friends, all males, could not anymore. What the *cazzo* was I gonna do?

Mauro and Francesco watched Luca challenge me, ill at ease. I noticed that Luca stared at Francesco, but Francesco looked down holding a hand on his arm, where a red scab reminded us all of my arrogance…or his; I was not sure.

I'm not Alberto, I told myself in the uncomfortable silence that followed. Maybe because I was a bit older, maybe because of personality, I led this bunch more often than not. After years of subjugation under Viola, I didn't mind at all. Was I just bossy? The air of mutiny offended me and reminded me of years of Viola's rejection and of all the other unkindness inflicted on me by my peers, especially in light of being a girl. The hell with it, I didn't need anyone.

I said, "Well, the hell with you, guys! You can do whatever you like, you always could. The Wolf Gang is over. Make your own. From now on, I'll be my own gang, *The Lone Wolf Gang*! Screw you all!"

I walked to my loyal yellow and blue cross bike. *Traitors. Who doesn't want me, doesn't deserve me.* But the wound burned. Oh, how it burned!

And all of this happened just because I was a girl? I thought of the quartet and I realized I was sitting on a time bomb. It was only a matter of time before they turned their backs on me as well. The warning signs were all over. Nico had made sure of that. I was condemned to a life of solitude, just like *the Little Prince*. At least he was a male. And sure enough he had abandoned his girly flower to its own thorny fate. I roamed around the Pro, brooding on my bad luck, going up and down the sidewalks with my bike, but I didn't quite feel like jumping.

"Lee?" Francesco startled me, peeking from behind a curve.

"What do you want?" I asked, trying to force anger in my voice, when in fact I was really glad to see him.

He fidgeted on his bike, looking at the asphalt. "Can I be a member of The Lone Wolf Gang?"

My heart leaped for joy, but I held myself back. "I'll have to think about it," I answered, eyeing Mauro, who lined up at Francesco's side, eyes downcast.

This meant that, somewhere, Luca the jerk remained alone with his resentment. This hurt me the most because, after all, Luca *was* my best friend and had always been a staunch ally. I hoped loneliness hammered some sense into his hard head. Sure enough, I saw his silhouette biking up to us from the bottom of the road. His eyes were sullen and he said nothing, but he lined up with the other two.

"If you want to be part of The Lone Wolf Gang, you have to pass a test, though." It wasn't going to be a free-for-all after their mutiny. They lightened up at my announcement, including Luca.

Yet, from behind the curve, Alberto's voice froze us in place. "Oh yeah? Can I try, too?"

Silence.

Me.

Alberto.

He was huge with his obvious fifteen years, male, a dark freaking stubble on his chin. His voice sounded deep and his arms were four times mine, maybe five. His bike was double the size of ours. He seemed twice as big as I remembered him, but his grin...his grin had not changed. At least there was no water in sight, yet I still felt like I was drowning. I was going to get a record beating. It had been a while.

My three acolytes hid behind me as if they thought I could somehow defend them from the beast. Silence carried on, turning into a question mark on my face because Alberto was waiting for an answer. I didn't even remember his question. Was there a question?

To my surprise, he lowered his eyes and blurted out, all in one breath, "Look, Lee, I'm sorry for the swimming pool. I was joking. I had no idea that you drank underwater. You didn't cry, and I thought it was just a game. I didn't mean to hurt you."

The vow I had made to never cry when I was nine came back to me. For the first time I realized how stupid it was to be ashamed of a signal so eloquent as tears, which in any language, at any time, suggested to the next person a state of fear or pain, or both. I looked at Alberto without the fog of fear and I saw a sad, misunderstood giant, maybe a little too lonely, just like Doggy-two, just like me, except that I was no giant, by far.

The three behind me were ecstatic. Perhaps my leadership skills were dictated purely by luck and circumstances.

"That's all right," I managed through my cottonmouth, mindful of chlorine and fear in a past not so distant. I hoped that no one noticed how shaky my voice sounded.

Alberto smiled, kindly. "Come on, I can teach you a couple of tricks on the bike!"

He took the lead, showing us how to get on the sidewalk with the back tire, then the front one. He taught us to do wheelies and other tricks. And you know what? I sucked. I was the worst of the whole bunch. I hoped that no one else noticed, but it would have been hard not to.

Life is so strange at times. I was on the verge of a great comeback, and instead I found myself panting behind my own gang, running after the lead of my worst enemy. I thought Alberto was a monster and that I would have never, never ever, been like him. Turns out that, after all, we were not so different.

"Dear Jesus, please, make sure that Alberto doesn't play with us anymore, he's nice and all, but it's much better when he minds his own business. And please, make it sunny tomorrow and let me sleep well, with no nightmares. Amen."

16

Boom

It was the last day of summer vacation. The golden sun of mid-September colored the first leaves crunching under the inexorable tires of my bike. I darted through the gate, always open. I turned around the house, preparing to hop down and rush inside.

Not on that day.

Too often we take for granted our lives to the point of degrading them to triviality. You never know when life is going to surprise you with a revolution, an event that will mark you for the rest of your days. Trapped in a vicious cycle, we blind ourselves with the forgetfulness of what we have, drowning our hearts in memories and regret for the things that we have lost instead. You should live every day as if it were your last, or your first, or the only day of your life, because even when nothing jolts you out of your tracks, *you* are different, changing by the minute.

Biking through my yard I rushed through the customary crunching of leaves unknowing that, from that moment on, it would have never sounded the same.

I turned around the back of the house and I found myself in front of the whole family: Mom, Dad, and Viola. They were staring at me, sitting around the table outside of the kitchen, where we had our summer meals.

"Hi?" Perplexity poisoned my greeting, received by the obvious calm before the storm: Dad was not at work. Viola's eyes were puffy.

Evidently, I was the last member of the family still navigating in the blissful ignorance of something dreadful and inescapable.

Mom said, "Sit down."

Merda.

I looked at the fourth chair, the very same one I had used to study the cycles of life in biology the previous spring: birth, growth, life, death. One event per each side of the chair. Maybe someone had died? Grandma? My gaze ran over the garden's fence, to the spot where many years before I had seen the paramedics' stretcher covered with the white sheet that had marked Grandpa's grand finale. Everything was still and quiet. Everything looked familiar, conventional.

I sat down. I would have much rather lingered in oblivion than reach the rest of my family on the bank of tragedy.

Instead Mom declared flatly, "Dad and I are separating."

Viola sobbed, face hidden behind her hands.

"Is Grandma okay?" I asked.

Mom looked surprised. "Yes, why?"

I remained puzzled because I didn't understand what Mom and Dad were going to separate, but I thought that it would be appropriate to cry. I remembered that Alberto the bully did not understand my discomfort because of my lack of tears. I saw the glossy eyes of the people dearest to me in the whole world, and I didn't even care what was going on. I just wanted them to know that their sadness was mine, and that there was no shame in their pain, whatever the cause. Indeed, tears began to roll down my face even though I didn't know why yet.

"What do you mean, you're *separating*?" I felt stupid.

"Ah, well, it means that Dad will go live somewhere else for a while. But, uh, you will be able to see him on the weekends."

"For work?"

Mom tried to be patient, but her words were strained and slow. I made a mental note about how Dad was not saying a thing.

"No, no. It's not about work," Starry added struggling but with kindness. "Things are, uh, not going well between us, you know? We need space and time…to think."

The concept was entirely foreign to me as if she had told me that the planet had split in two. Yet, the information sunk its sharp teeth in the place most vulnerable and hidden within me, my fear. I suddenly felt a huge sense of loss, abandonment, and lack, lack, lack.

"Starting when?" I begged, trying to hang on to something practical to escape the shadow of the feelings I did not understand.

"From today."

Coup de grace.

Dad was still quiet.

Dark feelings, cold, sticky and stifling, overwhelmed me, and I started to sob. Mom hugged me, and I wished I could say or do something to change the course of events, but the conversation was over.

Back in the house, alone with Viola, I asked, "Why did they decide so suddenly—"

"So *suddenly*? You're so dense sometimes, Lee!"

I didn't know if her reaction was to my question, their decision, the situation, or all of these mixed together.

She continued, "It's been months since they've been doing nothing but fight, didn't you hear them? What did you think they were doing locked in the kitchen every night?"

I had never heard yelling. *Loud talking, maybe.* Okay, very loud. I thought they were doing exactly what they had said: grown-up talk. I had never wondered. I had trusted them. I had seen what they had wanted me to see. Details came out of the haze: Viola storming in the kitchen, yelling at them, then running away, getting sick in the middle of the entrance; walking in on Mom and Dad arguing and going silent, way too often, for years; Dad's moodiness, his odd, pensive, remote grumpiness over the summer. Further back, I saw in a different light their sardonic choice of Christmas gifts: Mom had given Dad a brick *to show her love* just like Ignatz with Krazy Kat.

How did I fail to see?

I felt useless, a dufus. Viola was right. While I was busy with my sister, school, the quartet, and Ezio, my parents had drifted inexorably apart, leaving a crater where once was my family. No one had informed me, asked for an opinion, advice or comfort.

Dad came down the stairs with two suitcases.

Surprised, I found my feelings on his face.

We exchanged a big hug.
And then he was gone.

Part Three

SPRING

17

But Where Did Your Love Go?

Six months later. March 1989.

The timid sun of early spring filtered through the living room's window and lit up a corner of the brand new brown couch. Dad's study, emptied of colors, brushes, and canvases, had become Starry's, where she studied for her psych exams. Dad's obvious absence had been hidden behind new furniture.

Starry's first semester as a private student had been a huge success and she had brought home only excellent grades. Could Dad have been wrong about her *whim*?

Starry explained, gesturing at the freshly painted room "…And once I get my degree I will receive my patients in here."

"At *home*?" I asked.

"Yes. Many therapists dedicate part of their home to their practice."

"But it's also *my* home," I protested since it bothered me that no one ever asked for my opinion.

"Why, do you mind?"

"Well, doesn't it seem strange to you, having loonies roaming around the house?"

"Leda! We are talking about people, just like you and me. I also go to a therapist, so does Viola. Didn't you know? We all have issues, it's just that some of us don't quite know it yet." She gave me a meaningful look.

"*You* go to a therapist? And *Viola*?"

"Yep. I have been for years. She is the one that opened my eyes to a lot of things. That's why I wanna be a therapist; I wanna give back, you know?"

I thought about it, then said, "Okay, but to me, this will always be Dad's studio."

Starry deflated, but when she replied she seemed sincere. "I try to not think about it."

The old wallpaper had been torn off, and every room had been repainted. She had even gotten new curtains. The cleaning lady had changed too. The old one had stopped coming as soon as she had discovered my parents' separation, which had been morally unacceptable for her.

Personally, I hated the idea of a stranger looking after the house, but Starry always argued she wasn't going to spend her days cleaning after *my* mess. She had a point, since my room was a maelstrom of books, plush toys, and dirty socks that I consolidated, every so often, under the bed.

As usual since my parents had split, Dad picked me up after school on Saturday.

I jumped onto his new car, showing off my wrist. "Dad, do you like my new bracelet?"

"Sure, it's nice, but... Wait a second, what is it made of?"

A guilty blush betrayed me. I would have never thought he'd recognize the wire. "Well, I did go into your train room..." Dad had built throughout the years a huge electric train track with landscapes he had made himself. It was gorgeous, and it took a whole basement room.

Dad's face turned to anger. "You know I don't want you to play in there! It's electric wire you used to make your bracelet!"

I looked down. "I know, Dad. It's real sturdy, and I mean...not like you're going to use it anymore, right?"

He sighed. "I guess."

We looked at each other, his anger replaced by sadness. He had thought the separation temporary, but Mom had made it clear there was no going back. She had stopped talking to him altogether and she had forbidden Dad to step into the house. I had no idea what he had done to deserve such a treatment, and he seemed as clueless as I was.

Dad added, "Well, ready to go grocery shopping?"

"Yes!" I yelled. "This time focaccia for dinner, pistachio cream and chocolate gelato!"

Dad beamed. "Don't forget the whipped cream."

Finally Dad saw see me as an independent being rather than an appendage of Mom.

With the grocery in the trunk and fast food in our stomachs, Dad drove to the park of Monza. It was a beautiful spring day. Mimosa bushes exploded with yellow flowers, and the intense scent of the white, wild garlic blossoms covering the ground beneath the tall trees saturated the fresh air. The park was famous for its Formula One track, but Dad and I spent entire weekends exploring kilometers of paths snaking through fields and forests on rented pedal carriages and tandems, playing volleyball on the green lawns till dinnertime.

Dad and I entered his rented apartment in Milan around dinner time. He dropped the groceries on the floor and asked, "Wanna eat in front of the TV?"

"Hell yeah! *Odiens* is on!"

We enjoyed all the things Mom forbade, including watching silly shows like *Odiens* with bodacious showgirls like Carmen Russo.

I fell asleep on the couch with Dad scratching my back. I had never spent so much time with him in my entire life. It was a dream come true. Dad and I were finally friends.

On the following Monday afternoon and I tried to read in my own room, but I couldn't concentrate with Viola's music blasting its way in between the pages of *Pride and Prejudice*.

While I had been thriving after our parents' separation, she was not fairing well at all. She saw Dad sporadically, and when she did they argued. She had never been the sunny type, but things had gotten beyond gloomy. She spent days locked in her room blasting music. I saw her seldom, during the few meals she didn't skip. She never spoke and looked like someone who had lost her ability or willingness to smile, at least in my presence.

I hurled the book on my bed, marched to Viola's bedroom, and knocked on her door. I couldn't hear the noise of my own knocking over the loud music. I banged harder, with the anger of those who have tired of not being heard, with the frustration of those who are forced to listen to a pain that is not theirs.

The music stopped.

"What?" Viola asked from within.

I lost courage. "Ah, hi, it's me."

Unexpectedly, I heard the key turning into the door, which opened. Viola looked at me. She did not yell, she did not roll her eyes. For the first time in…I don't know how long, maybe ever, Viola just looked at me.

"Come in," she said, stepping aside.

I tried to hide my astonishment as I walked within Viola's lair, normally invisible to humans just like the fairy world of Afes. Her room was much bigger than mine, with a large window over the garden. It had changed a lot since the last time I had set foot inside. She had inherited Starry's old queen mattress (Starry had bought a new one when Dad had moved out), which was resting directly on the floor under the window.

She sat on the fuchsia love seat by the armoire. From the door, where I was standing, most of the mattress was hidden behind a bookcase and her desk.

Viola asked, "How are you?"

"Ah, I'm well. You?" I tried to keep a casual tone.

"*Really?*" Viola stared at me.

Wrong answer. Duly noted. "Ah, yeah. Why?"

"This thing with Mom and Dad doesn't upset you?"

Ah, that's what she's talking about. "Well, a little, sure, but it's been ages now and to be honest I see Dad more than ever, and if this is what they want…" Viola looked sad, defeated. She stood up. "And you?" I dared.

I couldn't recall having a similar conversation with my big sister before.

She walked to the record player and started the music over at a more reasonable volume."This song—" She cleared her quivering voice. "This song makes me think of them. Do you remember? They always used to listen to it together, in the car. It's *Hotel Supramonte* by De André."

I shook my head, a bit embarrassed because most of De André's songs were all jumbled together in my head after years of car rides.

De André sang, *"But where, where did your love go?"*

Sweet words melted in melancholy filling the emptiness in my heart, echoing through its growing walls. The more I got hurt, the more they got thicker. We are just as strong as the pain we are forced to endure.

When a sad violin ended the song, I would have liked to comfort Viola, but I did not know what to say. I had not understood the secret message behind the poetic words of the song.

"It's, uh, very sad," I said.

Luckily, often, what matters in times of great sadness and difficulty is not so much the words that are pronounced, but the feelings that push them to fill the space between two lonely people.

Viola looked up at me confirming, "Sad, yes, very sad, yet very beautiful. This solitude, this inability to understand each other…just like them."

"Yeah," I nodded, clueless.

I would have liked to continue to talk to Viola forever, to comfort her and let her know that she could count on me, but I was terrified that she might discover that I did not understand a thing about the song or the separation of Mom and Dad.

Yet, Viola started the song again, stepped away from the player, and spoke no more. Some silences take a long time to fill.

18

Meet the Devil

After dinner I snuck out to go to Grandma's to watch the cartoons Mom forbade. When Grandma was not in Afes, she was our neighbor in Arese. Our two gardens communicated through a small, rusty iron gate. I crossed it like Alice going down the white rabbit's hole. Spring was dressing Grandma's realm of flowerbeds, bushes, and fruit trees in all of its most vibrant colors, tinted by the evening light. It smelled like mud and new grass.

"Grandmaaaa! Grandmaaa!" I called.

"Here, Hon!" Her voice found me from the back of the yard.

I ran under the pergola covered with kiwi vines. Grandma was bent over double, digging into a flowerbed.

"Hi, Grandma! What are you up to?"

"Ah," she sighed, straightening up and massaging her back, "I just wanted to put down the peat before dark. I'm almost done." Grandma stretched, mumbling her unintelligible, classic string of curses, a mix of the French she had studied in school and her native *Milanese* dialect: "*Mon Dieu de la France, mi ne pö de pü!*"

"Why don't you take a break?" I asked.

"What break!" she barked. "If I don't slave, the garden goes to hell! Did you have dinner?"

"Yes, Grandma. I'm just gonna watch TV."

"Bah!" she uttered. "You're skinny like a stick!" she added bending over the flowerbed again.

I parked myself in front of her TV. With a bit of luck I found *Fist of the North Star*, which I was forbidden to watch at home because of its *excessively violent content*. No kidding, I smirked, as Kenshiro, the warrior with the seven scars, caused the heads of two minions to deform and explode in a splatter of blood.

I heard Gran coming back from the garden and she asked, from the kitchen, "Would you like some chocolate?"

"No, thank you!" I shouted back without taking my eyes off the show.

"Bread, butter, and sugar?"

"Yeah, yeah, whatever, thank you!"

Grandma reached me a few minutes later holding a tray. "What are you watching?"

"Ah...cartoons, Grandma." I tried to sound casual.

Grandma stared at the screen. "Bah! There's a movie I wanna watch in ten minutes, but it's not...suitable for you." Grandma smacked her tongue, indicating that she was excited about something, typically soap operas.

"Which movie is it, Grandma?"

"*The exorcist.*"

Thinking this was going to be one of Grandma's boring movies, I sat beside her reading the adventures of *Pimpa*, the happiest white and red pooch on the planet. Probably the *only* white and red pooch on the planet.

The film turned out to be a bit more eventful than I had expected.

Even if my eyes stared at Pimpa, my ears were haunted by the demons, screams and supernatural events that invaded the screen. *Fine.* I was almost eleven and I had seen real monsters, even if Mom insisted it had been nightmares, I could put up with a stupid movie. Plus, I wasn't even looking. Yet, somehow I could still see the images maybe because between me and hell-on-earth there was only Pimpa the pooch. She also seemed a bit concerned. After half an hour I could take it no more and stood up at the first ad break.

"Grandma, the devil isn't real, right? It's just a movie."

Grandma's eyes went wide and her nostrils flared as if she could not believe her ears. She raised a finger like an angry preacher and replied, "Are you *serious*? Of course it's *real*! The devil *does* exist! He lurks in the darkness waiting for your slightest weakness to damn you for good, Leda!"

My world crumbled into a thousand pieces. "But Mom said—"

"Your mother put garbage into your head! Blasphemy! She does not believe and will end up paying dearly for it! The signs are all over the place, but she refuses to see! What about that ridiculous snowfall in the January of '85? And in '86 when we got hail as big as tennis balls? God is angry! You must be God-fearing, Lee!"

Oh, I was fearing all right. I had seen the devil myself, and even Viola had been haunted. Not to mention Mom's friend flying on a stool!

Flustered, teary-eyed, I asked, "Grandma, what can I do to keep the devil away?" At least she didn't deny the obvious.

"Pray, Lee, pray. Pray to Jesus and he'll listen to you."

Good. Jesus and I went a long way back. I prayed every night, although it *did* rain sometimes. To get my mind off the devil, I ran into the kitchen. I climbed onto the counter to reach the wall-mounted cabinets. A meticulous excavation between medicines and other supplies led me to the "Effervescent Brioschi, citrus-flavored magnesia: digestive, refreshing, thirst quenching". I put a handful of Brioschi in my mouth. An immediate explosion of tartness burst on my tongue, filling my mouth with a citrusy, chemical foam. My eyes almost watered from the intensity, while I relished in the fizziness and the flavor. For a moment I let some white foam drool off my mouth pretending to be rabid.

"*Gross!* Cochi! What are you doing?" Uncle Bedo called, just back from work.

"Nothing!" I defended myself, half choking on the digestive and belching like a trucker.

Uncle Bedo chuckled. "If I catch you again I'll rat you out. Understood?"

I nodded. "Are you married, yet?" I whispered.

He blushed. "Soon. Speaking of which, how's your mother doing?"

Given their tense relationship, I was surprised he asked.

"Ah, okay," I answered.

"And what do you think of this *separation business*?" He wrinkled his nose as if the words stunk.

It took me a second to realize he was referring to my parents splitting. "Well, it's not great, but if that's what they need—"

Uncle interrupted me. "Are they getting back together anytime soon?"

It had been ages since they had split, six months already, and things seemed pretty settled. One of us had misunderstood the situation big time. I hoped it was me.

I replied, "I don't think so, Uncle. It seems, uh, pretty final. I mean, apparently they were arguing all the time—"

"Yes, but that's *their* problem. It's not for them to separate what God united. Marriage is a holy sacrament, you know?"

"Ah, yes. But what if it doesn't work?"

"You *make it* work. It's God's will. Your father should have put his foot down."

Uncomfortable with the topic, I said, "Well, I gotta go, Uncle, take care. BYE GRAN!" I yelled, hopping down from the counter and out into the night, watching my back just in case Jesus was busy. Scarier things were on my horizon.

We had just started to study English. 1989 was the first time it was introduced as mandatory into the elementary school system. Funny enough, our teacher, Ciro, was from Naples, and had a strong accent even when he spoke Italian.

No one was eager to be walled up in his classroom listening to incomprehensible gibberish when spring teased us through the window with a beautiful sunny day. Ciro, who normally was quite the congenial fellow, looked like he was going to lose it.

"ENOUGH IS ENOUGH!" he yelled, exasperated. "Flavio, give me that note."

"Which note?"

"NOW!"

Flavio did not budge, holding tight the note that Peo had just passed to him. Anguish devoured me maybe more than Flavio. He looked older than ten. He was the tallest kid in the school and his square jaw was set in an almost adult determination. His long hair fell in front of his angry eyes, challenging the teacher and letting him know he was no scared prey.

"Flavio, for the last time, hand me the note that Marco just passed to you, or I'll call your parents." Only teachers called Peo, whose last name was Partenopeo, with his first name, Marco.

Wow. A parent conference was just short of suspension. That seemed quite overboard! How could Ciro ask Flavio to betray his best friend? I was so disappointed in Ciro's behavior. He seemed so frustrated and angry, very much like most adults, and very much unlike himself.

I looked at Flavio who did not flinch, a wall of resentment proofing him against Ciro's request. The two exchanged a Cowboy stare-off that lasted several seconds; it felt like years. Was Ciro really gonna call Flavio's parents? As if they didn't have enough troubles. Flavio never talked about it, but his Dad, like many, had been laid off from Alfa Romeo, the car factory, and was still unemployed.

Flavio took his chances, burying the note deep into his pocket. Ciro made a show to write a note on the register.

In solidarity with Flavio and in protest against Ciro's typical adult, exaggerated, control-freak behavior, I crossed my arms and shut the hell up, which was no small feat, since I was the soul of his darn classes.

This was not just about Ciro. I was plagued by nightmares in which I was in a car but couldn't reach the pedals and I didn't know how to drive. Yet, the vehicle kept moving at a ludicrous speed on a winding road. Starry, as the good psychologist she was studying to become, had said it might mean that I didn't feel in control of my life. No kidding! The direction of my days was dictated by the yelling of adults, who had lost their compass. Well, screw it. That day in Ciro's class I decided not to play along.

My protest was quite successful. Ciro's questions lingered unanswered in a bored classroom. Nico turned around to smirk at me, giving me a thumbs up. He knew what I was doing and loved it. My heart made a little summersault. Nico looked dazzling when he smiled, which did not happen often. Every fiber in my being admired Flavio's courage, his strength, and his radiant personality, yet I could not stop staring at the back of Nico's head because he had bonded with my dark side, the one I hid even from myself.

Ciro scrambled to get a reaction out of the crowd. "Fine. Whoever answers the highest number of questions gets a secret prize," he promised. "How do you say *come stai* in English?"

Secret prize? I had to bite my tongue to remain stoic, judging Ciro as if I were his conscience. The class went back to its more normal, lively rhythm, the scene with Flavio soon forgotten by most.

Ciro declared, "Okay, kids. The winner is...Leda!" Cries of protest and disappointment rose from the whole class.

Stunned, I joined them. "But if I didn't even—"

Ciro interrupted me, "Yes, yes, I know. Come here."

Ouch. Did I get in trouble?

I crawled out of my desk and trudged toward him, everyone's curious eyes following my fate.

Ciro, who was very tall, bent down to put a plastic Smurf into my hand. It was playing the trumpet, just like Dad had when he was in the army. I didn't even like Smurfs, yet I gloated for getting the undeserved prize, even if I felt guilty.

Ciro bent over me like a wilted sunflower, whispering so that no one else could hear, "Listen, Lee, I heard about your parents' separation, it must be hard."

His words hit me like a cold shower, shoving me through time and space in a parallel world away from English, the quartet, school and the Smurfs, a world where my parents didn't live together any longer. How did Ciro find out? How did it fit into that sunny day at school?

I squeezed my hand around the Smurf, and I understood that this was a consolation prize, in the literary sense of the term, comfort from the ugliness of life and the end of love...with a plastic Smurf. Ciro obviously hadn't known of Flavio's Dad's unemployment. Maybe we would all be a lot kinder to each other if assumed people have reasons to act the way the do. All feelings come from somewhere.

Ciro's voice called me back to reality."Hem, Lee, there's more," he said. "Nico's father came to speak to you."

The blood drained from my face. Nico's father was as legendary as a unicorn but scary as hell. No one had ever met nor seen him, even from afar. Even for First Communion, the biggest deal on earth according to Gram, Nico had been accompanied by his brother alone. Then again, I had been the only girl sporting blue wool pants rather than a meringue dress.

In years of friendship we had only heard Nico's Dad's metallic voice, always dry, through the intercom, since we never played at Nico's because *his brother had to study*. Nico's discomfort in relaying the excuses constantly justifying the absence of his parents had deepened the mystery. Nico didn't want to talk about it, and let's be clear, if Nico was afraid, most certainly so was I.

Most importantly, why in the whole world would Nico's scary Dad come all the way to school to see *me*? My terrified gaze was betrayed by Ciro's, fixed on the classroom's door, toward which he pushed me, gently though firmly. I had no choice. I launched a quick, helpless, inquisitive look toward Nico who, like everyone else, was staring at me, perplexed. He knew nothing, and his gaze turned to alarm when he saw the fear in my eyes.

I was on my own to face Nico's terrifying father.

19

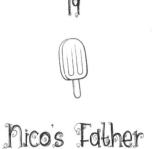

Nico's Father

Way too fast, I found myself in the hallway outside the classroom facing Nico's father, huge and gray like a mountain, but a lot hairier. He did not smile. He just stared, studying me.

After a moment's hesitation, I remembered my manners and I offered him my hand, muttering, "Lee. Nice to meet you."

His jaw dropped. His eyes widened and his nostrils flared a bit. He looked surprised, or maybe hungry. I was not sure.

"*You? You* are Lee?" he managed.

Surprised, not hungry. Thank goodness.

I nodded, at a loss. He was still holding the hand that he had shaken as if to stifle any thought of escape. He smacked his face with his left, dragging it to his mouth, rubbing it in a pensive gesture, still staring at me.

He finally spoke with a very strong Sicilian accent, "Lass, you were not what I expected, *miiii.*"

I giggled inside, recognizing Nico's typical exclamation. His observation took me aback, but I dared not investigate.

He continued to talk with a large, gray eyebrow raised, reminding me of a typical expression of my friend. "Was it you—was it you... who bit Nico?"

Ah, that.

I connected the dots, noticing his peculiar use of verbs, another southern affectation.

"Ah, Yes, Sir," I admitted, looking him straight in the eye. *Darn snitch.*

He looked even more puzzled. I surmised that he had come to make a scene but surprise had killed his steam. His thug son had been brutalized by a petite girl with a braid and green eyes. He came to defend his offspring and now felt ridiculous, which offended me a bit. Couldn't girls be badass, dangerous, ever?

He hesitated and then added as if trying to remember a spiel he had prepared beforehand, "Well, that was...*wrong.* You don't just go around biting people. Didn't your parents tell you?"

Okay. Now, I was furious. I couldn't believe that Nico had sung, the whimper, and I couldn't believe the nerve of this madman, who raised a savage and a snitch and wanted *me* to tell my parents how to educate kids.

I glared at him and retorted, "Well maybe, instead, *you* should teach your son not to go around fondling people's buttocks." I was still burning with indignation at Nico's offense. I was a member of the quartet, not some screeching floozy he could run after during recess. "Sir," I added to conclude my remark in a somewhat polite manner.

Meanwhile, he had let go of my hand and his jaw had surrendered to disbelief. He snapped it back shut and closed his eyes. When he looked at me again he seemed focused on a new resolve, a rekindled anger, but not against me. He turned his face into stone and concluded, "I am very sorry that I bothered you, *miss.* Rest assured that Nico will be disciplined."

Oh, merda.

I was no longer in the eye of the cyclone, but I felt sorry for Nico. While the gray monster trudged away, a shiver ran down my back, but it *was* Nico's fault. He could have shut his mouth, and none of this would have ever happened.

At recess I briefed Peo and Flavio about the meeting, omitting the most embarrassing details (how scared I had been and Nico slapping my sorry *culo*).

I said, "Nico snitched on me, the sucker. Can you believe him? I beat him up, and he went to whimper to his dad. But I gave his dad a piece of my mind…"

Peo and Flavio exchanged a skeptical look. I wasn't lying, but they were not dumb.

In the awkward silence that followed, I stole a glance at Nico. He was with Mario and some other guys, chasing the prettiest girls, who ran down the hallways screeching. First among them, Laura the Gorgeous: slender, long blond hair, and already a hint of breasts.

The girls laughed and ran away, while the boys chased them feeling them where they could. The odd behavior had started the year before, likely triggered by a combination of pre-puberty and spicy Italian comedies, pervasive on TV, where women were helpless in the face of males' predatory behaviors.

I was furious that Nico, even for a moment, had seen me as a girl and decided to slap my butt. Had he expected me to run away, giggling? *Stronzo*. He deserved the bite. Or maybe, if I had to be completely honest with myself, I was furious that he didn't *always* see me as a girl, that anyone else did not see me as a girl *ever*, and worst of all, that neither did I.

Instead of giggling and running away like apparently appropriate, I had torn the arm of the only fearless male that had shown me any attention. I was furious that I had never written to Ezio and that, likely, I never would. Since I didn't like myself, I couldn't fathom how anyone could.

I was furious that I didn't have the grace to be a girl, pretending to be stupid not to scare the boys away. I wanted to be smart, I wanted to scare the daylights out of them. I wanted them to respect me but, at the same time, I didn't want to feel so lonely. My heart ached. I was not a boy nor a girl; I didn't know what I was. I was furious that all of this seemed suddenly so important.

I looked at Nico running after Laura, his brown eyes bright with amusement. I would have liked to be able to wear skirts and earrings. I would have liked Nico to look at me the way he looked at Laura. When he did look at me, I was pretty sure he did not see *me*, anyway. By denying what I was, I had made myself invisible.

I looked at my jeans and my sneakers: blue canvas and white rubber, my favorite. My lowered gaze perceived a pair of sneakers right in front of mine, Nico's. I jerked my head up, my cheeks burning with anger and guilt. I tried to hide the shame and betrayal, but also the heartache for putting him in trouble. I gathered myself and shoved my gaze into his, challenging him. His eyes took me aback: sweet, sincere.

Nico tilted his head sideways a little. "Lee, I'm sorry. He saw the marks on my arm and your name came up. I had no idea he'd come to school."

My heart exploded with joy. He didn't snitch. Nico *was* my friend, a dumbass, but my friend. I could trust him, after all.

I smiled. "Now I understand. I'm sorry too. I hope I did not get you in trouble."

Nico, who still had his hands in his pockets, shrugged and said, "Eh, I'm used to it."

He sure was.

20

Delicious

It was the end of March, and Easter holidays had finally come. I went downstairs for breakfast around eleven and I couldn't believe my eyes: Starry was in the kitchen with the evident intention of cooking. She seemed, justly, very nervous. I didn't have time to open my mouth that she approached me, ladle in hand: a sight as rare as scary.

"Leda, I was just looking for you. Tonight a friend of mine from school will come over for dinner, and I want to make a good impression. Behave yourself, understood?"

I. Was. So. Annoyed.

She didn't even say hi.

She Leda-ed me.

She talked to me before I even got to have breakfast.

She was angry about something I didn't do yet.

And let's be honest..."Geez, it's not like I'm a savage, you know?" She looked at me sideways, and I didn't add much because I remembered recently belching the alphabet with Luca. "Where's Viola?" I asked.

"At Grandma's, studying Latin. Then she'll sleep over at Marta's. They have to babysit her little brother."

Marta's Dad had walked out on them when she was five. Her Mom had recently remarried and had a baby brother whom Marta adored. I didn't think that Viola ever babysat *me*, only her bestie's little brat.

I ate my typical Italian breakfast of milk and cookies, watching Starry sweat over Grandma Magda's recipe-book, one of the few traces left of Dad's previous existence in this very same house. I couldn't believe I had hung out with him in this very same kitchen, just a year ago. I saw my paternal Grandma, Grandma Magda, rarely, during boring, formal, Sunday lunches that Dad forced me to sit through. She was the opposite of my gardening, telenovelas-loving, dialect-swearing maternal Grandma.

Starry wore the immaculate apron we had given her years before for her birthday. It had been Dad's idea, to encourage her to take on more of the house chores that she shunned. It read *An old hen makes a better broth*, and showed *Lupo Alberto*, the famous wolf comic character, simmering his concerned, feathered girlfriend, Marta the hen, in a big cauldron. Starry hadn't laughed at the time.

Now she brandished the wooden spoon around the kitchen, reading a bit of the recipe, going to the fridge, then changing her mind and walking back to re-read the recipe and then back to the fridge. She opened it, took out the milk, back to the recipe. It was painful to watch.

"Starry, not to be mean, but if you want to make a good impression, why don't we order pizza? And it's eleven in the morning anyway. Isn't it a bit early for dinner?"

"Oh, shut up, Lee!" she blew up in frustration.

"Hey, I am just trying to help."

"Really?" She looked at me. "Maybe, then, while I start cooking the frozen peas, can you figure out the *besciamella* sauce recipe?"

That seemed an unfair subdivision of tasks, but we joined forces to decipher the cryptic recipes of Grandma Magda, who was an excellent cook but rarely shared her secrets. Her recipes were peppered with minimalistic clues like *just enough, until cooked* and the likes.

Five hours later, Starry's apron was no longer immaculate, and the table was a battlefield littered with explosions of flour, milk, chopped ham, and other unidentified befallen. What mattered though, was that the pasta casserole was baking in the oven and we were full of hope. It smelled like melting cheese and fried ham.

The *chicken in lemon jello* (which made me gag, but Starry would hear no reason because she had already made it once eight years ago and it had turned out edible) was in the fridge to jellify (yuck).

Fuzzer, our fat, house cat, circumnavigated the table, mewling hopeful.

Starry grabbed the pan with the chocolate pudding premix from the stove and looked into it, horrified, a revealing smell of burnt wafting off the dessert in generous smoky puffs. She threw the pan into the sink, and it sizzled. She slumped in a chair, defeated, head in her hands, staring into nothing with teary eyes.

I said, "Starry, ice cream is fine."

She lifted her head, searching my eyes. "You think so?"

"Of course! Who's your friend, a *chef*? What matters is good company, right?"

"Okay," she conceded. She got up to clean the table, still forlorn. Then, she almost gave me a heart attack. "WHAT? FOUR? IS IT REALLY FOUR ALREADY? I ONLY HAVE TWO HOURS TO GET READY!"

She dropped the apron on a chair and dashed upstairs screaming, "Do you mind cleaning up? And setting the table? With the good tablecloth!"

This friend had better be freaking awesome.

🍦

At half past six (unfashionably late), the doorbell rang.

Starry looked dazzling in a casual gray dress that accentuated her slim figure. Red sandals matched her nails, and black, heavy makeup made her big brown eyes huge behind the intellectual-styled spectacles.

I eyed her suspiciously. "Starry, spit it out. Is this guy a friend or a *boy*friend?"

"What boyfriend?" She jolted embarrassed, pausing with her hand on the door. "Are you sure that I look okay?"

"Yes, Mom. You look gorgeous. Just like three minutes ago, in perfect shape to open the door."

My irony was not appreciated. She fixed an auburn lock behind her ear. She had recently cut her hair short and dyed it a more reddish hue. She took a deep breath and finally opened the door for our much-awaited guest to make his entrance.

"Hi!" he greeted Starry with a kiss on the cheek.

I hated him on the spot.

The stranger was very tall, gray-haired, with two tiny, pale, blue eyes that looked evil behind spiffy blue glasses resting on his red, porky face. Not like he was overweight, just fleshy: red and fleshy and evil.

Starry glared at me, and I forced a smile in spite of the distrust that was filling me to the brim.

He turned to address little old me. "Hi, you must be Leda. I am Marco Soldanti."

Who would have ever introduced themselves to a kid using their last name? The Soldanti was suspicious.

The Soldanti added, "I brought you a gift."

Ah, corruption!

I had just met this Soldanti dude, and yet he had brought me a gift. Since he did not know me, I assumed he must have wronged me somehow, and brought the gift out of guilt. Something was cooking. I didn't like it. I didn't like *him*. I took the package, studying it, promising myself not to like its contents, no matter what.

"Thank you," I muttered out of politeness.

I unwrapped a white, brand new, professional Mikasa volleyball. This was a real volleyball, like the ones used by *Mila and Shiro* in my favorite cartoon, *Attacker You!* It was nothing like the cheap plastic ones Dad and I kept tearing apart, playing at the park. Against all odds and my own will, I felt my eyes twinkle. Maybe I had misjudged the Soldanti.

"This is amazing! Thank you so much! How do I inflate it?" He had my full attention.

"Ah, uh, maybe, I guess we need a needle or something?"

"Oh. Do you have one?"

"Ah, no. I'll bring one the next time," he answered evasively already focusing on Starry.

"Okay," I conceded, disappointed at the idea of having to see the Soldanti again to get my new Mikasa operational. I still couldn't shake off that first bad impression.

We started off with pre-dinner drinks and appetizers, all of Fuzzer's favorites. His mewling presence comforted me. The two of us choked on chips and olives, while the grown-ups chatted and drank red wine.

I had never seen Starry drinking before, if not for Veronica the Airhead's birthday party where, in the kitchen with the other moms, she had smoked multiple cigarettes at once in between cocktails.

Every so often the Soldanti dude questioned me about school, my favorite subjects, and my friends. I did my best to answer, looking sideways at Starry's urgent nodding and smiling since it was apparent that both the Soldanti and I couldn't care less about each other and were putting up a show for her benefit only.

At dinnertime, I couldn't wait to ravish the ham and pea pasta-casserole, one of my favorite dishes ever, a rare treat because it was one of Grandma Magda's recipes, yet not fancy enough by her rigid standards to make the Sunday menu.

We sat at the kitchen table, where we always ate. Starry carried the pan, just rewarmed in the oven. The pasta smelled and looked wonderful; a tarnished thin crust of cheese let you occasionally glimpse the velvety shyness of the *besciamella* sauce, penne peeking like waves in a sea strewn with islets of ham and peas.

The unmistakable aroma of melted parmesan filled my greedy nostrils, but I waited for Starry to serve the Soldanti and his fake smiles first. He reminded me of one of *Momo*'s creepy Men in Gray. Like them, he sure looked like he was trying to trick Starry into giving up something she should have better kept dear.

The Soldanti caught me staring and, unaware of my gloomy thoughts, declared with his unbearable nasal voice, "*Buon appetito!*"

I dug into my pasta, trying to get Starry's attention to exchange the nonverbal snarky comments that surely she was also thinking. Strangely, she didn't notice me. Her eyes were glued to our obnoxious guest, her fork hanging midair.

The Soldanti conceded, adjusting the glasses on his big nose, "deliiiciouuuusss," painfully dragging each vowel in that nasal pitch that sounded as spontaneous as *Raffaella Carrà*, the oldest talk show host on earth.

As the dinner progressed, the Soldanti kept repeating his theatrical comment, identical and condescending, with every dish presented to him. "Deliiiciouuuusss!"

Somehow this escaped Starry.

Normally, we would have secretly stolen ironic glances at each other, trying not to laugh out loud. Yet, our ever open communication channel was obstructed by the hideous presence of the Soldanti. At least the pasta was great. I couldn't speak for the Middle-Age-style chicken.

After dinner, Starry sent me upstairs, while she remained to chat a little longer with our guest. Even if I was elated to scram, I couldn't quite shake a chilling shiver down my spine. I didn't know what the Soldanti was trying to sell, but I sure hoped that Starry was not going to buy it.

The next morning at breakfast, Starry didn't even wait for me to have my milk to ask, "So? What did you think?"

Her eyes twinkled as she held up her tiny espresso cup.

I replied, "Starry, the pasta was amazing!"

"No, dufus, about Marco."

Finally we could get a good laugh out of this outlandish character.

"Who, the Soldanti dude?" I prodded, a smirk already giving away my amusement. I grabbed Starry's glasses and put them halfway down my nose, making a great show of adjusting them, while with an eloquent grimace I imitated the much detested: *deliiiciouuuusss.*

My personation was impeccable, yet Starry did not laugh one bit. Her castrated expectation congealed in the form of a bitter smile, just like the nasty gelatin on the chicken.

She asked, "Why? Didn't you like him?"

"Starry, not at all." Surprised and dismayed by her reaction I elaborated, "He seemed so fake, with those little eyes in the porky face with the strawberry nose."

"The *strawberry* nose?"

"Yeah. Big, red, and full of blackheads." Starry remained in an enigmatic, puzzled silence. Feeling bad I asked, "Why, do you have to work together? Is he selling you something?"

My words jerked Starry out of her catatonic state. "No. I know what it is. You are jealous."

"Jealous? Of the Soldanti dude? Why would I ever be jealous?" Starry blushed and looked down. I blurted, "NO WAY! Do you...*like* him?"

"Yes, *a lot*."

And all of a sudden, I lost my sense of humor too.

21

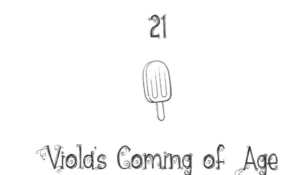

Viola's Coming of Age

A couple of weeks later, Dad dropped me back at the house on a quiet Sunday afternoon.

I was reading the first volume of *The Shannara Trilogy* into my bedroom when Viola's spite hit me full in the heart. She yelled from the bathroom, "You're just a dimwit, Lee! Can you at least flush, for god's sake?"

I could not believe my ears. As I marched to the restroom I yelled back, "What are you talking about? I always flush!"

She was staring at the toilet with her hands on her hips, her hair up in a messy bun. "A dimwit and a *liar*! I'm not gonna clean after *you*! Flush the freaking toilet, or I'm gonna tell Mom!" She stomped down the hallway and slammed the door to her room.

Furious, I stalked into the bathroom that I shared with Viola. In the yellowish water floated a lonely, cigarette butt, lipstick at one end. I was going to kill her.

"VIOLAAAAA! VIOLAAAAAA!"

"WHAT THE HELL DO YOU WANT NOW?" The scream came out muffled through her door, locked, as always.

"COME HERE!" I ordered, as peremptory as I could. This time she was not going to get away with it.

"Go to hell!" was her straight up answer.

I was going to kill her, I was going to kill her! I trotted to her door and kept knocking until the key turned and the door jerked open. "WHAT THE CAZZO IS YOUR PROBLEM?" Viola screamed.

"DON'T YOU KNOW THAT I HAVE TO STUDY FOR THE MATURITY EXAM? ARE YOU DONE WITH YOUR *STRONZATE?*" She slammed the door back into my face.

Never. Win.

Mr. Hyde kicked her door, and I left before he committed worse crimes.

I had two certainties: first, I did not smoke nor used lipstick. Second, if Starry found out that Viola was *still* smoking, she was going to lock her into her room from the outside and throw away the key, possibly with Grandma inside to tutor her in Latin and maybe even Greek. Why not, she could learn that, too, since I had just found out that Grandma had earned a degree in classic letters before going back to the housewife's forced labor routine.

So why, with tears in my eyes, was I going to flush the toilet? Because, after all, I preferred less hatred from Viola than the sweet taste of being right.

It was an important year for Viola. She was about to turn eighteen. The huge, terrifying maturity exam that she had to face to graduate from high school was the downside of much more pleasurable perks. She would have soon been inducted into the adult world, gaining her right to vote and to drive. Drinking had been happening, at least legally, since the age of sixteen.

To celebrate her coming of age, a traditional big party had been organized in a club in Milan, with all of her friends from the radio, her classmates, and Marta, of course. Naturally, I was not invited. I was way too young and *I would have been in the way*. I pretended not to care at all.

🍦

On the Friday of Viola's birthday, a few hours before the party, the doorbell rang unexpectedly. When I opened the door, I turned to stone. In front of my bewildered eyes, stood with a dashing smile and an orchid in his hand, Renzo, the light technician.

Without taking my eyes off the apparition, I screamed, "Violaaaaaa!"

I wondered if Renzo showed up at the birthday party of all the naïve girls he hooked up with weekly. Somehow, I doubted it. I had never even conceived that Dad could have been wrong. The idea that

Viola's crazy heart was right instead made me want to laugh out loud, really loud. Was Ezio going to show up on my birthday too? Then I remembered that, in spite of my promise, I had never written to him, and he didn't have my address.

Meanwhile, Renzo hopped on the stepping stones and reached the door. "Hi, Leda, how are you?" He planted a kiss on my cheek and handed *me* the orchid. "This is for delivering Viola's message despite all the perils. Thank you!"

Right behind me, Viola exclaimed in seventh heaven, "Renzo, I cannot believe it!"

I got out of the way as the two embraced. I ran off to the kitchen to put the orchid into a vase.

Starry intercepted me. "Is it really Renzo?"

It was Renzo to answer, stepping into the kitchen and kissing Starry's hand, "In the flesh! Miss Silvia, I am honored."

Wow, he was all out. Starry was completely taken with the gallant newcomer and offered him some coffee setting up the *moka*, the device to make espresso on the stove.

Viola protested, "How come *she* gets an orchid on *my* birthday?"

Renzo smiled. "Everything in its own time." Wow, he was good. He asked, "So, how are you?"

Viola replied, "Buried under way too many books, trying to survive the prospect of my maturity exam."

The confidential tone of their conversation suggested that they had kept in touch.

Tired of always hearing about it, I asked,"Why is this maturity exam such a big deal?"

Viola answered, "Because it's *huge!*"

"I get that. But how can it be worse than all the tests you take during the year?"

Viola explained, while Starry poured the espresso, "Well, first of all I don't even get to know if I'm admitted to the exam till June when everyone's grades will be exposed on public boards, so that I can be laughed at by the whole school. So, I get to study like a slave till then, even if likely I'll have to repeat the whole fifth year, since my grades are, uh…" She looked meekly at Starry. "Not improving as much as I'd hoped."

Starry kept puffing on her cigarette looking bitter, but she didn't interrupt Viola's spiel. My sister continued, "Then, *if* I am admitted, I get to *really* grind away for two weeks to prep for the written exams: two six-hours-long monsters: Italian composition first and then English after a couple of days."

I gritted my teeth. "Okay, I get it. That does sound appalling."

Renzo chuckled, but Viola continued, "But *soft*! The worst has to come yet!"

"It does?" I asked, missing Viola's literary quote.

"Yes, it does. *Then* they start the oral examinations, in alphabetical order, starting with one letter at random. A committee of ten teachers, of which nine you've never met before, get to grill you for about an hour on everything included in the program of the last year for at least two subjects."

I exclaimed, "Man! That's evil! Do you at least get to choose the subjects?"

Viola answered, "Yes, but they can decide to change one at the last minute. Isn't that ridiculous?"

Starry chimed in, "Oh, stop whining! In my time the oral examination was on *every* subject covered during the entire five years of high school!"

"NO WAY!" We all stared at her horrified. Indeed the big exam was changed every so often by a new reform, in an attempt to make it better. Somehow it always seemed worse.

Starry gauged our reaction, sipped some espresso, and then conceded, "Okay, maybe not all five years. I don't remember."

How could such an ordeal be ever forgotten?

"And when is it all done?" I asked, since Renzo's presence granted me answers, for once.

Viola answered, "By the end of July."

"Man! They screw up your whole summer!"

"Yep."

"Well, hopefully you'll get to go first, at least then you're done."

Viola's eyebrows shot up. "Are you *insane*? I need time to study! That is if they ever admit me in the first place."

Renzo, who had been sipping coffee, amused, asked, "Did you decide your examination subjects?"

Viola sighed. "Well, for the oral examination I ended up choosing English and Psychology."

Starry rolled her eyes and said, "I'm telling you, Viola, you're making a mistake!"

Viola snorted, frustrated in turn, rehashing for Renzo the discussion that she and Starry had gone through almost daily in the past week or two. "The psych prof is a hunk. Half the school has a crush on him and chose psych as their subject for the exam. This means that they'll change the subject for a bunch of people, and Starry's afraid it might end up being me."

Renzo joked, "Should I be jealous?"

"Of what?"

"The hunk."

Viola blushed and replied, "Of course not! I'm the only one genuinely interested in psychology rather than the teacher! If they change the subject to someone it had better not be *me*. I'd rather they did not admit me in the first place." Her face sagged.

"Does it really look so grim?" Renzo asked.

Starry took over. "If she only had studied from the beginning of the year—"

"And if only you didn't force me to go to Grandma for tutoring in Latin…" Viola interrupted. "I would have suffered less trauma!"

Renzo chuckled, and Starry added, "At least you have all of my understanding for math. I'd fail that, too."

I rejoiced because instead I was awesome with math, thanks to Grandma's forced labor learning multiplication tables by heart, in Afes, during the summer of third grade.

The doorbell buzzed again, and Starry jumped off her chair, brightening up. "It's Marco!"

I disappeared into my room to avoid the Soldanti. I had given up about the needle required to inflate the volleyball, which lay abandoned and flat in a corner of my bedroom.

At least some stories did have a happy ending, like Viola and Renzo's, provided Dad didn't find out. The Soldanti's insinuating voice molded a fake happy birthday for my sister, downstairs, and I was mercilessly reminded of more concrete, less happy realities.

Dad had always promised that he would have bought Viola a car when she turned eighteen. Maybe he thought the day would never come, and yet... After Viola's very successful party, there had been much pressuring and reminding Dad of his promise and they had gone to a dealer. They came back home with a brand new *Fiat Uno*, in a beautiful, metallic shade of teal. I greeted them from the backyard.

Viola did not seem happy. "I was just hoping for something a little more aggressive, that's all," she explained to me through the open window of her new ride.

"And I'm hoping you'll graduate with sixty/sixty," Dad countered sarcastically.

Viola parked in the garage and Marta climbed out of the back of the car, joining me in the front yard.

Dad said, "Viola, back out of the garage, for practice. It's not easy with the curved driveway."

"Dad, it's not a problem."

Viola knew that Starry was locked inside the house, waiting for Dad to leave to come check out the car. For some reason I ignored, she did not want to see him. They hadn't exchanged a word since Dad had moved out, except for the occasional, frigid two words required by the accidental intercepting of a phone call for Viola or for me. It was awkward.

Yet, Dad was not going to give up and Viola, reluctantly, climbed back into the car at his side, engaging the reverse.

After all, who would like to perform: 1-A difficult maneuver, 2-For the first time, 3-On their brand new car, 4-Paid for by their no-nonsense dad, 5-In front of the whole family?

Indeed Marta and I were standing in the middle of the lawn, Starry was secretly peering through her office's curtains, and even Fuzzer the cat was sitting under the shade of the big poplar tree.

Submissive, yet annoyed, Viola started the peristalsis out of the garage. A bit left. No, right. Too much. Forward, back again, right. Too much. Left. Back.

Through the open window, I heard Dad huffing, then he said, "Look at the rearview mirror!" He was in the front seat, holding on for dear life as if Viola were driving Formula One. His tension escalated. "STOP! EASY! NOOO! SON OF A WITCH! EASY, I SAID! RIGHT! RIGHT! MORE RIGHT!"

He made *me* anxious, and I was just watching. After numerous attempts, Viola managed to back the car out of the garage. She then had to turn, always backing up, following the narrow driveway and possibly centering the gate.

A first attempt ended up too wide on the lawn, causing Fuzzer to dart up the steps to the entrance. The studio curtain moved aside revealing Starry's frown.

At the third attempt, Viola nailed the driveway and headed toward the gate, but Dad kept gritting his teeth, emitting sounds of distress and frustrated half profanities that only exacerbated the tension. "Stop, OOOOH, STOP, I SAID!"

Viola slammed on the breaks. "WHAT NOW?" she demanded, exasperated.

"You're not centered, that's *what*! Look in your side mirrors!" Dad snapped back, just as irritated.

Yet Viola, who could take it no longer, hit the accelerator and the car jolted out of the gate with a screeching sound that chilled the blood in my veins. Distressed and defeated, Viola got out of the car to assess the damage.

Dad looked like he'd been shot right through his heart, hands in his hair and the face of one who knew that this would have been the inevitable, tragic epilog. I wondered if a different face could have, in fact, rendered the tragic epilog a little less inevitable. A series of silver scratches marked the impact with the gate on the right rear side of Viola's *Uno* car.

Starry disappeared again behind the curtain. Viola looked dejected, but Dad wouldn't let it go. "I told you to look in the side mirror—"

I interrupted him, "Oh, come on now, it's just a scratch! If you clean it a little, it'll come right off, see?"

I spat on the sleeve of my sweatshirt and rubbed the bruised buttock of the *Uno*.

"Really?" Viola looked at me, while Dad lost his voice for a moment, before adding,

"Yeah right. Forget it. It will take some hard cash to fix *that*."

Truly, we never found out because Marta, who had stayed stone-faced and silent till then, declared, *"Basty*, I think the scratch is beautiful. *Uno* cars are all the same, but now yours is special. You should leave the scratch and baptize the car *Scarred."*

The scratch remained in everlasting remembrance of that first, painful maneuver, marking my sis's vehicle as *Scarred*, forever.

Curious, I asked, "Marta, how come that you and Viola call each other *Basty* all the time?"

She lowered her eyes to find mine in spite of the black curls that crowded her face. "It's short for Bastard." At my quizzical look she elaborated, "There is no way that we are the blood of our supposed parents."

I asked no more. My undying terror of being adopted, given that I looked nothing like the rest of my family, confirmed that my sis and I were in very different phases of our lives.

22

Miami, Mee-amee

It was the end of May, and we were going on a school trip to visit the Borromean Islands of *Lago Maggiore*: *Isola Bella, Isola Dei Pescatori* and *Isola Madre*. We met in front of the school at 6:30 AM, dew covering the dawn-tinted grass with the mesmerizing scent of summer. The school grounds were otherwise deserted. Looking at the big doors without the crowd waiting to get in, filled me with a sense of surreal and forbidden as if I were in a picture of a familiar place from a different time where I didn't belong anymore.

I asked no one in particular, "Isn't it weird? Being here with no one around?"

Nico and Peo didn't say a word, while Flavio raised an eyebrow. Gesturing at our classmates, he replied, "Lee, what are you talking about?"

I didn't insist. I didn't want to seem weirder than I felt, somehow isolated in a crowd of yelling classmates. Most kids swarmed the *Broggi* bus, the typical rental for school trips, comparing their packed lunches.

Antonietta gathered us to roll call, which delivered me at Mario's side.

He prompted, "So? Ready to give up your sandwich, Lee?"

"Oh, go to hell, Mario!"

Antonietta yelled, "Leda, quiet! Everyone on the bus in single file!"

My sidelong glance to Mario betrayed the mortification of the unfair reproach.

The bus crooned off. A loud, cheerful choir covered its gentle hum. Only decent songs, however, because no one would have ever dreamed of disappointing Antonietta.

Mario didn't give up and grabbed my backpack. I snatched it back blurting, "Man, do you ever get tired of busting my balls?"

Mario hesitated for a second before replying, "No, it's my favorite pastime." I glared at him and stashed my bag between the window and myself. He asked, "Are you in a bad mood?"

"Not before I met you, I wasn't."

It was strange that Mario, of all people, would ask me such a thing, and it was even stranger that he was right; I was indeed in an awful mood.

The approaching end of elementary school terrified me. After five years together with the same classmates we were all going to be shuffled into the new middle school. I pretended to join in the singing that had erupted around me to avoid the searching eyes of Mario, that today more than ever, didn't want to mind his own business.

🍦

We had toured the islands of *Lago Maggiore* for the whole day. The ferry approached *Isola Madre* wading through the quiet, blue waters of the lake, which was surrounded by scattered villas and villages. Forest painted the inclines preceding the steep rise of the Prealps, littered with an abundance of colorful azaleas.

The island seemed larger than the other two we had visited, exploding in a fragrant display of wisteria, magnolia, and oleander. We were supposed to proceed in double file holding hands, but we were way too old for *that*, so we scrambled in a fluid flock, chatting. Nico kept straying and doing his best to get in trouble. Veronica the Airhead approached me on the right, probably just to be close to Mario.

Although we had been classmates since kindergarten, Veronica and I had never been close friends. We didn't have much in common. Everything about her was pink, sparkly and smelled nice. She had long curly blond hair and big blue eyes. With her characteristic sweet smile she asked, "What does your t-shirt say?"

I looked down at my favorite t-shirt, reserved especially for the field trip. It was white, with blue short sleeves, and a big American football on the front, but to be honest I had never read the lettering before.

I held out my shirt and read out loud, "*Super Bowl.*"

"What does it mean?"

"I don't know. I think it's English. Super means big. Bowl...maybe it's a very big ball?" I guessed looking at the football on the front of the t-shirt.

"You're so smart," Veronica flattered me.

I read the rest of the t-shirt, "*Super Bowl. Miami Dolphins, 1985.*"

I didn't know that in the faraway United States, in 1985, a team called Miami Dolphins had lost a very important sports competition and Italy was getting all the useless, pre-printed merchandise declaring them victors. I thought my t-shirt was the hight of American fashion.

"WHAT?" Mario yelled, outraged, at my left, where he had been quiet, lost in his own thoughts.

I repeated, "MIAMI DOL—"

"OF COURSE NOT! ARE YOU INSANE?" He turned purple and ran away, leaving me bewildered staring at his back, holding my own t-shirt.

"What's wrong with him?" I muttered while Veronica giggled.

A sudden epiphany downed on me: MIAMI... Mee amee... *MI AMI...* Do you love me?

I turned to Veronica, "Oh my goodness, he thought I was talking to him! He thought I asked him if... if he loved me!" I finished the sentence, face tingling, stomach dropping.

Veronica kept giggling. "He sure did. I'm glad he ran away at the news, but I hope he comes back soon," she added, her gaze longing after him. The girl was much quicker than I had given her credit for.

I yelled, "MARIOOO! I was just reading my shirt!" But he was already quite far.

I almost snapped my neck turning around, but Flavio was chatting with Peo and oblivious to what had just happened. I thought, mortified, that now Mario believed I had a crush on him.

Why would he run away otherwise? I felt so miserable and embarrassed. At least he wasn't going to talk to me anymore. I hoped he wouldn't start spreading rumors.

Nico asked smirking, "What the hell did you do to him this time, Lee?"

"Hell, nothing!" I hadn't seen Nico sneaking up on me. Veronica, startled, ran ahead to catch up with her girlfriends. Nico didn't notice or pretended not to.

I added, "He's just, uh, dumb."

He glared in the general direction where Mario had disappeared and answered, "If you say so." I wasn't quite sure what he meant, but he added, "I hope this time he doesn't come back."

I looked at Nico, a bit puzzled. "Yeah, me too."

"Good," Nico said.

"Good," I echoed.

This conversation wasn't going anywhere and it felt awkward, my heart starting to race for no apparent reason. I felt, weird, exposed and vulnerable.

Nico looked at the ground. "You have no clue, do you?"

"About *what*?"

Nico looked at me, and it felt like I had never seen him before, maybe because he was finally smiling, or maybe because after all of our years of friendship he had forgotten to hide behind his tough-guy mask.

I flinched. His mouth opened to say something, but he stopped mid-sentence. He looked down again, his black hair hiding his eyes. "Nothing. One day you'll figure it out, Lee." He kicked a pebble and ran after it.

Merda! Nico was starting to sound like a grown-up.

Back home Starry was excited to hear stories from my school trip. We were sitting at the table in our backyard in front of my favorite summer dish, so easy even Starry could pull it off, prosciutto with cantaloupe melon.

"Starry, really, it was nothing special. The flowers were pretty." I stuffed my face in melon, the saltiness of the cured prosciutto contrasting with the sweet pulp of the cantaloupe.

Starry studied me. "Mm. Is something wrong?"

I shrugged. I couldn't tell her about the big blow up with Mario and even less about my conversation with Nico.

Mom turned her eyes into slits before breaking into a smirk. "Tell me the truth, Lee, do you like someone?"

I felt my face on fire and hated myself for it. "*Like*? What do you mean?"

"You blushed!" I frowned at Starry and she sighed, bringing her hands to her heart and explaining, "I mean that when that special someone walks close to you your heart races and you feel edgy, flustered—"

"Awkward?" I interrupted her, my mouth going dry.

Starry chuckled. "Yes, *awkward*. I guess you could call it that."

Oh. My. God. Did I like freaking Nico the Thug? This was a disaster of cosmic proportions.

Starry prodded, "So who's the lucky one? Flavio?"

I gasped. "*Flavio*? W-why *Flavio*?"

Starry lit up a cigarette, leaning back in the plastic chair. "What do you mean *why*? He's so handsome, strong, the leader of your little bunch! He's funny and his grades are okay, too!"

"I guess…"

"Well, you'd be a perfect pair. You need someone strong-willed to manage that knucklehead of yours!"

"Hey!" I protested.

Mom smiled. "Don't get angry. You know I love you. By the way, look what I got today from a street vendor." She rummaged in the huge purse she always dragged around with her, full of cigarettes, lighters, and makeup to hand me a simple thread of red cotton. "It's a wish bracelet, Lee. This one is red for love. Choose your wish carefully!"

I stared at the cotton bracelet she had put in my hand. "And then?"

"Well, I'll tie it on and you can never remove it. When it breaks your wish will come true. It's so romantic." She sighed, her eyes dreamy.

"Oh." I stared at the magical bracelet. "And you can just buy them?"

Mom laughed. "Most people just take them off. It's not easy for wishes to come true." She winked. "You can't tell anyone what your wish is, but becoming Flavio's girlfriend could be a good idea." She winked as I offered my wrist.

Mom was right. Nico was bad news, always had been. Maybe I could make myself *like* Flavio instead.

"Dear Jesus, please make sure that Mario doesn't tell anyone about what happened today. And please make him forget so that we can go back to hate each other's guts. Also, make my awkward feelings go away, even more so if they're for Nico. It doesn't seem right, with him being a jerk and all. You know that better than I do. Please make me sleep well with no nightmares, and make it sunny tomorrow. Amen."

23

Unrequited Feelings

June was the best month of the year, but this was our last all together in elementary school. I was with the rest of the quartet at the bike racks. I looked at the orange wall, covered with familiar graffiti, and my gaze wandered to a bottom corner on the right where, under many layers of chalk, lay hidden a very tiny writing: L ♡ F.

I cursed the impulse that took me the damn day after the school trip, when I had stolen a piece of chalk and had come back, after pretending to go home, just to write it. I had immediately regretted it, writing on top of it all the letters of the alphabet, so that it was an illegible mess. Yet, I was still afraid that someone, somehow, might decipher it and make my shame public. If liking someone was awkward, not being liked back was going to be the death of me, much more so given that my own feelings were as messy as the darn graffiti on the wall.

Flavio was one of my best friends, almost a brother. I had always admired his imperturbable smile. No dad's unemployment or parent-conference got to him, nothing was too much to bear for Flavio's broad shoulders. Starry adored him and I had wanted to like him so much, but I still didn't feel about Flavio the way I had felt for Ezio during the previous summer. Not to mention the dark itchy feeling that crept under my skin every time Nico loomed close by.

Maybe because I had always seen Flavio just like a friend, it was weird now to try and see him in any other way, but I really, really wanted to. I ached to have something amazing enough to dare Dad's wrath, just like Viola and her impossible love for Renzo. They had been dating long distance for almost a year now.

Regardless, every time we were at the bikes I was terrified Flavio would see the stupid graffiti and laugh at my face or run away like Mario. Or worse, Nico might see the writing and humiliate me in front of the whole quartet.

Geez, I felt pathetic. It was hard to be a girl, but being a girl among boys, pretending to be a boy myself, was becoming impossible.

I huffed. School was almost done, and my secret was going to be safe for eternity.

Sadness overwhelmed me.

Getting everyone's attention, Nico taunted, "But I wonder, what's Lee staring at, looking so sad?"

My hair stood on edge as I tried to say something and failed, piquing my friends' interest even more. Everyone stared at the wall of shame. No way.

Now I'm gonna wake up. Now I'm gonna wake up.

Everyone turned back to me, waiting for an explanation. I fumbled with my bike's slippery lock and uttered, "Nothing, Nico. What are you talking about?"

Nico raised an eyebrow. "*Cazzate*, Lee. You know you can't lie to me."

He examined the wall, while I tried to remind myself that there was nothing left to read.

I finally mastered my lock. "Come on let's go!" I jumped on my bike, ready to clear the grounds.

Nico protested, "Wait just one second, what's this? There's something down here in the corner that someone tried to erase big time."

You've got to be kidding me.

I pedaled toward home, and Peo and Flavio, thank goodness, followed me inciting Nico to do the same. Cold sweat.

Nico reached us at full speed and fell in by my side. "You can't run forever, Lee! Was it a heart I saw under all that chalk? You can tell me who is it that you like."

"Screw you, Nico!" I didn't sound too convincing. Could he read my mind? He was always the source of all of my troubles.

Laughing as he veered away to get home, he warned, "Sooner or later I'm going to catch you!"

I didn't know how I felt about that prospect. Had he been *flirting*? Was he making fun of me? I said goodbye to my friends and pedaled home as fast as I could.

🍦

Later that afternoon, Flavio and I were getting to his laundry room, where his mom kept the board games, when he stopped midway down the stairs, turned, and asked, "Do you know what *tarzanelli* are?"

Peo and Nico were not around yet. I almost bumped into Flavio's chest. He was still taller than me, despite the fact that I was on a higher step.

I increased the distance between us. "What-*Tarzans*? *Small Tarzans*?" I replied, puzzled.

He chuckled and resumed his descent. "Yeah, *small Tarzans*...you really don't know?" I shook my head feeling belittled.

Flavio explained, "It's when you go take a dump and a dingleberry of poo hangs from your butt, neither going up or down, hanging like Tarzan from a vine. What do you do?"

I was shocked by the terrifying possibility that such a thing might ever happen to me, but above all, by the knowledge that Flavio evidently saw me as a male, a brother, a member of the quartet, and *not* a possible girlfriend. Didn't I know that already? After all, I loved that he trusted me with such a private question, and I did my best to address his concern without laughing.

I answered, "Well, try to get rid of it with toilet paper?"

🍦

Two weeks later, our finals were done, elementary school was over. Kids poured out of the building, running and screaming.

In front of our bikes, Nico looked me in the eye, at a loss for words. He was the only one sharing into my melancholy. Maybe the two of us had lost enough in the past to gauge the breadth of what we were about to lose. Flavio's happy-go-lucky attitude feared nothing or no one, and Peo was quiet.

"Lee," Nico finally uttered looking emotional, which was unsettling in itself, but Peo hit him hard on the back, and for a second I thought Nico was gonna spit up a lung.

Peo said, "Shut up! We'll be in the same class in middle school, I know it."

Flavio seized Peo from behind rubbing his monk-head really fast with his knuckles.

"Ow, OW, *OW!*" Peo protested, fighting Flavio's grip.

Flavio said, "No school for three months! We're free, *free!*"

He let Peo go and danced away, Peo running after him, grumbling. I stared after them until I realized that Nico was still beside me.

I turned to him. "Have a good summer, Nico," I said with my heart in my shoes.

"Yeah. You too, Lee. I'll see you…in the fall."

I sure hoped that was the case as I watched him turn around and bike away.

Nico's silhouette had just disappeared behind the school when Mom's *Panda* car pulled up at the curb to pick me up and drop me at Dad's.

My unease must have been obvious, because Starry inquired, "So? What's wrong?"

I thought about the cactus that I was holding on my lap, I would have done without it, but that was not the problem.

Getting teary-eyed, I explained, "I think I'm sad because in middle school I might not be in the same class with the quartet."

"Mm, and who says so? Aren't you all going to the same school? Plus, you live so close! It will not be difficult to keep in touch, right?"

"It wouldn't be the same, Mom. One thing is to see each other every day at school, sharing everything, another thing is living in the same town."

"Well, the world is full of potential friends! You'll make a lot of new ones in middle school, maybe even better than the quartet, right?"

Heresy. I could not believe my ears. "Starry, are you *insane*? It takes forever to make friends, you don't just *find* them. Remember the fox in *The Little Prince*?" I wiped a tear from my left eye.

Starry weighted her words. "I sure do. But, if I might say, you are still quite the rookie. Wouldn't you agree? I met my best friends in middle school. Did you know that that's where I met Vanna, my friend in Padua?"

Starry stayed at Vanna's every time she had to go there to take her finals.

"Really?" I asked.

"Yeah," Starry confirmed, hands on the wheel and cigarette in her mouth. "Many years ago she lived in Milan and we were in middle school together. Think about that, she even moved away, yet we are still friends after all these years!"

"True. But you hadn't talked to her in ages before you went back to college."

No matter how she put it, I could still taste the bitter flavor of our goodbyes. I remembered the deserted school door, on that early morning of the field trip. The same melancholy and sense of not belonging engulfed my heart. Those doors would never open for me again.

Starry asked, "So, care to share about the cactus?"

"Oh, *that*. Nothing special. Mario just gave me a souvenir of his hatred for my birthday, if you can believe it."

"Of his *hatred*? *Lee!*" Starry chuckled, taking me aback. Okay, maybe *hatred* was a strong word, but Mom knew I liked big words.

Starry elaborated, "Mario has a huge crush on you, forever!"

"*What*? Where did you come up with *that*? He spent *years* harassing me, and now he gave me a *cactus* for my birthday. He even wrote *say it with flowers* on the card! And what's with all this *liking-talk*, suddenly?"

"Oh, Lee! It's just that you're growing up! At your age it's hard to find the maturity to express feelings. Kids are shy and insecure. Mario gives you attention as he can. If he hated you, he wouldn't remember your birthday, weeks in advance, and even less give you a gift. Don't you think? What he's trying to say with flowers is that he *likes* you, dufus!"

Starry's words began to permeate my disbelief. The *Miami* skit on the school trip took a whole new meaning. Was that what Nico had meant when he had said that I was clueless? Had he known? I thought about my own behavior toward Flavio and Nico: the denial, the shame, the fear. Things were, indeed, complicated.

"Maybe you're right," I agreed.

Starry pulled in front of Dad's building. "And doesn't that make you happy?"

"No," I answered. "Why should it? What does Mario have to do with the quartet? I'm sad because I'm not gonna see my friends anymore."

"I see. I was hoping that maybe you liked Mario back. After Flavio, he's my second favorite, with those big brown eyes and the wild blonde hair…"

"No, I don't! And why do you always want me to like someone?"

Starry flinched. "Geez, take it easy. They're cute, that's all. Why don't you invite one of your friends to Grandma's in Afes? You could spend a bit more time together."

"*Really?*" I lit up like a firework as I got out of the car. The idea of spending a week with Nico made me giddy and incredibly uncomfortable all at once, except that… "Nico will be in Sicily, though."

Starry beamed, "Good! I mean, that's too bad, but I'm not sure that Grandma would have been up for handling Nico. You know what I mean? How about Flavio?"

Nobody was ever up for handling Nico. Somehow that made me miss him more. I shrugged. "Sure, Flavio would be awesome."

"All right. We'll call him tomorrow, once you come back."

And so Mom managed to organize my one week vacation in Afes with Flavio. He had been as excited as I was, and his mom had loved the idea, given that with her husband premature *retirement* they hadn't planned any vacation at all.

It was settled. We were going to leave at the beginning of July, in two weeks. I stared at the red bracelet on my wrist and wondered if I had chosen my wish wisely.

Part Four

SUMMER

24

Milestone

My departure for Afes with Flavio was a couple of weeks away, so I spent my first few days of vacation with The Lone Wolf Gang. When I got home from Luca's on an early summer's evening, I found Viola slumped on the stairs with Starry trying to console her.

"What happened?" I asked.

"Mind your own business!" Viola burst in tears, stood, and ran up the stairs, slamming the door of her bedroom.

"What did I say?" I wondered.

Starry sighed. "Nothing." Yet, she was livid. She reminded me a bit of the cartoon cowboy *Lucky Luke*, with that stern gaze and the cigarette butt hanging from her lips. She added, "She was admitted to the maturity exam."

"And isn't that great?"

"Yes. But they changed her subject, just like I predicted."

"No way! Starry, you jinxed her!"

Starry squinted at me. "Right. Now it's *my* fault."

"Psych?" I asked. "With what?"

"Italian literature." The words choked in her throat, already rough from smoking. Starry swallowed. "The amount of stuff she would have to study is ridiculous. There is no way she can get ready. They should have failed her. Now she's forced to study all summer to likely repeat the year anyway."

"So?"

"So, that's it. We'll see what happens. She won't have to apply for college until August anyway since it starts in October." She stood up and walked into her study.

One week later, I woke up drenched in sweat at 3 PM. I had slept fifteen hours.

My repetitive, almost obsessive dreams made me think I was running a fever. I heard Viola's voice coming from Starry's bedroom. Starry was laughing. I rolled out of bed, I felt okay. Maybe I had just been tired. I opened my door and reached them across the hallway.

Viola exclaimed, seeing me, "Lazarus!"

She must have been in a pretty good mood to make biblical references.

Mom asked, "Lee, are you okay? You do sleep a lot, but I was getting worried."

"I'm good," I replied, looking at the blue sky outside Starry's window. The silver maple was bathed in sunshine. I couldn't wait to go play with Luca.

"Are you sure? Your face is red like a Japanese lantern. Go get the thermometer."

I got back, thermometer under my armpit, and I lay down on the bed next to Mom. Viola was sitting on the ottoman in front of Starry's vanity table.

Mom added, "Get at least under the covers!"

"But it's warm!" I protested.

"That's a good sign."

Viola resumed the conversation I had interrupted. "So, I'm thinking to follow in your footsteps. I wanna go to the University of Padua and major in psych. Not as a private student like you though, I want to attend courses and everything."

Starry answered, dismayed, "Isn't there a college you like in Milan?"

"No, Starry. Psych is only in Padua."

"I know, but how about philosophy, maybe?"

"No way. That's *so* boring, I barely passed."

"Well, did you tell *your father*, yet?"

Since they had split, Starry referred to Dad only as *your father*.

Viola shrugged and Starry urged, "And where are you going to live?"

"Starry, I don't know. I might need to share with roommates."

"Maybe I can try to ask Vanna," Mom suggested referring to her old friend, "she lives there and might know where to look. Meanwhile, focus on the maturity exam."

Bored, I crawled inside a pillowcase, from which I had removed the pillow. From there I exclaimed, "Fetus!"

Starry chuckled. "Lee, aren't you a bit too old to play fetus?"

"Fetus!" I replied.

Viola added, "I can't believe you still fit in the pillowcase. How do you even do it?"

I was very good at fitting in nooks and crannies, but I just rehashed, "Fetus!"

The phone rang and Starry picked up. She pressed the receiver to her chest and whispered to Viola, "It's Prof. Polenghi!"

Polenghi was Viola's ancient, Italian teacher. She had ignored Viola for the entire five years of high school, except for when Viola had passed out during the Vienna field trip. Since they had changed Viola's exam subject to Italian literature she checked on my sister regularly, sharing tips, quizzing her (with disastrous results), and inquiring about her progress.

Viola's face blanched as she gestured with both her arms and her head a flustered *no, no, no, no!*

Starry made up, "I'm sorry Prof Polenghi. Viola is… in the bathroom."

Through the handset, we all heard screaming loud and clear, "The *fanciullino*! Good lord, tell her to study the *fanciullino*! She *must* know Pascoli!"

click!

Viola buried her face into her hands.

"I CAN'T TAKE IT ANYMOOOOOORE!" she wailed. "I will never pass, and next year I'll have to repeat this whole nightmare! I'll never go to college!"

She stood up and rushed out of the room, leaving Starry and I stunned, staring at the door through which she had disappeared.

"Fetus?"

"Yes, fetus, okay, hand me the thermometer."

My little hand peeked out of the pillowcase holding the verdict tool. "Mom I'm fine. Can I go play with Luca?"

"No, today you'd better stay in—*what the hell*! 40.5 °C! Run to your bed, *right now*!"

It was the highest fever I had ever had, too bad it was not during school."But Starry, I feel okay and I just slept fifteen hours!"

"Read a book, okay? I'm gonna call the doctor."

"Can I bring up my computer and hook it to your old TV?"

"Can you do that?"

"Oh yeah. That's easy." The cables could only fit in a couple of places. There weren't too many options.

After a moment's hesitation, Starry conceded, "Fine, but just because you're sick. As soon as you're well, it goes back downstairs."

"Thank you!"

I spent the following thirty-six hours playing *Space Invaders*, which, according to the doctor, was not a bad solution.

At the end of June, I turned eleven. It seemed like a huge milestone, maybe because in September I was going to start middle school. For the first time since I could remember, I didn't get to spend my birthday at the amusement park. Without Dad it wouldn't have been the same, and Starry said it was a long way just to get cotton candy since I didn't dare to go on the rides for fear of passing out, just like my sister had.

Therefore, I spent my birthday at the pool, which was great, but it was also like any other day. Roberto, the hairy lifeguard, announced a swimming competition organized to celebrate the beginning of summer. Bathers hesitated. Someone stepped forward. Roberto tried to recruit me, but the other participants were grown-ups, and I would have rather saved myself the humiliation. Luca and Francesco, however, encouraged me, "Come on, Lee! It's your birthday! You swim like a fish! Show them!"

It was true that I was a very good swimmer. Because of my slightly crooked back, I had been taking swimming lessons for years and, as much as I hated doing endless laps in the indoor pool during the frigid winter months, I had joined the agonistic team though I never competed. I had no interest in swimming more than I was already forced to. However, I would have loved to show Dad the gold medal, for once. So, I eventually caved in.

I stood on the pool edge with the other contestants, fidgeting, uncomfortable with everyone's attention. I looked at Roberto, who was standing with a raised hand and a whistle in his mouth.

FWEEEEEEEE!

And so it began. I jumped into the water, swimming as fast as I could, without seeing a damn thing. I hoped I was going straight, but I had no idea because there were no lanes. The race was very short, only one lap. When I hit the opposite wall I stopped, dazed, trying to gather my bearings. To my surprise the other participants had not arrived yet.

I was first.

The crowd was roaring. Ecstatic, I looked at them, smiling. They seemed a bit *too* excited. Several people shouted at me, moving their arms up and down. The next contestant hit the wall, jumped out of the water, and crossed the finish line. A second one followed, while I remained stunned. In my excitement, I had missed some important explanation on the modalities of the competition. Full of bitterness, I got out of the water to win the third place and a bronze medal, awarded during a brief ceremony.

Ronda Fachuskich, the wife of our hideous neighbor Marcus, approached me laughing out loud, and exclaimed for everyone to hear, "Silly Leda! Didn't you understand that you had to get out of the water? You really are all muscle!"

Her shrill phony voice, all soft Rs, would have sickened even *Giumbolo*, the silliest, happiest cartoon character on earth. She even tried to knock on my empty head as a jest, but I didn't let her, stepping aside and glaring. People around me laughed at my stupidity, or maybe at the *all muscle* comment since I had the physique of an anchovy.

Great. But that was not all. At the height of my humiliation, I saw Viola approaching: Viola who hadn't been at the pool in years, Viola who had been locked up in her room for weeks to study for her maturity exam. Of course, fate would have arranged for my sister not to miss the pitiful spectacle of my fiasco. It was the worst birthday of my life.

"Congratulations!" Viola smiled, no irony in her voice.

Incredulous, I objected, "But I finished third."

She looked at me, surprised. "Truly, you won. I don't care what their stupid rules say. You're a ten-year-old shorty, and you beat two grown-ups, by quite a length too!"

Ecstatic, I corrected her, "Eleven. I'm eleven *today*."

"Yeah, yeah, whatever." She rolled her eyes. "You're still a shorty. Come on, I'm gonna teach you head dives."

She threw her bag on the grass and shed her clothes under the unwavering, adoring gaze of The Lone Wolf Gang, their eyes glued to her yellow bikini and everything it did not cover. We sat together on the edge of the pool, and she showed me how to raise my arms above my head, palms adjoined, plopping into the water. Then we dove by a kneeling position, and then from standing. It was the best birthday ever.

Who would have ever thought?

When we got home, Starry was waiting for us with my birthday cake, which she bought at a bakery and she kept referring to as *dinner*. Fortunately she had respected my wish and the Soldanti was not around. While we were binging, the phone rang. Dad wanted to wish me a happy birthday.

Still elated after my afternoon with Viola, I couldn't wait to share my enthusiasm.

"Dad, I came in third at a swimming race! They even gave me a bronze medal!"

"Never first, huh?"

"Yeah, I know," I answered, my mood dampened.

"Well, come on, third's pretty good, right?" he added. "How many participants were there?"

I hesitated, my heart in a swamp. "Three, Dad."

My humiliation was reflected in Dad's disappointment, or perhaps vice versa. To break the heavy silence I asked, "Dad, what's bronze?"

"It's an alloy of copper and another metal, usually tin."

We said goodbye, both grateful to end the conversation away from our discomfort.

I had just put down the phone when it rang again. I thought Dad had forgotten something.

"Hey!" I said.

"Lee?"

"Nico?" Surprise washed over me like a tsunami.

"Yeah. What's up?"

"Uh, not much, aren't you in Sicily? How are you?" I answered, bewildered. Nico had never called me from Sicily before. We chatted often during the school year when he called to know the homework, which was weird because he never ended up doing it anyway, but this was a first.

He answered, "Yeah, same old here. Uh, Happy Birthday."

"Wow, you remembered? You're not the jerk they say, after all."

"I am. I'm just making an exception."

I could picture Nico's smirk as if he were right in front of me. For once in my life, I felt special and it was all because of Nico the Thug.

"Thank you," I answered from the bottom of my heart.

"Gotta go," he answered.

"Bye."

Best. Birthday. Ever.

"Dear Jesus, please, make this year wonderful, starting from my vacation in Afes with Flavio. Make Dad love me even if I never win first place. And please have Viola be my best friend from now on. And let me sleep well with no nightmares, and make it sunny tomorrow. Amen."

25

The Quartet in Two

Flavio and I chatted for the whole three hours of the car ride to Afes. Soon the road became familiar, and I tried to share with Flavio the excitement of seeing the red house, the broken window, or the church by the big tree. "That's it! See? The apple orchards!"

Flavio took it all in and I wondered with a knot in my stomach if he was going to love the Valley of Not as much as I did.

Starry's Panda stopped in front of the big, green gate. As I ran to open it, however, its characteristic squealing was not followed by the familiar cries of welcome. It was too early in the season for the family to be around.

Grandma's head peeked from behind the house. "There you are! Weren't you supposed to be here two hours ago?"

"No, Ma," Starry answered laconically.

"Grandmaaaaaa!" I yelled.

Grandma hugged me, covering me with kisses, *bleah*. Then she raised her head to greet Starry and Flavio, whom she had known for years.

Grandma led us to the kitchen and started her rosary of complaints, loading the espresso maker. "Silvia, why would you leave in such a hurry? Tomorrow already, to go waste your money when you could stay here for free!"

Starry answered, "It's with my friends…"

But Flavio and I were not interested in their conversation and went out running to explore the garden.

There is always a slight anxiety in sharing with someone dear to us the things we love most. What if they don't like them?

Unfortunately, that was the case with Flavio. He had never loved tree climbing, and even less reading, which I thought we could be doing together, hiding in my favorite shrub. The branches gave him a nasty rash. The quartet in two did not work very well, maybe because Flavio was used to lead and here he had to follow me instead.

We entered the house and I rejoiced, filling with Afes' familiar smell of old wood and empty rooms. For once I was happy when Grandma called us inside and asked us to go buy groceries.

Flavio and I walked along the state road, immersed in the apple orchards separating Grandma's house from the rest of Afes. We passed the first building on the right, a newer construction with an awful fresco on its side showing two fat kids with bright red eyes gathering fruit, apples and pears, from laden branches.

"How ugly!" Flavio commented. "They almost seem to have demonic eyes!"

I looked at the fresco. "Wow, I never thought of the connection, but a few years ago my sister and I discovered a bright red pentacle, you know, the star of the devil? It was painted on a boulder in the middle of the little pond in the woods. Can you believe it?"

Flavio laughed. "Not really! Satanic rites? In this tiny mountain town? You're pulling my leg!"

"All right, I'll take you there tomorrow if you want, so you can see it with your own eyes!"

Meanwhile, we arrived at the store, across from the church. We got a cart and worked our way through Grandma's list, which included far more items than we had anticipated. While I stayed in line at the counter for the bread and Tyrolean salami, my favorite, Flavio went searching for milk and vegetables.

I reached him at the cart, where I noted that Flavio had grabbed commercial 2%. Good thing I had noticed, Grandma would have suffered a full meltdown, and us with her. I pulled the milk out of the cart as Flavio approached, a bag of potatoes in his arms.

"What are you doing?" he asked, raising an eyebrow.

"You took the wrong milk! Didn't you hear Grandma going on and on about getting fresh milk of the valley, not commercial 2%?"

Flavio smirked. "Yep."

"Then why would you get the wrong one?" I asked waving the carton under his nose.

"I didn't," Flavio insisted against all evidence, throwing the potatoes in the wrong cart.

"Flavio, what the hell are you doing?"

Flavio chuckled. I looked at the cart in which he had dumped the potatoes, by the rest of our groceries. I looked at the empty cart from which I had freaking stolen the 2% milk. A very perplexed old lady was holding it, giving me the stink eye.

I put *her* milk back into *her* cart, heat rising to my face. "I'm so sorry, Ma'am!"

As I slid into a side aisle, she kept glowering at me with the wariness typical of small-town folk. Flavio was bent over double laughing so hard I considered punching him in the face, but I couldn't stay angry, it was all too funny, and I cracked up too.

Have you ever laughed so hard that you could not breathe, that you could not stop? So hard that your legs became weak and couldn't hold your weight any longer? That you got teary-eyed? Isn't that a strange contradiction? Crying because of laughing?

Bent over double in the aisle of a grocery store in the middle of the Valley of Not, I wondered if it truly was impossible to separate joy from pain. After all, even the happiest moments dragged along the awareness of their transience. I wondered if my laughter roared out of control in an attempt to exorcise my fear of separating from Flavio and the quartet, the pain of my Dad moving away.

As we both gasped for air, we wiped the tears from our eyes, still uttering a few giggles. We had been through a lot together. The porn mag, First Communion, befriending Nico, discovering our base on the poplar tree, the hillocks, Peo flying on the bike like E.T., the (almost) death of Nico, dingleberries, pissing on the sub's car, fighting Ciro…Yet, as soon as we had been alone it had looked like we had nothing in common.

I almost asked Flavio what he felt about the end of school, if he was afraid, but the checkout approached and I pulled out the food from our cart instead.

"Dear Jesus, please let Flavio and I have fun tomorrow. Make sure that Nico is having a good time in Sicily, but that he misses me, too. Please keep us safe as we investigate the satanic rites at the pond, let me sleep well with no nightmares, and make it sunny tomorrow. Amen."

When I opened my eyes on our first morning in Afes my Casio told me it was 9:30 AM. As usual, I slept in Grandma's big bed. Flavio had settled in uncle Bedo's small bedroom since Uncle was still in Milan for business. I realized when Flavio had asked me that I had no idea what Uncle did for a living. I was so used to the grown-ups in my life that I had never considered that while they shared most of my world, I seem to know little of theirs.

I jumped out of bed just in case Flavio was already up. I ran down to the kitchen. Motes of dust danced in a sunbeam. The quiet was interrupted by the buzzing of one big black fly. I stepped out into the yard through the open glass doors. The crisp morning light was reflected in the vibrant greens of the willow tree in Grandma's huge garden.

"Grandmaaaa! Grandmaaa!" I called. Grandma's head sprouted out of the herb garden and I trotted toward her. It smelled like mint and basil. "Have you seen Flavio?" I asked.

"Good morning! I haven't. He might still be sleeping. Your Mom instead took off already. Bah! She said to give you lots of kisses."

"Thanks!"

While I waited for Flavio to get up, I settled in front of the TV.

Grandma trudged back inside and asked, "Do you want some breakfast?"

"No Grandma, thank you. I'll wait for Flavio."

"Why don't you wake him?"

"It's only ten, Grandma."

"I think you should wake him up, or at least have breakfast. What are you gonna do here by yourself with an empty stomach?"

"Grandma, I'm not gonna die, I promise. I'll just wait."

"Are you sure you don't want some breakfast?"

"Grandma, *yes*! Thank you, I'm sure."

"Bah! Whatever you say. What do you want for lunch? And for dinner?"

"Grandma, I don't know, whatever."

"But what does Flavio eat?"

"Anything, Grandma, just like me."

"Are you sure?"

Fortunately, behind Grandma, Flavio made his bleary appearance. "Ah, good morning. I hope I didn't oversleep."

Grandma opened her mouth to confirm Flavio's fears, but I was faster. "Of course not! Wanna have breakfast?"

It took some time to convince Grandma we didn't need lunch after such a late breakfast, yet she still managed to force two Nutella sandwiches in my backpack. Flavio and I started up the steep slope beside Grandma's property leading up to the woods.

The forest was mostly pine and beech trees with an underbrush of wild cyclamen and berry bushes. Wild heather covered the ground around the narrow path. We got to the sports center and crossed the real road to get to the pond trailhead. I could not believe my eyes; an incredible amount of *sanguignoli* littered the pinewood. *Sanguignoli* mushrooms were rare, valuable and tasty, not quite like *porcini* but close, definitely amazing with polenta. I shared all the knowledge I had inherited from Dad and Grandma with Flavio, explaining how rare they were and that most often they were *matti*, crazy.

Flavio repeated, "*Crazy?*"

"Yup. Not edible. They might kill you or make you crazy." I explained drawing circles in the air by my forehead with my finger. "The only way to find out if they're good or not is to see if they bleed."

"*Bleed?*" Flavio stared at me wide-eyed.

Full of pride I proceeded to demonstrate. "See, if you break a little piece of the cap, just like this, it might bleed red or white. Red is good…" We looked at the milky liquid oozing out the broken cap, "… white's *crazy*." I threw out the tiny piece of mushroom.

Flavio exclaimed, "No way!" jumping onto the next mushroom to test it himself. We had a ball checking out all of the mushrooms, yet they all turned out to be *matti*.

Surprises were not over yet. The once thin trail to the pond, hidden between grass and undergrowth, was now wide enough for a trailer to go through, although still covered with grass and pine needles.

A large wooden sign read,

TOWN OF AFES
EXERCISE TRAIL
1988

"Ha. This is new," I commented, miffed as if I had expected someone to ask for my permission to plow through the woods. "They must have built it last fall."

"The last one's a *picio*!" Flavio quoted Nico, shooting past me till the next sign, where he did ten push-ups as indicated on the wooden post and ran to the next stop.

I followed Flavio as fast as I could, cheating on most exercises to keep up. He still arrived first to the reeds that announced the water. We were both exhausted.

The pond, once black and quivering with water striders, was of a milky, unnatural teal. In a couple of spots the banks revealed a tarp peeking from the dirt, betraying the artificial nature of this new pond empty of tadpoles or any other bug.

Flavio mocked me, "It's nice here and all, but not quite *satanic*, I'd say."

No one was around. I wondered for whom they had put all the pretty benches that now surrounded the water.

I gestured to the boulder in the middle of the pond. At least that was the same. "That's it! Let's go check it out from the other side!" We walked around and I stared at where once was the cursed pentacle. "I guess they washed it away, or something."

Flavio frowned. "Yeah, right."

We sat on one of the benches by the side of the pond. Everything was quiet, except for the wind whispering through the pine tops. The forest surrounded us with its gentle murmurs. The sunlight barely filtered through the tall branches, creaking in the breeze, lighting up patches of dry needles on the forest floor. It smelled peaceful, earthy and familiar. The water was still and the sky was a blue oval above it. Every so often a bee or a fly buzzed by investigating our presence.

Yet our silence grew strange. Flavio was *never* quiet or still. I would have liked to say something, but I didn't know what. I would have liked to know what Flavio was thinking, if he believed my pentacle story or if he thought that I had brought him here under false pretenses.

Does he think I have a crush on him?

Then I remembered that even I didn't know if I had a crush on him, and I didn't feel better. I swallowed hard.

I looked at the bench where we were sitting on. It was full of inscriptions, names, hearts, *go Trento,* but mostly names and hearts. Flavio turned around and looked at me, strangely serious.

Oh, *merda.*

I lowered my gaze to my red bracelet. Sometimes a second can seem like a year, and Flavio *was* still staring at me.

I wanted to disappear, run away. The whole situation felt wrong, very wrong, and then, unexpected, came my salvation.

"Look! A pentacle!" I yelled, pointing at the bench. Just below it, an inscription in the wood read, *NEVER DIE.*

We jumped up to examine our find. The rustling of the leaves sounded louder, more urgent. We inspected the whole bench, but could only find more names and hearts. The wind died, and the forest went quiet. Then, a sudden thud followed by a loud crunch scared the daylights out of me. Flavio jumped up and ran, and I followed him for dear life.

We stopped at the pinewood, among the disfigured *sanguignoli* mushrooms. I was bent over double to catch my breath.

Flabbergasted, Flavio exclaimed, "What the hell was *that?*"

"I have no idea, maybe a dry branch fell?"

"So loud? And the crunchy noise?"

"I don't know. The pentacle on the boulder was years ago, but the benches have been added only last year."

Flavio wiped the sweat from his brow, his breath slowing. "This means that someone keeps coming to the pond to do some kind of rite. Or do you think it's a coincidence?"

We sat on the swings behind the bar of the sports center discussing the mystery and eating our Nutella sandwiches. then we set out to explore the woods on the way back home. After about half an hour of roaming, I saw something in the distance. "Hey, what's that?"

Flavio squinted. "It seems like a tiny cabin."

We approached the shack like the pro ninjas we were, creeping from tree to tree. The structure was a small stilt house, about one and a half meter from the ground. A wall was missing entirely while, on the opposite side, a small window overlooked the forest. Inside, a bench and a tiny table were all the furnishings in the maybe three-square-meter space.

Flavio asked, peering inside the small structure, "Do you think it belongs to someone?"

"It seems like it's been abandoned for years. Maybe hunters use it?" Beyond a few birds, I had never seen any wildlife in Afes' woods.

Flavio's face lit up with a huge grin. "It seems to me that we have just found us a new base!"

"Awesome! From here we can fight the enemy!"

We both laughed and got to work to fix the shack. I knew now that Flavio was an amazing friend, but nothing more. I had wanted to feel that crazy high that I had experienced when I had fallen for Ezio, but this was not it. Flavio was a steady, reassuring presence in my life, like Peo.

Nico was also a steady presence, just not reassuring, more like unsettling in fact. In spite of that, I couldn't wait to have him at my side again, even if he made me angry more often than not. They were my friends, we were the quartet, even if now I was pretty sure, I was indeed a girl.

🍦

Every day was an adventure at our new base. We gathered acorns and berries *to get us through the winter*. We collected bark to use as plates, piled dry wood to be able to build imaginary fires, and explored the forest around the stilt setting booby traps to catch our enemies and game.

We found a broken, dried up bamboo reed near a swampy stream and we used weeds and sticks to give it legs and arms. The reed became Diana, our companion of adventures. We had to take care of her because she was wounded and had to stay at the hut while we scoured the woods, running as if possessed, climbing trees, and eating the Nutella sandwiches that Grandma prepared for us.

Every evening, when the sun turned golden, we bid goodbye to Diana and started toward home. It did not matter to me if Flavio was just a friend or more, but as I was about to discover, it mattered a lot to somebody else.

26

Magic and Butterflies

We only had two days left in Afes. The sky, clear in the morning, had turned gloomy. I hoped our vacation was not going to end prematurely.

Flavio asked, "Did you hear that thunder?"

"Hard not too. It's so loud. Should we go back?"

We had been at our base just a couple of hours at most. We hadn't even eaten our Nutella sandwiches, yet. Another thunder, longer and more powerful made our decision inevitable.

We headed toward home at a good pace, speeding up a bit with each new crack of thunder. The sky was growing dark, angry, and scary. We began to run on the trail in the forest. We avalanched down the fields toward the state road at breakneck speed, avoiding capitulating flat on our faces by breaking our descent with long, regular jumps.We made it home just as the first fat raindrops fell.

"Thank God!" Grandma welcomed us. "I was starting to worry! What would you like for dinner?"

"Anything Grandma, we still have to get to our sandwiches."

As she listed dinner options intermingled with complaints about our imminent departure (even if Grandma knew I was going to be back in August) we rushed out into the garden. Better drenched than soul numb. Yet, the sky was opening up. Thunder rumbled in the distance, where the dark clouds had moved, meanwhile.

I said, quite annoyed at the mercurial weather, "Well, maybe it *did* rain at the base."

"Hopefully we didn't get too much damage," Flavio surmised.

We sat on the short stonewall nearby the clematis laden with purple blossoms to eat our Nutella sandwiches.

"Leeeeedaaaa! Leeedaaaa!"

I rolled my eyes and exchanged a meaningful look with Flavio before heading to the kitchen. Grandma was restless. She looked strange, uncomfortable. Obviously there was something on her mind.

"What's up, Grandma? Did you call me?"

"Ah, yes. So, what is it that you two do together all day long in the woods?"

Her inquisitive look baffled me since I had spent my days in the woods with Viola and my cousins since I could remember, and Grandma had never raised objections before. Was this so urgent that she had to call me in to ask? Couldn't we chat about it at dinner?

"Nothing Grandma, we play in the woods," I answered, still puzzled and feeling a little guilty, because I was not quite sure if our appropriation of the base was legitimate, and I would have rather not talked about it.

Grandma, who was a guilt-hound, must have smelled something because she did not relent. Maybe she was afraid we might get hurt, but she seemed more annoyed than worried as she added, in a tone I did not recognize, "Make sure that you don't stay too close to *that Flavio there*," nodding outside with her head.

That Flavio there? My best friend that she had known for years? I was bewildered at her sudden bitterness. "What do you mean, Grandma? Why?"

My lack of understanding turned rapidly into confusion and alarm. I had no idea what Flavio might have done wrong, especially without me seeing it.

"Leda, because he's a *boy*! And you *are not*. Don't you have *girl friends*?"

I couldn't believe that Grandma had joined the crusade to convert me into a princess, and I couldn't hide my hurt. "No, Grandma, you know that. My friends are males, *all of them*. Flavio, Peo, Nico, Luca, Francesco, Mauro. What difference does it make?"

"Well..." Grandma chose her words. "It's just that...you've been here for days and...Flavio has never had a bath!" she concluded a bit too fast as if she had just thought of it.

Her face looked like a question mark as if she had thrown the bait and were waiting to see if the fish bit. I had no idea where she was going with all of this, but I sure breathed a sigh of relief. *Lord knows what I was thinking.*

"Oh, Grandma, whatever! Who cares? I didn't either. We're always in the woods anyway."

Unfortunately Grandma's expression hardened further while she added, "Well, don't stay too close. Don't touch him. He's...*dirty.*" She seemed to be improvising, ill-at-ease. "I mean, he's...*dirtier...* than you. I made his bed this morning and it was dirty with poo."

Eeew. I remained speechless. I couldn't believe my ears. Obviously, Grandma was not being completely honest. I had no idea why she would invent such a story. I just felt anger and confusion. "Whatever," I said, running outside with what was left of my Nutella sandwich.

I reached Flavio, still sitting on the wall by the purple clematis. I bit into my sandwich and managed to say, a bit embarrassed, "Look, maybe take a bath tonight."

He dismissed me. "Nah, I'll be home in a day or so. I'll shower there."

He licked his fingers, brown with Nutella. Everything mixed into my head: his fingers brown with Nutella, Grandma's disgust, dingleberries, and his allegedly dirty bed. I felt a repulsion like never before and didn't know how to express it. It just burst, first as a bitter wave inside of me, then as words.

"You're *gross!*" I yelled as I watched him with eyes full of Grandma's reproach.

For the first time in our friendship a gap opened, a misunderstanding, the pollution of adult malice, partial and unjust. Why couldn't adults speak openly about sex, when it seemed to be all they worried about? I was drowning in my ignorance mixed with the fear of grown-ups, a sense of foreboding that something nasty and inevitable was going to happen, turning me into garbage. Everyone knew that I was about to make a huge mistake, yet nobody bothered to warn me about what it was.

Flavio was startled by my aggressiveness. "Huh?"

Followed the embarrassed silence of half-truths and things unsaid, the moldy world of adults. Full of a shame that shouldn't have been mine I got up and ran away.

And then the storm came.

$$\text{🍦}$$

"Dear Jesus, please make Flavio forget the stupid things I said today and make it so that we're always friends. Make our last day in Afes memorable and please let me sleep well with no nightmares, and make it sunny tomorrow. Amen."

One of my wishes was not going to be granted.

$$\text{🍦}$$

On the morning of our last day in Afes, I tried to focus on the positive things: the sun was shining and it was quite hot, Flavio seemed in a good mood and completely oblivious to the scene I had made on the previous day. He didn't even seem to notice my melancholy due to the fact that this was our last day together before going home, summer, middle school, and the rest of our lives.

I was quiet as we walked through the woods to get to the base. Diana was waiting for us. I looked at Flavio's broad smile as he declared, "We have to close shop. Let's hope the hut keeps through the winter!"

I forced a smile back, even if we would never be back to check, not together, anyway. Our game was over soon.

I suggested, "Wanna go get a *Calippo* ice pop?"

"Sounds great! It's so hot today," Flavio agreed.

We hiked to the bar, and then we walked around the building to sit on the swings eating our treats in peace. Mine was lemon-flavored, Flavio's orange. Peo would have chosen cola and Nico lemon, just like me.

I asked, "Doesn't it seem weird to you that after tomorrow we won't see each other anymore?"

Flavio slurped on his ice-pop. "What do you mean?"

"Well, we'll go home, on vacation, then to middle school. It's not likely we're going to be in the same class again."

"Who knows?" Flavio shrugged.

Compared to his Dad's unemployment my concern must have seemed outright stupid. Yet, my parents had split, and I still would have rather not lost my buddies on top of that.

He added with a big smile, "Meanwhile, there's the summer camps' trip to *Gardaland*."

"*Summer camp?*"

"Yeah, you should try, it's such a blast!" As I looked at him unconvinced, he added, "Well, at least you have to come for the field trip to *Gardaland*."

Gardaland was the biggest amusement park in Italy, right over *Lago di Garda*. My brain replayed the TV ad with *Prezzemolo*, Parsley, the mascot dragon, the huge roller coaster with three death spins and the final catchphrase: *The dream of every child*.

Not this child.

I loved amusement parks, and I would have liked to go, but I had never been on a real ride before. Given Viola's inner ear defect and her passing out on a ride in the spring, it probably was a good idea that I never try. We *were* related, after all. Starry had sworn I was not adopted.

"Maybe," I replied evasively, finishing my *Calippo*.

I threw the wrapper in the trash close by, and I picked up speed on my swing, to escape from my loneliness, from my fears, and from the conversations I did not want to have with Flavio. When I was going as fast as I could manage, I let my head dangle backward and I watched the world turn upside down. I loved the intoxicating sense of vertigo from the sudden change in perspective. Could it be my inner ear's defect?

Flavio, who had also gathered momentum tried to do the same, immediately pulling his head back straight. "WOHA! Lee, you're crazy!"

I laughed. "Give it a sec, your brain gets used to it."

"I'd rather not, thank you very much."

Still at full speed, I announced, "I'm gonna jump."

"Are you insane?"

But, just like a million times before during my many summers in Afes, I let go of the swing and took flight. I rotated my arms in the air for balance and landed, feline, bending my knees to ease the impact, a good eight meters away.

Flavio blurted, "WOW! Are you hurt?"

"Of course not, *chicken*! Come on!"

Flavio picked up speed, yelling, "I'll give you the chicken! I'm gonna crash you, Lee!"

He leaped off, yelling the Japanese battle cry we had learned from the *Gialappa's band* TV show, "BANZAIIIIII!"

He landed in a heap, but at least half a meter farther than me. He gathered himself, turned toward me and raised one fist, shouting, "SCOOOOORE!"

I pushed him not too hard, just because he was being obnoxious, but he stumbled backward on the brick border separating the gravel from the woods and ended with his butt on the dried pine needles. I chuckled, but he grabbed my ankles in revenge and I landed right on top of him.

I rolled off him, and we just lay on the forest floor, both laughing hard.

Flavio asked, "Have you ever explored up here?" He was pointing uphill, where the sparse tall grass around the swings peppered a sweet ascent toward the top of the mountain, dotted with pine trees that became progressively denser.

I shook my head. I was a bit skeptical about exploring the mountain since the forest was thin and too close to the sports center to hide anything interesting, but I followed Flavio since it was our last day together. We hiked through the green blades of grass, clapping our hands to scare away eventual snakes.

An intense blue sky patched with clouds filled the space between the pine tops. The sun came and went, crawling from bush to bush. Flavio and I clambered up, side by side, a few meters away from each other. There was no path to follow anyway. The slope was becoming steeper.

"Hey, Lee! Is this a trail?"

I moved closer to him to check out a thin path snaking uphill, hidden by the vegetation. "I don't think so. It seems quite vague and it's not marked by paint splotches on the trees."

"Let's try to follow it," Flavio proposed. "We're going up anyway."

"Sure," I conceded, looking at the petering out trail.

Yet the path continued. As we walked ahead, more of it was revealed beneath the undergrowth, snaking higher and higher and widening, revealing a bit of ground pierced by small boulders and carpeted with pine needles. The scenery became more and more beautiful, rocks, pine trees, and blue sky.

We emerged from the trail on a small plateau and were stunned.

In front of our mesmerized eyes unfolded Neverland. A gorgeous grassy glade, flooded by the sun, cut in half by our zigzagging path and colored by countless wildflowers; white, yellow and pink. The place was alive with a sea of butterflies. It was clearly enchanted. I had never seen so many butterflies all at once, or probably ever. Orange, white and yellow, iridescent blue: they fluttered in a playful summer chorus of crickets and wind.

The only joy greater than making an incredible discovery is to share it with your best friend. When I recovered from the astonishment, I turned to look at Flavio, and I found him still mouth agape. He turned around to look at me and smiled, eyes full of flowers, magic, and butterflies. "WOW!"

It looked like we had found the secret fairy world of Afes, after all.

We continued on the trail, breathing in every scent, looking at each butterfly, listening to every cricket and trying to make as little noise as possible, terrified at the prospect of breaking the spell. After the clearing, the path curved behind a hill and climbed farther.

On the very top of the hill, between the tallest pines, someone had built a throne of wood on which we climbed incredulous to watch the sunset. It was so wide we could both sit side by side.

"This is incredible!" Flavio exclaimed, still in awe.

"Incredible," I echoed.

And then we didn't say anything else because sometimes words just aren't enough.

When I came back home to Arese, Luca was on vacation. Viola had taken a break from studying and had gone with Marta to see Pink Floyd in concert, in Venice.

I didn't want to go to the pool by myself, so I spent my days perched in the wisteria hedge that surrounded our yard, reading Kafka's *The Trial*. Viola had liked it very much but said I was too young to appreciate it. She had been right, but stubborn as I was, I didn't give up, forcing myself through the pages. Nonetheless, I kept getting distracted. The field trip to *Gardaland* was tomorrow.

I hopped off the hedge and went to call Flavio, determined to find an excuse not to go on the roller coaster.

Garda Lake was gorgeous, green and emerald, surrounded by little towns and gorgeous villas. The park was right by it, huge, arranged with incredible flowerbeds, people flocking around the dancing mascots. I turned to share my surprise with Flavio, but he had run along with some other kids toward the roller coaster, his favorite ride.

My heart fell into my sneakers, but Jesus had my back. When I reached them in line, I spotted a sign announcing that only kids one meter-fifty and above were allowed on the ride. Masking my relief with regret, I pointed the sign to Flavio.

He laughed. "Lee, who cares! No one's gonna check. Plenty of shorties in the line," he gestured to the crowd ahead of him.

I switched to my consolidated adult tone as I explained, "Yes, but I'm *way* less than one-fifty. You guys go ahead. I'll look at you from here." I wasn't going to be the party pooper who passes out in front of everyone turning the day into a tragedy.

Flavio shrugged, and I walked out of the line with the younger kids.

The same story repeated itself for most of the day. I was just one of Flavio's many friends, one who could not ride roller coasters. He was much better than me at making friends, actually most kids were. That's where Nico and I were more alike. I tried to keep up with Flavio, but a slow sadness filled my heart. It was the end of an era, it was time to change. I didn't want to be like poor Nora anymore, hidden in the closet waiting for someone to look for her.

I looked at Flavio's back for the last time, my fists squeezed with a new resolution, it was time for a new Leda.

27

Pole Position Marcus's Style

Back in Arese, our house was quiet in the heat of July. Starry was studying and Viola was too. The random letter choice had put her maturity oral exam at the end of the month, giving her a slim extra chance of passing at the price of dooming her summer.

Nothing suggested my imminent departure for the seaside with Dad: no swearing while loading the luggage in the car and no waiting in the garage to defend the legitimacy of my belongings. A strange melancholy invaded me like a sudden tide. I looked out of the living room window waiting for Dad's car to peek from behind the curve, hoping that seeing him would bring my mood back to that annoyed, trivial routine I had taken for granted for so many years. I would have never thought I'd miss it. I just stared at the heat, at the emptiness, empty in turn, almost lost in the lack of something I couldn't quite pinpoint.

Dad was still a mystery to me. I had no idea of what he thought and felt, but I loved him dearly. The weight of the separation from Mom had taken its toll from him. It had started with denial, as he had thought the separation temporary. Then he had switched to anger and sadness. He barely spoke to me about it, but Viola had mentioned horrific discussions, where Dad vented to her as if she were Starry.

Needless to say, my fragile, crushed sister had not benefited from such sessions. Eventually, Dad had resigned to Mom's decision. He had moved into a bigger, more permanent apartment, had called up a bunch of old friends, and had begun a new life with the resolve of someone who was not going to give up on happiness. I silently watched him, hoping he found whatever he was looking for, and wondering what had caused my parents' big fallout in the first place.

Finally, Dad's car turned the corner, and I ran to greet him. Already furious, he almost ignored me, glaring at the suitcase behind me. "Lee, how much stuff can you possibly need?"

His sour comment could not have made me happier. At least a few things never changed. "Dad, it's my usual luggage, and this year it's only the two of us. It should be a piece of cake to fit it in the trunk, right?"

"Ah, actually, the Fachuskiches are going with us. Didn't I tell you?"

My blood turned to cement. *"What?* And since *when? Why?"* The hideous Fachuskiches, owners of Doggy-two, nightmare of children, were going to poison my vacation with Dad.

Dad shuffled stuff in the trunk while I stared, in shock. He said, "You'll see, *the more the merrier,* right? There's the whole family, including their kids and Ronda's brother. So, we will not feel lonely."

I couldn't hold back a whispered, "Better alone than in bad company."

"What?" Dad asked, soaked in the sultry heat of July while pushing my suitcase in a space half its size.

"Nothing. I'm gonna say goodbye to Mom."

"Yes, but be quick! We're already late."

I rolled my eyes, unseen, and I ran back inside. When I got out of the kitchen in the backyard, Starry put down her book. "Ready to go?"

"Starry, did you know that we're going with the Fachuskiches?"

"NO WAY!" Starry was as outraged as I was, she also couldn't stand the odd family. "I sure don't envy you."

Tears welled up in my eyes. I didn't even know that Ronda had a brother. If he was like her, I would have been better off shooting myself in a leg.

Mom melted into a big smile spreading her arms in an embrace. "You'll see, it will be fine, you'll have a great time, I'm sure."

I held back the tears, gave her a kiss and ran out.

Dad was gone. The car was abandoned in the sun. "Dad?" I called, perplexed.

Maybe he had been sucked into the trunk like Alice down the white rabbit's hole. The trunk, however, was closed.

I walked around the bend toward Luca's, and I saw Dad trotting out of the Fachuskiches' gate, with two bags on his shoulders and dragging a further piece of luggage. His face was scrunched in a massive frown.

"I can't freaking believe it!" he said. " We have to leave, and they're setting the table for lunch! Marcus had the nerve to ask me if we wanted to join them!" Dad's anger was diluted by his disbelief. "I was very clear! Departure at 11:30 AM! Marcus even mentioned that it's only 11:20! As if they're gonna be ready in ten minutes! AARGH! And who the hell eats at 11 AM anyway? Darn Austrian people!"

Italian lunch time is around 1 PM. When Dad, sullen, leaned back against the car, crossing his arms, I realized the ridiculousness of our situation. We couldn't wait inside the house because Dad hadn't crossed the threshold since he had left with his two pieces of luggage, yet if we accepted the Fachuskiches' invitation we would never leave on time.

"So, what?" I asked, wanting in on his plan.

"So, *nothing*! He thinks he can do whatever he wants, but he'll see. If he's not here at 11:30 sharp we're gonna leave him behind. We're *not* gonna miss the ferry because of Marcus, that's for sure!"

The midday sun baked us mercilessly. Fate's irony forced me to wait at home as if we were already on the cement grill of Genoa's pier.

At 11:50 Dad, who had remained stoically embalmed against the car if not for the frequent and increasingly intense glances at his wristwatch, blurted out, "That's it! He's gonna get a piece of my mind!"

He started down the street at a good pace toward the Fachuskiches' residence. Resigned, I resumed reading *Petersburg Stories* by Gogol.

After ten minutes he was back. "They're still sitting at the table. Can you believe them? He said to go ahead, that they'd catch up on the highway. Marcus is quite the speeder, too. Let's go."

I barely had time to buckle up that we were off toward the highway. *Bennato's* last cassette played at full volume.

🍦

We arrived at the burning pier of hell with only two miserable hours to spare (before boarding of course, not departure). *Lucio Dalla* sang *Piazza Grande*.

While driving toward our dock Dad surmised, "They must have passed us on the highway. They're probably ahead, already waiting in—WHAT THE FUSS! Look at *that* line! And it's all Marcus's fault!"

Dad got in line, livid, after *at least* thirty cars. They didn't seem like much to *me*, but we were sure far away from the much-coveted *pole position*.

Dad turned off the engine. "I'm going to see if they're up ahead in line. Wait here."

As if I had an alternative. I tried to visualize the beach and the sea between the mirages emanating from the asphalt, focusing on the soothing sound of the seagulls in the harbor, imagining crystal clear waters reflecting a cloudless sky, the fine sand, and the shells. But instead I kept thinking of Viola, home studying.

Dad returned frowning, got into the boiling car and sat down without saying a word. After half an hour Lucio Dalla's tape resumed from the beginning.

Dad muttered, "I knew it, I told him so. He's gonna miss the ferry. Son of a witch! He's not to be trusted. We should have left together." The muttering became louder with the passing of time.

Ten minutes before boarding the Fachuskiches were still missing from the snake of cars that was growing around the pier at exponential speed.

A metallic voice announced through a megaphone, "Good afternoon! Please prepare for the boarding procedures."

Still, there was no trace of the Fachuskiches. I feared Dad might pop a coronary, as he gripped the steering wheel gritting his teeth in the immobile line of cars.

Suddenly, a rogue vehicle sped along the endless column. With horror, Dad recognized Marcus's car, hurtling down the line. "What the hell is *he* doing?"

It all happened in an instant. After a brief shock, the horde of lined up vacationers reacted. Tired, sweaty, and frustrated after hours under the inclement sun, they got to vent by slamming onto their horns, glued to their seats not to lose their place in line.

Some leaned out of the windows, waving their fists and shouting words I had never heard from Dad's lips, only on the school bus.

Dad was frozen, arms outstretched to the wheel and eyes wide open. Marcus was going to be lynched by the crowd. The Fachuskiches, fortunately, didn't see us and moved past, all the way up to the top of the line, where they stopped aside the vehicle in pole position as if nothing had happened.

Marcus exited from his car with his hands up, and a wide smile, "Come on folks! Two lines, please, move up in two lines! Come on forward friends, there's room for everyone!"

The doubt that he was a charlatan with no right whatsoever to tell anyone what to do was overwhelmed by the greed to grab a better spot in the virgin row. The anger of the vacationers imploded in a fast and furious reassembling operation amid shrieks and curses, while Marcus, radiant, got back to in his car, in pole position, just on time for boarding.

Dad said nothing and did not participate in the battle over the new row. By looking at his grim face, I thought he did not approve. Nonetheless, he couldn't help the hint of a smile every time we moved a tad ahead because of a defection to Marcus's row.

28

The Engine and Other Appendages

Two days into our vacation I was already fed up with the Fachuskiches.

The two kids, Alessio and Daniele, were already in college. Both were incredibly handsome and boring: longer, wavy brown hair, blue eyes, and athletic. Both played tennis semi-professionally and spoke of nothing else. Because of our age difference they treated me like a little *girl*, and I emphasize the girl part, which made them also a bit irritating.

But not all the Fachuskiches were bad. Sergio, Ronda's brother, treated me like a person rather than *a little girl*, in spite of the fact that he was thirty-two. Indeed, we started quite the friendship due to our common passion for books.

Both Dad and Marcus had brought their engine dinghies, and every day we set out to explore new shores. On the third morning of our vacation, we were aimed toward Budelli, a beautiful beach reachable only by sea. I loved so much sprinting on the boat since I craved to feel the speed on my face. Also, every time I looked at my shadow hovering on the sea I noticed a halo of light behind my head. I never mentioned anything because I did not want Dad's scientific explanations to tear apart my illusion that I was special.

The boat slowed down, tearing me away from my musings. We approached Marcus's dinghy and the captains consulted.

Dad argued, "No, Marcus. That's a bad idea, it's full of shallow areas, we're gonna get stranded. Let's go around it."

"No way, Carlo. I know it like the back of my hand. Follow me and we'll soon be at the beach. Full steam ahead!"

Marcus left without giving Dad the chance of a retort. Dad chanted a tune made up of his peculiar swearwords but followed.

After less than five minutes my thoughts were interrupted again by a sudden and cacophonous thump, followed by the death of our engine.

"WHATTHEFUSS! SONOFAWITCH!"

I dared not ask. Dad sported a massive frown and kept cursing while examining the engine and trying to restart it.

Marcus turned his boat around and, looking amused, inquired, "Problems?"

Dad stopped swearing. With the laconic air of one who's above reiterating that he was right, he pulled up the engine's powerhead to show our poor propeller, blades twisted by the impact with a rock.

Instead of apologizing, Marcus used Viola's technique; he blamed, and he did it with style, skill, and a good dose of mockery. "I told you to follow me! If you had *followed* me…"

Dad nipped his comment in the bud with a look that I made a mental note to learn.

Marcus towed us to shore, and Dad and I went to the closest small town to look for someone to fix the engine. It was a hot, Sardinian afternoon and the town was baking, deserted, in the aroma of eucalyptus and oleander, the sea a faraway, blue stripe at the horizon.

We had no luck. Disconsolate and bored, I left Dad to rest on a bench, while I approached the shop windows under the porticoes surrounding the *piazzetta*. Quite unexpectedly, I saw the most beautiful plush toy in the universe: a small, white bunny with a muzzle like a cartoon character.

"Do you see anything you like, *Chubby?*"

Gasp, Dad had snuck up on me. "Oh, no. Well, there. That bunny's really cute."

Dad said, "Aren't you too old for plush toys?" Was I? Was anyone too old for plush toys? I shrugged. Dad smiled and continued, "Come on, I'll get it for you."

"*Really?*"

Dad didn't normally just *buy* stuff. He pushed the door of the store, which didn't budge. "Ah, it's closed. Of course, it's two o'clock."

"Well, never mind Dad. Thank you, anyway."

He sighed. "Lee, how come you became such great friends with Sergio? He's so much older than you."

I shrugged. "Similar interests, I guess. Why?"

Dad shrugged in turn. "It just seems a little weird that you spend so much time together, that's all. Let's go home now. We wasted enough of this beautiful day."

I couldn't have agreed more. Dad put his arm around my shoulders and my troubles melted away.

He had changed...*a lot*. He had always been right before, he had never wasted money, and he had never been too physical. Splitting from Mom had knocked some of the certainties out of him, smoothing his edges. He had become more grateful for what he still had, and although he was still right most of the times, at least according to him, he didn't dismiss everyone else's opinion scoffing like he had once.

His newfound uncertainty and vulnerability made him more approachable, human, lovable. It was almost as if he had been crystallized in a life he thought perfect, without being able to see its flaws. Only the earthquake of the separation had jarred him awake, jerking him back into the race to make things better.

🍦

A few hours later, I got out of the water and sat on my towel on the beach near Sergio, who was reading *Thus Spoke Zarathustra*. He was ascetic-thin, with long, smooth, jet-black hair, and dark and curious eyes.

Sergio was weird. This was evident from the way he was treated by the other members of his family who, when he spoke, rolled their eyes not listening to what he had to say. To be honest, they behaved with me in the same way. Yet, Sergio was an adult, seemingly very interesting, sensitive, and intelligent. He didn't seem to mind too much his family's odd behavior. He spoke only if you listened to him, otherwise he stopped talking, and listened to you instead, something I had never seen before, in adults or children. He had a pure look to himself, not like me, Flavio, or Luca, who were naïve and sometimes didn't see things as they were. It was more as if he saw everything, but chose what to look at as if he expected nothing from life, but took everything it had to offer.

I asked, "Where's everyone?"

Sergio looked up. "Daniele and Alessio are playing tennis at the courts. Marcus is asleep in the shade." He nodded toward a tree where Marcus was slumped on a chair wearing his ridiculous mirrored sunglasses and a t-shirt wrapped around his head as if it were an Arab turban. Sergio continued, "Ronda went home to prep dinner, and your Dad, I think, went back to town to look for a mechanic."

I felt like I had deserted Dad in his impossible mission, plus I felt a bit lost without him, surrounded by the Fachuskiches. Thank goodness there was Sergio.

Around 8 PM we went back to the apartments. Since there was still no trace of Dad and I had no key to our place, I had to accept political asylum in Fachuskichian territory. I sat on the carpet in their living room, looking absently at the TV.

Daniele, sitting on a couch right across from me, was watching a game of tennis, of course, while Alessio read *La Gazzetta Dello Sport* at the dining table. With a certain anxiety, I thought about De André's kidnapping. Or maybe Dad had gotten himself arrested again, like that time with the U.S. MPs.

I tried to pay attention to the game, but my eye fell instead on a very strange thing. Between the legs of Daniele, sprawled on the couch, a monstrous excrescence protruded from the side of his swim shorts. I wasn't entirely dumb, I knew that males had penises, I had seen Luca naked by accident a long time before, and I had seen the porn mag, but this was not on paper.

I shot another guilty, fleeting glance. It was a red, giant protuberance, looking awfully wrong. Of course I couldn't ask, but I couldn't stop dropping my eye either. I wondered if all the males became so monstrous after a certain age. Fortunately, the door opened, and Dad made his entrance.

"Dad!" I ran to hug him. He was all sweaty and clearly tired but sported a victorious smile.

As soon as he put me down, his smile widened even further, "Lee, look what I found in town!" He presented me with the plush bunny.

I was overwhelmed with joy. Dad had remembered and returned to the store just for *me*. He had changed, indeed. I had never felt so loved by Dad, before. I thanked him from the bottom of my heart.

As soon as we sat down to eat, Dad told us he had dropped the engine at the farm of a certain Asile.

"Did he fix it?" Marcus asked.

"Not yet. He scowled and asked me for *fifty-thousand liras now and fifty after.*"

"No way!" Marcus interjected. "You didn't give him the money, did you?"

Dad scoffed. "Of course not! I'm not an *idiot*. We only had his donkeys as witnesses. I told him he had the engine as collateral, and I'd pay him when the job was done."

Dad was a real tough guy. I asked, "And what did Asile say?"

Dad shrugged. "He glared at me and went back inside."

Marcus gulped some soda and asked, "And when would the engine be ready?"

"He didn't say…anything, in fact." Dad answered. "I yelled after him I'd be back in two days, but that was that."

"In my opinion," Marcus said with his mouth full of spinach, "they are going to sell your engine on the black market."

"OH, SHUT IT! Don't jinx it."

Ronda, bored to death, asked me out of the blue, "So Leda, what did you name your bunny?"

"Uh, Dennis." What did she care?

Ronda seemed taken aback, "Danny? And there I was, thinking in ten years you would marry Sergio! Who would have thought you had it for Daniele?"

It was hard to tell who reacted worst. Daniele turned purple, like his penis. Sergio's eyes opened wide with surprise. Dad choked on the coke he was drinking, and I felt heat rising to my face while stammering, "No, no, Ronda. Dennis, like the cartoon: *Dennis the Menace.*"

Obnoxious Ronda laughed out loud. Marcus kept chewing spinach without batting an eyelid.

Dad yelled, "Ronda, please! Leda is barely *eleven*! I doubt she thinks of marriage, least of all with Sergio or Daniele. I mean, no offense—"

"Oh, come on, Carlo," Ronda interrupted in her most mundane tone, "I was only joking. But rest assured that one way or the other we *are* gonna snag Leda into the family!"

Hair bristled on my neck. I felt like the one hundred and second Dalmatian invited for dinner by Cruella Devil. Images of Daniele's horrific appendage overlapped with the evil laughter of Ronda, disturbingly similar to that of Cruella.

The ease with which Ronda imposed on me her conceited assumptions hurt, but Sergio bumped his knee into mine under the table. I recovered from the shock and turned toward my friend who was eating, serene, already forgetful of the indelicate exchange that had just occurred. He must have been used to it, poor guy. He looked at me and, pure as morning, he smiled and winked, making me understand that if I was still immune to the malice of certain grown-ups, somehow he had been cured.

29

When Things End Up in the Wrong Places

Two days went by. Without his dinghy, Dad sat on the beach looking bored and forlorn.

"Hey, Dad! Want to go for a swim? We can look for sea urchin's shells!"

"Mm, no thanks. I think I'll go windsurfing instead."

I followed Dad's gaze scanning the bay, where several windsurfs cut the waves zigzagging fast in the distance.

"Wow. You know *how*?" I asked bewildered. In my eleven years of life, I had never seen him touch a board.

"Of course. It can't be *that* hard."

Oh, boy. I rolled my eyes. "Yeah Dad, just like breakdancing, piece of cake."

Dad actually *laughed*, and with a smart-ass demeanor added, "Exactly. I'll show you one day who can breakdance."

He stood up, shook off the sand from his swimsuit, and walked toward the rental hut. When he came back he announced, "I have enrolled in the beginner class!"

One hour later the whole clan watched him in the knee-deep water, trying to climb on the board, balancing, and straightening the sail. Just like all the other beginners, Dad kept falling into the water with increasing frustration. When the class ended, Dad was as wet as he was angry.

Marcus exclaimed, "So, *champ*! Not so easy, after all, huh?"

"Oh, shut up, Marcus! It's just that my hands hurt! If I had proper gloves it would *really* be a piece of cake."

Ronda and Marcus burst out laughing, followed by their offspring. Sergio read his book, and I pretended not to see nor hear what was happening, maintaining a sympathetic, stoic face. Dad, however, did not stop at our beach umbrella but kept walking past, still soaking wet.

"Dad, where are you going?" I wondered alarmed, looking at his gloomy expression.

"To get my engine back!"

Now I *really* started to worry.

Fortunately, Dad came back within a couple of hours, just when we were about to leave the beach.

Marcus, amused, asked, "And the engine?"

"Well, " Dad seemed reluctant to spit out what had happened, "no one was around."

"Even the donkeys?"

"Oh, no, they were there."

"Then you were in good company!" Marcus laughed out loud. Then he added, "Come on, there's still hope! Even if they sold your engine, I doubt they made enough money to leave the island. You can always kidnap the asses for a ransom!" Followed theatrical laughter. "You're lucky you didn't lose more."

Dad mumbled, annoyed, "Yeah, yeah, very funny. I'll pick up the engine tomorrow."

Marcus looked like he could not believe he was going to laugh even more. "We shall see. We're off in two days, Carlo. But what do you have there?"

Dad's murderous glance confirmed he did not share Marcus jocular mood. He tightened his fist around a pair of yellow leather gardening gloves. *Oh, God.* I thought the gloves were just an excuse blurted out to absorb the humiliation of his windsurfing debacle. I never thought Dad would have followed through with it. He waved the yellow gloves on Marcus's amused mug, and announced, "Let's see tomorrow who'll be laughing!"

To which Marcus replied immediately, glinting mirth, "I sure can't wait!"

The next morning Dad showed up punctual to the windsurfing lesson, wearing his yellow leather gloves and a swimsuit. He looked a lot like Mickey Mouse, he only needed black round ears on his jet-black widow's peak. The clan had gathered on the beach to enjoy the show. Ronda lay on her chaise in the sun with sunglasses and a straw hat. The boys sat on the sand, shoulder to shoulder. Marcus was slumped on a folding chair under the red beach umbrella with his mirrored sunglasses and his blue t-shirt as a turban. Sergio read his book by my side, sitting on a beach towel.

I wondered why in the world would Dad consider Marcus a friend. Then I remembered of Flavio's behavior on that distant day at *Gardaland*, and I thought that sometimes things change, even if we don't want them to.

Meanwhile, Dad ignored Marcus's ironic remarks and stalked to the sea, chin up high, proud of his yellow gloves, mindless of the other beginners falling around him like flies fried by a bug lamp.

He climbed on the board, grabbed the sail, and shoot off toward the horizon.

Bewildered and full of pride, I yelled at him, "GO, DAD! YOU ROCK!" Then I turned to the clan. "Marcus, you're not laughing anymore, are you?" I mocked, gloating at the sight of Marcus leaning forward in his chair, lowering the mirrored sunglasses as if he had seen Carmen Russo topless.

For once, Marcus shut his mouth. He grabbed his crossword puzzle and retreated in a monastic silence. Too bad Dad was not there to enjoy it. Ronda remained impassive on her chaise. Sergio read his book, and the boys played soccer on the sand.

I redirected my proud gaze on the bay in search of Dad, who had already become a dot on the horizon. I lay on the towel warmed by the sun and fell fast asleep, wondering if Dad could really breakdance.

Sergio's voice woke me up at one o'clock. "Leda, you're getting sunburnt."

I rubbed my eyes, assessing my rosy skin: I was going to be lobster-colored by the evening. "What happened to Dad?" I asked.

Sergio updated me with a vague concern in his eyes, "I don't know, he never came back."

"*What*? It's been two hours! I'm going to ask."

I walked to the rental hut, where a tanned beach hunk tended to the boards and pedal boats. I asked, "Excuse me? Did you happen to see my Dad?" At his confused gaze, I added, reluctantly, "Hem, the guy with the yellow gloves."

"Oh, *him*! A phenomenon! He shot into the bay like a rocket and never came back." Based on his northern accent, the guy was not from Sardinia. "Don't worry girlie," he added. "There are no sharks here!"

Adults can be real dumb sometimes. "Listen, he's either hurt or in trouble. It was his first time. Can we go look for him?"

"Of course, girlie. Turiddu! TURIDDUUUU! This girlie here really wants to go for a ride."

Luckily, Turiddu turned out to be a member of the coastal guard emergency medical service. Turiddu, Sergio, and I climbed on a small engine boat and started the search.

Turiddu asked with a heavy Sardinian accent, "Don't you worry too much...What's your name?"

"Leda."

"Well, he probably lost his balance in the deep water, and there, with the wind, it can be quite challenging to pull up the sail."

"But it's been hours. He must be exhausted."

"We shall see."

My anxiety grew as time went by. Sergio was quiet. We could find no hint of Dad's passage, or his windsurf, anywhere in the bay. Other daredevils challenged the bigger waves in the open sea, but none of them wore yellow gloves.

"Should we go back?" Turiddu asked after a good forty-five minutes of fruitless searching. "He probably went back while we were out here looking."

Sergio suggested, "Can we check the next bay? It seems unlikely, but maybe he ended up a bit farther than he meant to."

Turiddu nodded, and we approached the beach separated from our own by a long, rocky promontory. There, on the sand, Dad sat beside his windsurf still wearing the yellow gloves.

As we moored, I jumped off the boat running toward him. "Dad! Are you okay?"

When he saw me, a huge smile of relief widened on his burned face. "Lee! What are you doing here?"

"We came looking for *you*, Dad! I was worried sick, you've been gone for hours!"

"Well, I'm very good at going left, but I had no idea of how to turn around so I just kept going. I was just resting for a moment before turning back."

"So, you're okay?"

"Of course! In great shape!" Dad exclaimed slapping a yellow-gloved hand on his thigh and wincing.

Turiddu, who had observed the whole scene with his arms crossed over his chest, said, "If you want, you can surf your way back. We'll see you at the beach."

"Ah, no, thanks. Since you bothered to come all the way here—"

We all burst out laughing, even Sergio, and Dad had no choice but to join us.

Turiddu added, "I'll tell the lifeguard to drive your windsurf back at the end of his shift."

Dad apologized and thanked him profusely.

As we watched Turiddu conferring with the lifeguard I asked, "Dad, how come you're still wearing your yellow gloves?"

Dad looked at his yellow hands. "As a matter of fact, I am not."

He pulled out the gloves from his trunks' pocket. The leather had leached dye deep into his skin and Dad sported bright yellow hands, just like Mickey Mouse, for rest of our stay.

On our last day, the boys were busy playing tennis, and since the rest of us could fit on Marcus's dinghy, we set out for a last trip. We spent the day by Molara Island, where the water is so clear the place is known as *Le Piscine*, the swimming pools. Marcus's engine did not lift up like Dad's, so his dinghy couldn't be hoisted to shore. To leave, we had to wade in the water, bags over our heads. I threw my bag on board, ready to jump in.

Marcus offered, "Do you need a hand, Lee?"

"No, I'm fine. Thank you."

Nothing was easier than jumping on the dinghy from the water. I leaped, clinging with my arms on the raft to pull myself up. But Marcus, stubborn as ever, grabbed my butt to push me on board.

It was a moment. I didn't know how or why, but one of his fingers slipped *in* my butt.

I wriggled away and turned to look at him. Both of us seemed puzzled, but no one spoke. The interaction had been very inappropriate, and I felt as if it were *my* fault.

The unaware clan climbed aboard and we headed back, but I kept thinking about the strange incident, ashamed, wondering if Marcus had noticed the strange rash on my left buttock when he had grabbed my behind.

🍦

That night at dinner, Marcus asked, "Care to tell us what happened to your engine?"

Dad stopped chewing and put down his fork. "I have it," he answered.

"Fixed?"

"Nah, they didn't have time."

"Oh well, at least they didn't rip you off." Dad looked down at his plate and chewed a little faster. "Or did they?"

"Asile asked me fifty-thousand liras for the trouble."

"NO!" we all exclaimed outraged.

"And what did you do?" I asked.

Dad hesitated, "I paid. What else could I do?"

"You could have avoided the rocks to begin with," Marcus replied and I thought Dad would throw something at him. Unfortunately, he didn't.

🍦

"Jesus please, make sure that I never have to see Marcus again, and that Sergio and I stay friends forever. Please make Viola pass her maturity exam, let me sleep well with no nightmares, and make it sunny tomorrow. Amen."

30

Time Passes, Seasons Change

When I came back to Arese from the seaside I couldn't wait to hug Starry and find out about my poor sister's fate. I ran into the house and in my mom's embrace.

"How did Viola's exam go?" I asked, as soon as she let go of me.

Starry smiled. "Believe it or not, she survived. They asked her—" she stopped, smirking at me and creating suspense, "*Pascoli* and *The Fanciullino*! Thank goodness for Prof Polenghi and her tedious phone calls!" We both laughed. She added, "The boards with the results will be made public on Tuesday. Now she's at the seaside with Marta and her parents, in Liguria."

"*Really*?" Marta hated her stepdad and did not get along with her mom either.

"Yep, the girls deserved a break after the exam and you know how they're inseparable."

"Nice. Do you think she passed?"

Starry shrugged. "Tough call. I don't even know how they admitted her in the first place with her grades."

"Let's hope for the best. When are we leaving for Afes?"

"Wednesday. I will not stay, but Viola and Marta will tag along."

"Really?"

Again, I was quite surprised. Viola had become more of a sophisticated city girl, not in a sissy way, more like a musical punk, dark beauty. Marta was different, quite alternative but in a more graffiti, urban, artsy-vandal kind of way, still not Afes material.

Starry explained, "Yes, really. Grandma made a scene when Viola said she wouldn't go to Afes, this year. So your sister gave up on the condition that Marta would go as well. Grandma couldn't deny her since you brought Flavio."

It seemed so far away, and for some reason I couldn't wait to see Nico, rather than Flavio, hoping with all my might that we would all be in the same class in middle school.

🍦

On the following day, the entrance door slammed open and Viola's voice announced her return, "CIAOO!"

I ran downstairs, intercepting her and Starry, who was just coming out of the kitchen.

"Hello!" we greeted her in a happy chorus.

I sat on the bottom step of the stairs, while Starry gave in to the temptation of trying to hug my big sis. Viola's gaze went from cheer to annoyance, then panic. "Eew, Starry, please!"

Starry was so happy to see her that, rather than taking offense, teased her, pursing her lips and sending Viola lots of little, playful kisses, waving her arms, pretending to grab her.

Viola retracted behind a wall of embarrassment and discomfort, making hissing noises like an angry cat. Eventually, Starry joined me on the step, still spurting joy from her every pore. She asked, "So, how was it?"

Viola answered, "Oh, it was great!"

"And how was the house? And her parents?"

"Hem…well. The house is gorgeous! Perched on the rocks with a little stone stair winding down to the beach. Why can't we buy a house by the sea, rather than going to Afes, the *asshole* of the planet?"

Starry sighed. "First of all, the house in Afes is Grandma's, not ours, and she's happy there. Second, we are in no position to buy *anything*, right now. We're struggling to make ends meet as is."

"Whatever," I meddled into their conversation. "I love Afes. In July I had a blast!"

Viola muttered moving past us, dragging her suitcase upstairs,"Yeah right, with Flavio you would have fun even on the moon."

"Shut up!" I retorted.

"You shut up!"

"Back to the routine, I see, " Starry commented, lighting up a cigarette.

🍦

On the day that Viola's results were to come out, I sat around with Fuzzer the cat, petting him to offset my anxiety, waiting for my sister and Starry to come back with the news.

At a quarter to four, I heard the unmistakable sound of Starry's Panda car. The front door slammed open to Viola's cry of, "FORTY-TWO! FORTY-TWO! I'm a legend! FORTY-TWO!"

I had no idea what she was blabbing about, but it certainly sounded like good news. I rushed to the foyer, where Viola danced ecstatic, humming, like in a trance, "forty-two, forty-two, forty-two!"

When she saw me, she stopped, planted her eyes on me, and with the biggest smile I can recall ever seeing on her face she declared, "Not only I passed, but I didn't even get the lowest grade!"

I asked, "And what's the lowest grade?"

"Thirty-six!"

"And the highest?"

"Hem...sixty."

Starry stepped in then. "Yes, it's great you passed, I agree, but forty-two is a sucky grade. As smart as you are, if you only studied a bit more during the year—"

Viola interrupted her, *"Starry!* Forty-two! No preaching, today! Even that bitch Monica got a forty-two and she studied her butt off all year! Oh, and Marta passed too!"

She danced to her room to spend the next few hours over the phone. This too had come to pass.

🍦

It was the August of 1989. I lost myself in the reading of *Zazie in the Metro* until the road to Afes colored with memories under the wheels of Starry's Panda car: the red house, the broken window, the church. I felt as if knowing what was going to come behind a curve in the road gave me a right to that land so far away that, nonetheless, I felt so close. There, among apple orchards, beneath the shadow of the great mountains, I finally felt like I belonged.

A couple of hours after our arrival I tried to persuade Starry to join me hiking.

"Come on, Starry! You've got to check this out! It's wonderful! It's a secret trail into the forest, full of flowers and butterflies, it's gorgeous, and you *have to* see it!"

"No way, Lee, you know butterflies scare me pantless." She shivered at the thought.

"But Starry, it's beautiful! There's such a view—"

"No, Lee, forget it. I'm glad you had fun with Flavio, but I'm out."

"Starry, *come on*! Why are you so afraid of butterflies, anyway? They're so pretty."

To my surprise, Starry thought about it. Then I remembered that she had been studying psychology for a whole year, already.

Eventually, she explained, "Well, I think it's because when I was a child, my brothers had me pin butterflies on a board to collect them, you know? They were, uh, still alive and…BLEAH!" She shivered.

"Oh God, Starry, it doesn't matter. I understand."

Her face broke into a bitter smile. "Speaking of…Did you know that Uncle Bedo got married to Teresa in June?"

I nodded, proud of my intel. Starry looked surprised and added, "Well, guess what. They split."

"*What*? But they only just got married! And wasn't he the one all up in arms about *your* separation?"

"Oh, you heard about that, too? Apparently she ran away during the honeymoon. I'm not sure what the heck he did to her."

"No way."

"Yeah. I tried to call her to see if she was okay. I hated how Dad's family never checked on me after the separation."

"But their Dad's family!"

"Well, for twenty years they were my family, too." She glared. "Anyway, Teresa sounded frantic and asked to never call her again, then hang up."

Wow.

Starry joined Grandma into the kitchen for coffee, while I stayed on the steps right outside, sitting in the sun, pondering about Uncle

Bedo's broken heart. To be honest I was more concerned with sweet Teresa.

Starry was saying to Grandma, "I know. I'm sorry I can't stay longer, but Vanna has a place in Sardinia and she invited me to join her. It's a great opportunity to relax a bit without spending money."

Grandma retorted, "To relax from what? You've relaxed all summer, hanging out with your friends to do God knows what. And here I am, alone for months, slaving away in the garden, planting flowers that no one ever sees."

Starry called, "LEEEDAAA!"

I almost fell off the stoop. "Starry, I'm right here. No need to scream."

She blurted, "Didn't you want to go for a hike?"

"Sure, but I thought you said—"

She interrupted me, "Come on then! It's getting late. Sorry, Grandma, I did promise to go along. We'll chat later."

"Bah!" was all that Grandma had to say.

Starry then looked at me, "Let's at least drive till the sports center, okay?"

"WHAT DO YOU WANT FOR DINNER?" Grandma yelled after us, but Starry pretended not to hear, trotting to the car with me in tow.

Starry parked in one of the five spots by the pine trees, all available. First I took Starry to the pinewood to show her the *sanguignoli* mushrooms, but to my disappointment, they were all gone.

"Starry I swear! I had never seen so many. They were everywhere!"

"Maybe they just withered, it's been almost two months."

"It has," I considered. "Come on! I'll show you the trail."

I walked past the swings and we searched for the secret trail. It took me a while, but finally we started up the mountain.

"Lee, slow down. I can't keep up!" Starry wheezed. "It's such a steep climb, let's go back!"

"Come on, we're almost there," I lied.

After several cigarette-breaks and at least an hour of climbing, I saw the top of the slope, announcing the magical glade.

"Mom, it's right there!" I pushed ahead with my heart in my throat.

When Starry reached me, she found me transfixed in front of a patch of plain, dry, yellow grass. Everything was quiet. Everything seemed dead.

I said, "I swear it was right here, all green and flowers everywhere, and lots of butterflies." My voice quivered.

Starry bent over double, catching her breath and sweating profusely. She collapsed to sit on a rock. After a few minutes, she lit another cigarette. "Lee, I believe you, but it was early July. Now it's late August. Time passes, seasons change, flowers and mushrooms dry out. Even butterflies, fortunately, don't live too long."

I sat next to her in silence, wondering if I had killed the magic of the place by bringing a grown-up.

We drove back home in silence. Things were indeed constantly changing. Flavio was not as similar to me as I had hoped. Instead Nico, who had crashed into my life like a cataclysm, had proven to be a loyal friend, a jerk at times, with some dark spots in his past, maybe, but I felt the same way, didn't I? I couldn't wait to see him in the fall.

Nothing ever stays the same. Mom and Dad had split and had started new lives for themselves. Mom was going to be a psychologist, and Viola was going to follow in her footsteps. Her impossible love story with Renzo, the decrepit light technician, had been a dream come true. So what was going to happen to me? What was I going to be? The possibilities were as scary as exciting.

31

The End of Childhood, the Beginning of Everything Else

A couple of days later I heard a familiar voice calling me through Grandma's yard, "Cochi!"

I ran to hug Uncle Bedo, puffing on his giant, inseparable cigar. "Uncle! How long are you staying for?"

"Until tomorrow. Then I go to South Tyrol for a series of piano concerts."

"So soon! Are you going by motorbike?"

"Yes. Want to come?" He winked.

"You know I'd love to. When are you coming back?"

"Just in time to drive you, your sister, and her friend, back to Arese."

"Oh, thank you." I stared at him at a loss for words, then managed to say, "Uncle, I've heard—"

He stopped me in my tracks with a peremptory gesture of his hand as his face turned bitter. "I don't want to talk about it. Women are like *that*. She'll be back. Remember what I said. No one can separate what God united. Speaking of which, now that you don't live with your Dad anymore, I hope you don't lose your way like your mother did. Are you still going to Mass?"

I fought the impulse to roll my eyes. "Of course, Uncle, every Sunday." At least when I spent my weekends with Dad, I omitted to say.

"Do you even pray?"

"Of course!" I answered full of pride. "I pray every night!"

He was not quite sold yet. "Oh, yeah? And what do you pray for?"

"Well, it depends of course, but typically to sleep well with no nightmares and for a sunny day."

Uncle Bedo burst into a fit of laughter. "*You do?*"

"Yes," I answered, offended. "Why?"

He chuckled a bit more, then said, "And what if God listened? What would we eat if it never rained? What would the farmers do? We're lucky he doesn't listen to *you!*"

I stared at him in shock as I realized that I had prayed most of my life for drought and famine.

Uncle seemed suddenly startled. "Did you hear that?" He puffed at the cigar and put a hand to his ear.

"*What?*" I asked.

His alarmed look freaked me out. Then he began chanting, "DON DON DON"

"Uncle, come on! I'm eleven and two months, now!"

"DIN-DON, DIN-DON, DIN-DON"

"Uncle, I'm a grown-up! I'm not afraid of Assenzio anymore!"

Despite my own words, I found myself running like hell for the kitchen steps just before the fatidic, "DINDINDINDINDIN!"

Some things never changed, and Uncle Bedo was one of them.

Days went by slow. Bored to death, Viola and Marta dug out Grandpa's old moped from the basement. It was a Piaggio *Ciao* at least twenty-years-old, which had been abandoned under a white sheet, just like Grandpa last I had seen him, leaving the house on a stretcher.

The clunker hadn't worked for ages but Marta, who knew her share about engines, had fixed it. The two girls had then painted *FLAT OUT* on the side of the jalopy in flaming big letters. *Flat out* was the battle nickname of the old thing, since the only way to go faster than a pedestrian, especially in two, was to push the throttle all the way forward. These clandestine activities occurred in the basement behind the laundry room, where Grandma rarely came.

Grandma's wrath befell the girls anyway. I was sitting in the living room watching TV on a late morning, when I heard a loud crash, then stomping.

Grandma yelled, "What's going on?" She stomped upstairs, then yelled louder, "What the hell have *you* done? One must be careful, even more so when they're a guest in someone else's home! Doors are very expensive!"

I rushed upstairs and saw the glass door to the bathroom shattered on the floor. Marta, mortified, blabbered, "Ma'am, I'm so sorry."

Viola had also run out of the bedroom she shared with Marta. "Grandma, it's not like she meant it! It was an accident!"

Grandma thundered, "Are you drunk?" She sniffed Marta like a hound.

Marta tried to explain, muttering, "No, of course not! I've no idea what happened! I just got dizzy and fell right through the door." It was a miracle that she hadn't hurt herself beyond a couple of scratches.

Grandma was furious."Even in your bedroom, you moved the beds around, and who gave you permission, huh? Did you see the marks on the floor? Who's gonna clean *that*? And what are you always doing locked up in there anyway? What are you hiding? I remind you that this is *my* house! From now on I get all the keys and that's that!"

For once I was not to blame since I slept in Grandma's big bed. Actually, for the first time ever I had noticed that she snored quite a bit for someone who suffered from insomnia. In fact, she snored soundly all night long.

Viola huddled close to her friend. "Grandma we can move back the beds."

"Bah!" Grandma replied, stalking away.

As Grandma left, still fuming, Viola's eyes glinted with mischief. She glared at me and threatened, "You'd better not say one word about Flat Out. Understood?"

I nodded. Not only Grandma would have lost her mind, but if Mom or Dad were to find out, they would have locked my big sister in a dungeon. And one day she would have come back to hunt *me* down. The thought of snitching did not even cross my mind, yet their little secret was going to have the most unexpected consequences.

🍦

It was our last day in Afes. Viola and Marta were out with the moped and, since Grandma had sequestered the key, their bedroom was open. I could not resist sneaking in and snooping around. In spite of Grandma's blow up, the three full beds were still joined into one big island, close to the window. I rummaged in the drawers of the desk where I found a sketchbook full of doodles. One was particularly gorgeous. It was a woman with amazing green eyes, smiling and looking away as a breeze mussed her long wavy hair.

My heart stopped when I read the inscription below the drawing, in Viola's handwriting. It read, "Freaking Leda at eighteen."

What? Hadn't my sister noticed I was the ugliest on the planet? I stared at the page in shock, confused, till a realization dawned on me. Was it possible that all of Viola's unkindness had been due to jealousy?

The girls' voices startled me and I rushed to put the sketchbook back.

The door opened, and Viola asked, "What the heck are you doing in here?"

I turned my back to the desk. "Ah, I was waiting for you."

"Whatever." Viola plopped on the joined beds and Marta followed her while I sat in a corner, hoping they wouldn't kick me out. They ignored me, continuing their conversation.

Marta said, "Here, this is the best part!" She pushed a button on a small voice recorder and her voice crackled out of the device, "The best thing in the world? Taking a dump, man! Everyone knows *that!*" followed by loud guffawing and Viola's recorded opinion,

"No way! The best thing in the world is *sex!*" more laughter.

Startled and embarrassed, I wondered what Viola knew about sex, and if she had just said so to be a smart ass, the way Nico would have. Then I remembered Starry's outrage at reading her secret diary and wondered again.

Marta asked me, shaking me from my thoughts, "And in your opinion, Lee?"

Flattered, yet terrified to give an answer not up to par, I said, "Nutella?" To my delight, they burst out laughing.

The door flung open and the three of us jumped.

"Uncle! You're back!" I yelled, jumping up to go greet him, but his deranged face stopped me dead in my tracks.

He stared right through me, at Viola and Marta, his lips trembling with anger. I had never seen him like that, and I had no idea what to do, what to say.

"Who. Did. This." He sort of asked. He was clutching the white sheet that had covered Flat Out.

We just stared. His eyes shone, maybe with a hint of tears. He turned to look at me and added, overwhelmed with sadness, "That scooter was my father's. My father's! You defiled it!" He stalked out dragging the sheet behind him.

Whose fault was it? Innocence. Lack of experience. Sometimes its beauty can be a little too blinding. I would have never guessed that Uncle could have felt that way, that adults had their Mr. Hydes, too. I was about to find out a lot more.

🍦

At the end of our vacation, Uncle Bedo, taciturn as ever, dropped us back in Arese.

After thanking him, I jumped out of the car and took my luggage. I left Viola and Marta to say their goodbyes in the front yard, rushing into the house to see Starry, expecting an epic hug.

She was in the kitchen, amazingly making risotto. I don't think she heard me coming, because she gasped, and when she turned I saw tears streaming down her face.

I had never seen my mom cry.

I didn't think that adults ever cried at all. Why would they, if they always knew what to do, what was right and what was wrong? But did they? My parents separating, Marcus's abuse of me and anyone around him, deluded teachers, Grandma's tantrums...I was not so sure anymore.

Starry jerked back to the risotto, wiping her eyes. When she turned toward me again, she had a huge smile on her face.

"Come here!" she said, spreading her arms to welcome me as if nothing had happened. I sank into her embrace, but couldn't erase what I had just seen.

"Starry, are you crying? What's wrong?"

"It's nothing, really, onions. Everything's fine."

I protested, "But you hate onions! You never use them!"

"Shh, it's okay," she crooned, without denying her little lie, just adding to it with another obvious one.

Until that moment, the truth had been very clear to me, held and dictated by maternal and paternal wisdom, indubitable, glossy and transparent like a glass marble. Up until that moment, the world had been divided into good and evil, my parents the referees, I, Flavio, Nico, and the other kids rookie players. Breaking a bike or eating radioactive pistachios triggered the fear that the world would end, that this time there would be no forgiveness by the beholders of truth, love, and justice until the accident was forgotten and everything went back to normal. But on that late August afternoon, my mother's tears tore the illusion, defeated the magic, and cracked the perfectly smooth surface of the mirror that for years had told me who I was.

If Mom was lost, who was gonna find *me*?

Her hug felt different, more to receive than to give. I knew that things were not okay at all, and the truth hit me in a very slow second, like in the cartoon *Captain Tsubasa,* when the kids ran along an infinite soccer field brooding over their whole life and the goalie never came.

Adults' *great truths* were nothing but assumptions and big leaps of faith.

There.

I found myself alone, looking for answers when I didn't even know the questions. Monsters didn't disappear when you grew up; adults just assumed they were something else, something *possible*. I understood that weaknesses were to be hidden, problems covered up, just moving forward and hoping for the best. Perhaps, more importantly, I received the confirmation that words were not necessary to communicate, in fact they were often in the way, describing things as adults *wished* they were. An infinite soccer field, an eternal second, like a feather of antimatter.

I hugged my mom back as tight as I could, determined to find out what was wrong with her. Lots of changes waited ahead. Some were expected, like the beginning of middle school, some not at all, including the best summer of my life. Of course I had no idea then, all I could think about was my mom crying.

It was at that moment that I ceased to be a child, or better, that I started to build upon my child's soul a new layer of uncertainty and awareness, fragile and ethereal: the beginning of my adolescence. I had finally accepted that I was a girl, and I was determined to learn to behave like one, not according to everybody else's expectations but to my own. For some reason that made me think of Nico and I felt heat rising to my face.

END OF BOOK 1

Leda's adventures continue with book 2, "Out of the Nest, an Italian Summer" as paperback, audiobook, or ebook! Check it out on Amazon now or keep reading for an excerpt!

HELP ME OUT?

If you enjoyed *An Italian Adventure* please take the time to leave an honest review. Only about one reader in a thousand leaves a book review and yet, reviews are one of the most important factors in helping readers choose their next novel.

PLEASE LEAVE A REVIEW!

Good places to leave a review are Amazon, Book Bub, and Goodreads. Good or bad, your review will be just as valuable to me as to other readers looking for books that fit their taste. It can be a one line or a long one, it does not matter.

Thanks from the bottom of my heart!

Keep reading for an excerpt of the next volume in *the Italian Saga*, "Out of the Nest!"

EXCERPT FROM OUT OF THE NEST, AN ITALIAN SUMMER

September 1990, Arese, a small town in the Milan province, in northern Italy

As I stared at his face, I understood the question he dared not ask.

He glued his gaze on me, a slight blush betraying feelings I had not suspected. We had always been friends. I had never looked at him that way, but I allowed myself to: he was so darn handsome. His wild hair made him seem like the rebel he pretended to be. Instead, he was sweet and sincere even if, on one occasion or two, he had done rather questionable deeds. Boys will be boys. I knew he could be a jerk. His mesmerizing eyes, locked on mine, held no promise of that. He interrupted my catatonic state with his question.

"Lee, do you want to be my girlfriend?"

Was it possible that the love of my life had been there all along?

ACKNOWLEDGEMENTS

J.K. Rowling invented the term Horcrux to refer to an object enchanted to hide and protect a sliver of a human soul. In creating the Horcrux, the human may become weaker, but their soul will live forever in the enchanted object.

After publishing nine novels, it is apparent to me that each one of them is a Horcrux. The people closest to me have been watching me pour myself into each page for the past few years, offering unrelenting support and unwavering confidence. First among them, Seth Amman, source of most of my magical powers and constant recharge for my overspent soul.

If you find a sentence where the order of the words is "Italianized," it was a stylistic choice approved by editors and proofers alike. On that vein, my most heartfelt thanks to Renni Acre, Rodney Garrison, Dan Stripp, and Carol Amman.

Would a book still exist, if it had no readers? Probably, it would only in the broken heart of the author. Therefore, thank you so much to you and to all the readers who have entrusted me to take them on this new adventure. Your support and kind words have been essential through hectic days, editing marathons, and blanc-page panics. May this story give you reason to grow and be happier, from my soul to yours.

—Gaia B. Amman

ABOUT THE AUTHOR

Gaia B. Amman was born and raised in Italy. She moved to the United States in her twenties to pursue her Ph.D. in molecular biology. She's currently a professor of biology and the Chair of the Biology and Mathematics Department at D'Youville College in Buffalo, New York, where she was voted "the professor of the month" by her students. Her research and commentaries have been published in prestigious, international, peer-reviewed journals, including *Nature*.

A bookworm from birth, she wrote throughout her childhood and won two short story competitions in Italy in her teens. Fluent in four languages, Gaia is an avid traveler, and many of her adventures are an inspiration for her fiction. Mostly she is passionate about people and the struggles they face to embrace life. Her highest hope is to reach and help as many as she can through her writing and her teaching. She authored the sci-fi fantasy *Linked—Will Empathy Save the United Terrestrial Democracy?* and *The Italian Saga* of which you just read volume eight. The books, light-hearted and funny at first sight, deal with issues like sexuality, divorce, addiction, mental illness, abuse, first love, and self discovery.

Among Amman's favorite authors are J.K. Rowling, Jandy Nelson, Neil Gaiman, Kristine Cashore, Chuck Palahniuk, Kurt Vonnegut, J.R.R. Tolkien, Antoine de Saint Exupèry, and many others.

To receive a notification about GB Amman's new releases, click the FOLLOW button on her author page on Amazon, or follow her Facebook Page.

More books by Gaia B Amman:

- Linked, Can Empathy Save the United Terrestrial Democracy? (2017)

The Italian Saga

An Italian Childhood Duology
- An Italian Adventure (2015)
- Out of the Nest, An Italian Summer (2016)

Italian Teens Duology
- Forget Nico (2016)
- Sex-O-S (2016)

Italian College Duology
- Finding Leda (2017)
- Happily. Ever After? (2018)

Woman Scientist Trilogy
- The Immigrant (2019)
- Singles (2019)

Connect with the author on social media if you like to nerd out about books, music, movies, and science!

Register for the (more or less) monthly newsletter at http://www.gaiabamman.com/

Or check out:

Blog: http://www.gaiabamman.com/
Goodreads: https://www.goodreads.com/author/show/14233144.Gaia_B_Amman
Facebook: https://www.facebook.com/GaiaBAmman/
Instagram: https://www.instagram.com/gaiabamman/
Book Bub: https://www.bookbub.com/profile/gb-amman
Twitter: https://twitter.com/GaiaBAmman
Tumblr: https://www.tumblr.com/blog/gaiabamman

DISCUSSION QUESTIONS

- In the first chapter of the book we learn that Leda does not want to be a girl. What reasons does she provide? After reading the whole book, can you pinpoint some other reasons why Leda might have preferred to be a boy? Does she want to try and be a girl at the end of the book? Why? What changed?
- How are Leda and Nico similar? How are they different? Why do you think they become friends? How does their relationship change throughout the book?
- One of the big themes of the book is the inability of adults to discuss sex with children. Why is that so hard in your opinion? When is this evident in the book? What episodes in the book deal, somehow, with sex?
- Do Leda and Viola get along at the beginning of the book? How does their relationship change throughout the book?
- The Chernobyl disaster took place in Ukraine (at the time Ukrainian Soviet Socialist Republic) on April 26, 1986. What happened? What were the consequences? Was there a more recent nuclear incident that broke the news worldwide? Search the internet for answers.
- From what you can infer from the story so far, why did Mom and Dad split?
- When Mom and Dad split, how do Viola and Leda react in the short term? And in the long term?
- Does the separation change the relationship between Leda and Dad? How?
- How does Dad change after the separation?
- "Time passes, seasons change". How does this sentence apply to Leda's life?
- Marcus grabs Leda in a very inappropriate way. She thinks it's an accident. What do you think? How does Leda react?
- Religion and superstition seem to mix quite often in Leda's

world (think of Grandma, for example). Discuss episodes in the book

- How are women viewed in Italy at the end of the 80s? Discuss with examples from the book
- Can you recall some of the Italian customs you learned from the book?
- Leda is a bookworm and she mentions many books throughout the story. Was there any you recall or that you read?
- Sometimes, in the book, Leda lies. Can you recall some examples? Why do you think she lies?
- Mom reads Viola's secret diary because she is concerned about her. What would have you done in Mom's shoes? And in Viola's? Do you think that Mom had the right to read Viola's diary?
- The story takes place in the late 80s. Were there any references to old technology you were not familiar with or that is not in use anymore? Provide examples
- Many things happen in the book, but in the last chapter there is one specific event that triggers the beginning of Leda's adolescence. What is it?

CPSIA information can be obtained
at www.ICGtesting.com
Printed in the USA
JSHW031030070420
5010JS00001B/99

9 781516 916207